WALKING DEAD GIRL

A VAMPIRELAND NOVEL

BY LILI ST GERMAIN
WRITING AS

JESSICA SALVATORE

WALKING DEAD GIRL

ISBN-13: 978-1974455898
ISBN-10: 1974455890

Cover Designer: Regina Wamba at Mae I Design
Formatting: Champagne Book Design

Other Books by Jessica Salvatore

THE VAMPIRELAND SERIES
Walking Dead Girl
The Vessel

Writing as Lili St. Germain
THE GYPSY BROTHERS SERIES
Seven Sons
Six Brothers
Five Miles
Four Score
Three Years
Two Roads
One Love
Zero Hour
Alternate (short novella)

THE CARTEL TRILOGY
Cartel
Kingpin
Empire

THE CALIFORNIA BLOOD SERIES
Verona Blood
Burn in Your Blood
In Cold Blood

THE SKULLS CARTEL SERIES
The Prospect
Queenpin

STANDALONE NOVELS
Gun Shy (Psychological Thriller)
Afterward (Contemporary Romance)

And till she come, as truly as to heaven
I do confess the vices of my blood

– Shakespeare, OTHELLO

ONE

DRINK.

That was the first thing he said to me.

I opened my eyes. Naked save for a bloodied white sheet, my tender skin covered in sticky red blood. My broken body somehow, *impossibly*, repairing itself.

I felt something warm at my lips. *Blood*.

“Drink,” he repeated.

I did.

“Be grateful,” he said later. “I saved you.”

I hated him for it.

This is not a story about love. There is no happy ending. There is only darkness, and the struggle to avoid being consumed by it.

This is a story about survival.

I don't really know where to start, but there must be a place. A place before the world went dark, before I learned of the horror that existed on this earth. Back when I was just a girl—though that seems so long ago, I sometimes wonder if it was just a dream.

I could start at the beginning, but where is the beginning? Was it the night I was taken? Or the balmy summer I spent falling in love, the last summer that I walked under the sun without it burning my flesh?

Maybe I should start with the night innocence came to a crashing halt. The night I was taken. Yes, I will begin my story there, in a frozen parking lot with a silent scream.

I was seventeen years old the first time I died. When I was first taken, I thought that my ending had arrived, a smirk on his mouth and bloodlust alight in his eyes. I waited to die, to be torn apart by sharp teeth and vicious hands.

And I did die.

I just didn't expect to wake up afterwards.

But here, now, lying in a pool of my own drying blood, naked and alone, the only comfort when he brings me that thick, syrupy liquid that burns and cools my throat all at once?

I wish I could go back and tell myself that death was the very least of the things that I should fear.

THEN

It was the final week of first semester in our senior year. I had just finished a mammoth session filling out college applications with my best friend, Evie. I remember little details—the way the last few falling blossoms from the Northern Red Oaks on campus looked like drops of fire on the early December snow; the way my fragile human heart hummed with excitement that school was almost over; the way everything looked clean and new blanketed in snow. Most of all, I remember the stab of worry I had felt at taking the shortcut through the deserted football field to get home.

Blair Academy was smack in the middle of Blairstown, New Jersey. A hundred and fifty-something-year-old institution that sprawled luxuriously over four hundred manicured acres. It was preppy and expensive, and I was there because my father had attended school there, and his father before him. My father was dead. My mother was a high-powered corporate attorney who spent most of her time in her New York loft apartment with my stepfather, Warren. She had never really wanted children, and thought she couldn't have any. She had lucked out with me—although she probably didn't see it that way—and so I had never really had much to do with her. My father was everything to me. My mom moved to New York a few months after he died. She was meant to come home every weekend after her long week at work. She never did. I didn't really mind. I didn't resent her for not being my mother—I had never known or expected anything more from her, and I knew she loved me despite her maternal shortcomings. After Dad died I usually split my time between living on campus during the school week and spending weekends at our house, a few miles from school.

What I loved to do more than anything else was run. I was on the track team and when I was in the middle of a run, it was like I could fly. The college scouts had been at our annual running meet, and I had just filled out my application to a handful of elite track programs.

My best friend Evie was as poor as I was wealthy. She was on a full scholarship right through high school, and she was *smart*. She whipped my ass in most things academic. I had always been bright, but next to her I—and the rest of the general high school population—looked like a bunch of dumbasses. Needless to say, having a best friend who was a genius made study *much* easier. The girl had a natural talent for teaching and mentoring. Her parents weren't dirt poor, but they struggled, and to have Evie at a school like Blair Academy made them so happy. Really, they were like my adopted family. People always asked if we were sisters, I don't know why. We were both short and sarcastic but she was strawberry blonde to my brunette, curly to my straight and had green eyes that were nothing like my blue ones. I had skin that turned brown after a day in the sun, where she had pale alabaster skin that practically glowed.

"You okay to get back to your room?" Evie asked, jerking me out of my idle thoughts.

I stopped as I realized we were standing at Evie's car. She shook her set of keys and looking at me expectantly.

"I'm not going to my room," I replied.

"Going to suck face with Jared?"

"You make it sound so endearing, Evangeline," I said petulantly. "And yes, I am going to see Jared. I will most likely suck his face at some point tonight."

"Gross," Evie said. "He's like my brother. I've known him for*ever*."

"So have I," I reminded her. "And I sure am glad he's not my brother." I raised my eyebrows suggestively and laughed.

Evie made a face. "Get out of here before I throw up on you."

I exchanged goodbyes with Evie and made a beeline for my own car. Teachers and day students got to park right at the entrance of Blair but most live-in students had to trek almost a mile to the regular boarding school parking slots. Sighing, I hoisted my bag higher on my shoulder and walked past a Crown Victoria, a Bentley and a Fiat before reaching the average-looking old clunkers in the student parking lot.

As soon as my feet touched the snow-covered oval, all thoughts of trigonometry and English lit dissolved. A jolt of adrenaline hit my stomach as I thought about finals, about Jared, about my eighteenth birthday in a few months. Everything was going *so well.*

Trudging through the silence, I began mentally making lists for an end-of-finals party at my perpetually parent-free house. Keg. Food. Decorations. New clothes. So, naturally, I wasn't even looking where I was walking when the hot guy stepped out from behind a shiny black truck. He was so close I almost tripped over him. I jerked back to reality, cursing myself for being so inattentive.

He was wearing jeans and a black sweater, and looked kind of like a thirty-something Calvin Klein underwear model with dark blue eyes, a hint of European heritage in his olive skin—Italian, maybe?—and black hair cut close to his skull. He was the furthest thing from threatening I'd ever seen—during the day in a crowd I'd let my eyes linger on that handsome face—but at midnight in New Jersey, anything was possible. I averted my eyes and veered to the left, quickening my pace. My thoughts instantly shifted from beer and clothes shopping to serial killers and the can of bear spray in my handbag.

Pulse quickening, I passed hot dude and kept walking towards my car. *It's cool, he's probably just a new teacher in the wrong lot.* And then he spoke.

"Mia!" He called after me. I froze for a moment, then began to walk again. Faster, pushing my strides longer. *Just get to the car.*

He laughed, a deep, throaty chuckle that sounded like caramel and in any other situation would make me melt. Instead, it made me shudder inwardly, adrenaline spiking into my muscles.

"Sorry, gotta run!" I mumbled awkwardly, almost at my car.

"Mia Blake, don't you remember me?" He padded casually after me, while I scurried like a timid mouse. I was almost embarrassed by how uncool I was being. "I'm Ryan. We were in Bailey's drama class together last semester."

Bailey was a washed-up ballerina who liked to yell at her students. Of course I knew her, but I definitely didn't know this *Ryan*. He looked kind of old to be a student—not to mention, *way* too hot for me to forget. I might have had a boyfriend, but girlfriend had eyes, too.

I turned to face him, but kept walking backwards towards my car. The Honda Element sat less than twenty feet away.

"Oh, sure," I lied. "How's things? Sorry, I can't stop." If he's a student, then I am so freaking rude right now.

Ten feet to my driver's door. *I'm probably just being stupid*, I thought, an unfortunate side effect of growing up two hours from New York. We might have been in a nice suburb, but even so—nice people generally didn't loiter in parking lots and teenage girls rarely walked to their cars alone. Blairstown was a place where everyone was still on alert after 9/11, even me, and I'd only been a child when the towers had fallen. Three girls had already gone missing from high school parking lots in New Jersey that year.

I am such an idiot. I should have gotten a ride with Evie.

Five feet. Walking backwards was harder than it looked, and my silver ballet flats were getting ruined in the damp snow. Not that I cared about my stupid shoes. My mother always berated me for not wearing boots in the snow, which is why I wore the flimsiest shoes possible. Can you tell I didn't really get on with my mother?

"Well, gotta go." I slid my key into the door of my car and unlocked it with a satisfying *thunk*.

"That's not a bad idea," he said, stepping so close, so *fast*, that I jerked back in fright. I heard the click of a car door opening nearby, and two more guys started to walk towards us.

I pulled the can of bear spray out of my handbag, the safety switch already off. Ryan grabbed my wrist faster than I could push the nozzle down to spray a load of mace into his face, and squeezed so hard I could feel bone crunching on itself. I gasped and let go of the can. It bounced on the asphalt and rolled underneath a blue

Camry a couple of cars away from us.

"Help!" I yelled to the empty lot, kneeing him in the groin.

He barely reacted. *That figures*, I thought to myself. *No balls.*

"Let go of me!" I demanded. "Help!"

"Stop struggling and be quiet," he said calmly, his grip like an iron vice on both my wrists. He smiled, showing straight white teeth and matching dimples.

I opened my mouth and screamed as loud as I could, then fell hard against the car behind me as a fist slammed into my face. I saw stars and choked, warm blood dribbling from my nose.

Great, he probably broke my nose.

I looked up to see the taller of the two offsiders pointing a gun at my face. "No more noise," he ordered in a thick accent. Was he Mexican? I couldn't figure it out, but then, I'd just been punched in the face, so there was that.

With my eyes half shut, I gestured to my handbag. "Take it," I said numbly, not feeling anything but utter shock at the turn of events in my otherwise normal night. "Here, take my grandmother's ring. It's worth at least -"

"Mia," Ryan cut in. "Honey, I don't want your ring, or your Canal street knock-off."

My heart dropped at what that could mean, and bile rushed up in my throat. Before I could swallow it back, I *threw up* all over his expensive-looking black loafers. I bet nobody had ever done that to him before.

"Goddamn it!" he swore, looking at the mess I had made. "Ford, get a towel or something."

The shorter of the two guys—the one *not* pointing a gun at me—high-tailed it towards a black van, moving so fast my eyes couldn't follow. *Man, he really hit me hard.*

I stared in shock as he zipped back to us with a pink rag covered in oil, knelt down, and started *wiping* Ryan's shoes.

"It's not a knock-off," I protested. "My bag. It's genuine."

Nobody said anything. Why was I defending a fucking bag? Why wasn't I fighting harder? The world started to spin lazily around me, and ironically, Ryan's grip was the only thing keeping me from falling into my own vomit that lay splashed between our feet.

"My boyfriend is gonna kick the shit out of you," I gasped. Even as the words were coming out of my mouth, I couldn't believe what I was saying.

"Boss, we need to get going," the one with the gun urged.

Ryan nodded, kicking Ford's hurried hands away from his feet. "Dose her!" he barked, and something sharp stabbed into my forearm. My mouth formed a horrified O as I saw the taller guy pressing the plunger down on a syringe that was already deep in my skin. He'd moved so fast, I hadn't even had time to scream.

How did he do that so fast? "What-" I spluttered through a mouth full of cotton wool.

A thousand broken threads of thoughts ran through my addled mind, but I couldn't move. Couldn't yell out. Couldn't even close my stupid mouth. I was literally frozen.

They are going to rape me and kill me and I am going to die.

They are going to bury me in the woods under the snow and nobody will ever know what happened to me.

Or maybe they'll keep me alive in an underground basement.

Or maybe they want my kidneys.

I am so screwed.

But one terrified thought rose above the rest.

I don't want to die.

The stuff stung like a bastard as it made its way into my bloodstream, but the pain was short-lived. I didn't even have time to collect my gaping jaw from the pavement and close my mouth before blackness descended over my vision and I crumpled like a rag doll. Rough hands carried me through the night air, and I landed somewhere that smelled like oil and cigarettes.

The last thought I could form before the darkness closed in was *I should have run when I had the chance.*

TWO

DAMPNESS. I SMELLED DAMPNESS, AND THE COPPER SCENT OF old blood.

My wrists ached. My arms burned, tied above me in an impossible knot, and I came to with a violent jerk when I realized I wasn't waking up in my own bed. Opening my eyes, I found myself chained from a wooden rafter, crucifixion–style, in a tiny, dark room that had no windows and moss–stained limestone walls. My toes barely touched the cool ground. For a few seconds I struggled with the chains that dug deep into my wrists, but vertigo slammed into me at the slightest movement. Groaning involuntarily, I peered around the room that held me prisoner. The memories of the parking lot, of being taken, rushed at me all at once, and I shuddered.

My face throbbed where I'd been punched. My nose made a sickening scraping noise with every shaky inhalation. Silently, I began to cry, salt water blurring my vision. Things like this didn't happen to girls like me. But this was happening, and it seemed like every bit of good luck I'd ever had was coming back to bite me.

I couldn't get free from my bindings, so I tried to come up with a plan of escape …

… and drew a blank. Every plan I could think of had the initial step of being untied. With no foreseeable hope, I started to panic, my silent tears turning into heaving sobs.

After a few minutes, my sobs slowed to a steady, silent weeping. Fear churned in my belly as my shocked brain tried to find a way out. I surveyed my dungeon in greater detail, able to swing around on my chain a little to get a three-sixty view of the room. It looked like a small storage room, with one small window behind me that was covered entirely with old plywood, a pile of old rags and blankets underneath. All four walls were made from the same water-stained cinderblock and covered with tufts of moss and green slime. A beige-colored door with an old-fashioned brass keyhole and no handle stood in front of me. An identical door, this one with a handle and no keyhole, was to my left. The room was a perfect square, devoid of furniture, roughly twelve feet by twelve feet. Dull cherry-colored stains littered the concrete floor. I tried not to think of what they could be from.

Under the window, the pile of rags started moving. I screamed.

"Be quiet!" The pile of rags hissed, suddenly moving and sitting up and becoming a girl. Fuck! I'd figured I was alone, and I wasn't sure whether to scream or be relieved that I had company.

I shook my hands, rattling the rusted chains that kept me suspended. "Help me!" I hissed back.

The girl—who I could now see wasn't a pile of rags, just a very skinny girl—shrugged her blankets off, stood and came over to me. She was young, maybe thirteen, with massive green eyes and dirty, straw-colored hair that fell almost to her waist. She wore a green t-shirt that matched her eyes, though it was covered in dirt and bloodstains. Her jeans were just as filthy. She peered at me, as if trying to decide whether to punch me or give me a hug.

I smiled weakly, gesturing with my hands. "Please?"

She continued to stare at me, unblinking.

"What's your name?" I tried again.

"Kate," she answered automatically. "You one of them?"

"One of who?"

She raised her eyebrows in disbelief. "One of them vampires."

Now it was my turn to raise my eyebrows. "Um … no?"

She narrowed her eyes. "You ain't got no bites on you. You must be a vampire." She glanced disdainfully at my chains. "A sick–in–the–head goddamn vampire. Is this some kinda joke? Tie yourself up so I can let you bite me?"

Jesus. Vampires? They didn't exist, at least not in real life. The closest I'd come to a vampire was lining up for Skarsgard's autograph at Comic-Con.

"Kate," I said slowly, "I don't know what happened to you, but I was taken." Images of the guys in the parking lot, the heavy fists, the bumpy car ride, flashed through my thoughts. Images of that smarmy motherfucker who called himself Ryan. I couldn't believe I'd thought he was attractive. The first chance I got, I was going to rip his balls off and stuff them down his throat. At least, that's what I wanted to do.

"I was walking to my car. I don't know where I am. *Please help me.*"

She appeared unsatisfied, but reached up with a reluctant look on her face and started tugging at the chains that pinned my wrists. Before I could blink, I was on my ass on the floor.

"Ow!" I cried as my tailbone screamed in protest.

"You're welcome," Kate said sarcastically. She retreated to her pile of rags and huddled into the corner of the room, hugging her knees to her chest.

"Thanks," I muttered. "How do we get out of here?"

Kate laughed, and it was such a horrible, dejected laugh it made me shiver.

I looked at her questioningly. "What?"

Her face immediately settled back to a blank. "Why don't you got no bites on you?"

"I don't know!" As I said it, I realized the sores I was seeing all over her arms and neck were a combination of bite marks and deep, straight gashes. "Holy shit," I gasped. "What did they do to you?"

Her steely composure fell momentarily, and was replaced by acute sorrow. "You must've just got here," she said softly. "I'm surprised they didn't bite you already. You look *fulla* healthy blood."

I shuddered.

"There ain't no gettin' outta here," she answered my question. "So quit tryin'. It makes them mad."

I tried not to freak the fuck out as I thought of my options.

"Are we in New Jersey?" I asked.

Kate shrugged. "I'm from Kansas."

Where the hell were we?

I thought about that for a while. In the middle of Kansas and New Jersey there was ... about a billion places. *Shit!*

"Hey Kate?" I asked.

"Mmm?"

"How long have you been here?"

She sighed. "Today makes ninety-three days."

I choked on the impossibility of that number. Ninety-three days. I would die if I had to stay there that long.

"I can't believe they haven't killed me yet." She continued softly. "Thirty is usually the limit before they kill you."

I swallowed back tears and screams. "What–why do you think they let you live this long?"

The age and weariness in her tiny voice was almost too much to bear. As were her words. "Apparently," she said with finality, "the young ones taste better. And he… likes me. He calls me his pretty baby." Her eyes filled with tears. "Sometimes, afterwards," she whispered, her chin trembling, "he lets me sleep next to him for a little while."

My chest tightened painfully as I read between her faltering words. She'd been cut. She'd been bitten. And beyond all uncertainty, she'd been raped. By Ryan? The one who'd brought me here?

My hatred for him dialled up to eleven as I imagined him pinning her down and taking everything from her.

"Thirty days?" I said quietly. "How do you know?

"Because," she replied, "you're the fourth roomie I've had."

I replayed her words in my head, over and over again. *Young girls taste the best. Thirty days.* They'd bitten her until she bled. Jesus, she was barely a teenager and they'd raped her, and she was grateful for being able to sleep in a real bed for a couple hours afterwards? What were they planning for me?

"You got pretty eyes," Kate said, looking at me oddly. I smiled sadly. My turquoise blue eyes were my best feature, according to my mother, and people always commented on them.

"Thanks," I said.

You're the fourth roomie I've had.

Where was I? How was I going to get out of here? I didn't once consider the possibility of not getting out. Only stupid girls got murdered. I would find a way to get out, a way to outsmart these guys … they just had to come and open the door first. Or the window.

If they were even coming back for us. I'd heard starvation was a nasty way to die.

The sun rose the next morning, through a tiny split in the planks of wood that boarded the solitary window. I had slept on and off, not from choice but from pure exhaustion. Still nobody came, and my stomach rumbled loudly in protest. Kate didn't talk or move much, and spent a lot of time completely passed out. I wondered if it was the blood loss or the lack of food. She really did look like crap.

I used the long, empty morning to explore every inch of our shared cell. I had since discovered the door with the handle opened into a bathroom. The faucets had been removed, but there was a nondescript toilet, a rusted bath, assorted bugs and mildew. There was nothing in the way of weapons. Even the heavy-looking lid of the toilet cistern was screwed on tight. Frustrated, I paced from one tiny room to another, racking my brain for an answer that just didn't seem to exist.

I spent the rest of the day watching a sliver of sunlight move across the floor and dreaming up ways of escape. But still, nobody came. As the sunlight waned and my captivity approached 24 hours, I really did wonder if I would live to see my family again.

My second night in the dungeon, someone finally made an appearance. Two of the guys that had taken me—one, whose name I knew was *Ryan*, and the other, the guy Ryan had called *Ford*, the one who wiped my vomit off Ryan's shoes. Ford immediately stormed in, grabbed Kate up off the floor, and dragged her out into the hallway. The door slammed shut and I was left alone with the one who had broken my nose. My heart was beating so loud, I could barely hear anything over the roaring of my blood.

"Stand up," Ryan said, tossing me a plastic bag full of stuff. I peered into the bag, seeing—and smelling—cold-cut sandwiches, potato chips and a plastic bottle of water. Mouth watering, I left the bag on the floor and stood on rubbery legs. I didn't want to obey him, but I sure as hell didn't want him to kick the crap out of me if I stayed sitting down.

"Where am I?" I asked. "What is this place?"

For someone that took young girls and bit them all over and raped them, he sure didn't look too excited by my presence.

"What do you want?" I kept throwing questions at him. "Who *are* you?"

"You're exactly where you're meant to be," he answered sharply. "If you keep asking questions, I'll kill you."

"You broke my nose," I said accusingly, narrowing my eyes. "I liked my nose."

He raised his eyebrows, coming closer, peering at my nose. "I could punch you again, straighten it up?"

I pulled my head back, just out of his reach. "Screw you."

"Do you need anything? More blankets?"

I stared incredulously at this teetering Jekyll and Hyde who wanted to punch me and get me a blankie in the same conversation. "I need to get home," I said slowly, as if I were speaking to a moron. "I have my geometry final in two days. My mom is going to kill me if I don't call her."

His tone was dry. "Somehow, I don't think that's going to be a problem anymore."

Fear shot up my spine again. "Look—" I started.

"No, *you* look," he said dangerously, putting a hot hand around my throat and squeezing. "I didn't come in here to make casual conversation."

I gasped and choked for air.

"Just do what you're told. Cooperate. It'll be over soon enough."

I nodded weakly, still choking. He released his grip and I fell to my knees, coughing as I held my throat with both hands. He waited, staring at me blankly, as I found the air to speak.

As I asked the question I wasn't sure I wanted answered.

"Are you going to kill me?"

He laughed, but his mask slipped a little, because he faltered. "Of course not."

"Well then you're pretty stupid," I shot. "Letting me see your face. Your license plate. Your *tattoo.*" I pointed to the black, luminous symbol etched onto his wrist that looked like a pair of eagle's wings.

"Are you trying to talk me into it?" he asked with a smirk.

I glared at him.

"I know what you're doing, sweetie. You're trying to provoke me."

"How am I doing so far?"

He grinned like the smug bastard he was. "Not bad."

There was a scream from the hallway. I looked past Ryan, to the open doorway, and then back to him, trying to figure out a way to *just get past him.*

"Did you bite her?" I demanded. "Did you..." Damn, I couldn't finish my question. I didn't want to think about *that.*

He raised a hand to the side of my head and fisted a handful of my hair; not hard enough to hurt me, but enough to send a message—if I moved an inch, he'd tear my scalp off. I felt my breathing quicken, a thin sheen of sweat gathering over my chest as I fought the urge to strike out at him. I liked my hair, and I didn't like my chances of being able to hurt him in any way. My heart sped up like a jackhammer, filling my ears with the roar of my own blood.

I whimpered as he brought his mouth down to my neck and grazed his teeth ever-so-slightly against my skin. Something about the way he held me compliant was so utterly overpowering, I couldn't begin to try and protest.

"Please," he said against my neck, "finish your question."

I couldn't.

"Did I," he nipped lightly at my neck, "bite her? Or did I fuck her?"

I breathed rapidly, my limbs like butter, melting into the wall, *into him.* The room spun. Would I pass out? No. I very much did not want to pass out in his cruel embrace.

"I don't kiss and tell," he drawled, pushing me away so my head smacked against the wall. My knees buckled and I leaned back, splaying my hands against cool limestone for support. He pointed to the bag of food. "Now be a good girl and eat *all* your dinner." Before

I could respond, he turned and left the room, locking the door behind him.

Holy Mother of God. I wasn't sure if he'd been about to kiss me or kill me, but I was glad he was gone, because I'd been *thisclose* to peeing my pants or bursting into tears.

I forgot about him for a moment. I was starving. I dived at the bag and grabbed the water first, dying to wet my tongue. I opened the bottle and took a small sip, swishing the water around my mouth. It tasted fine, but the seal had been broken, as if it had been refilled. I wondered if it had been drugged and vowed to drink as little as possible.

The sandwich was typical truck–stop fare, white slabs of bread jammed with low–grade salami, but after going so long without eating, it was the best thing I'd ever tasted. The bread, soggy from too much cheap mayonnaise, melted on my tongue as I bit, chewed and swallowed with unnatural speed.

I wondered how it could be that they would feed me if they were going to kill me, and then the door opened, and Kate was thrown back in to the room. I dropped my sandwich and rushed at the door as it was slammed in my face.

Kate was bleeding *everywhere*. I dropped to my knees, helping her to sit up as she trembled violently. Her eyes were blank and unseeing, as if she were staring at something that wasn't there, something I didn't even want to guess at. And her shirt was torn open. She had fresh bite marks on her chest, oozing blood, as if her filthy white bra had been yanked down just long enough for someone to sink their teeth into the flesh of her small breasts and suck.

"Kate!" I said. "Kate!"

She looked straight through me.

"What happened?" I asked, as I pulled her onto my lap.

And something weird happened. She smiled up at the ceiling, and I tried not to hyperventilate as my palms stuck to her bloodied skin.

"Why are you smiling?" I asked her. "Did you find a way out?"

"He promised me," she replied dreamily.

"Who promised you? What?"

"His name is Caleb. The Chosen One. He promised me."

I pressed my hands to her bleeding throat, trying to help her.

"What did he promise you, Kate? Did he say he'd let us go?"

She began to cry. "He said he'd let me die, soon."

I pulled my hands away and tried to see it from her point of view. How, if I'd been stuck in this room as long as she had, maybe I'd rather bleed to death, too.

THREE

Once upon a time, I was just a girl. My name was Mia.

I wasn't the first girl that was taken.

Sure, I had heard all about the girls who were missing, and even though they were only 'missing' I knew in my heart that those girls were dead. And my heart broke for them, for their families, just for a moment. Until the thought was replaced by something else, something different, because I couldn't bear to think about those poor dead girls any longer.

I felt sad for them. But more than that, I felt *glad* that they had been strangers—not someone I knew, and certainly not me. *Things like that didn't happen to girls like me.*

They always happened to someone else, and *that's* why I barely blinked as I made my way across an empty football field, through a snow–laden parking lot, to meet a fate I had arrogantly assumed was reserved for *other people.*

I was a stupid girl.

And I paid for my stupidity with my life.

FOUR

Time was agony. My stomach twisted in a knot for days on end. Kate wouldn't wake up anymore. She wasn't dead, but she may as well have been.

And me, I was so full of anxiety that I threw up every day until there was nothing left but clear bile that burned my throat, my tongue. I wasn't even hungry any more, not even after I had nothing left inside of me. I was just waiting.

I got a food delivery once a day, the highlight that broke up the long emptiness. Sometimes it was different people, but most of the time it was Ryan. I tried to talk to him. Bargain with him. I asked him how the weather was outside in the place I didn't know of. After a few days, two things occurred to me: Firstly, that I was becoming used to this ritual. That, even as afraid as I was, the pattern, the routine, brought me a sense of great relief. Mere days, and I was already a compliant slave, waiting against the wall for my daily visit.

And secondly, more disturbingly, that I enjoyed Ryan's visits, looked forward to them, even.

That realization was terrifying. The fact that this had become my 'normal'. The fact that I would rather be with a crazed kidnapper than be by myself.

It felt like I had been there for ever and ever.

I kept the water bottles lined up on the edge of the decaying bath. One morning, with sun streaming through the crack in the boards that covered the window, I counted them.

There were twelve. And if Kate had been right about me…

I had eighteen days left.

FIVE

Any day now, they're going to break me out. Somebody is going to come for me. Somebody is going to save me.

Nobody came for me. Nobody saved me.

I don't know why I thought they would.

SIX

DAY NUMBER THIRTEEN, MY LUCKY NUMBER, SPARKED A change in my routine. Along with my morning meal I got another plastic bag, this one packed with fresh clothes. A pair of jeans. A red t-shirt. Clean underwear. A bar of soap. A toothbrush. And a faucet fitting.

I stared at the bag in horror. Someone wanted me clean, dressed nicely, and with minty-fresh breath. It sounds so trivial now, but I *agonized* over whether or not to clean myself up and change my almost two–week–old outfit. Kate watched me, barely awake, but she didn't offer any explanation. And I didn't ask. I was tired of her. She never had anything good to say.

He appeared again in the doorway, dressed impeccably as always in a pair of dark blue jeans and a black shirt with rolled–up sleeves, the whites of his dark eyes the brightest thing in his ensemble. He still hadn't spoken more than five words to me since that first day when he'd pressed up against me and threatened to punch me in the face again, but equally, he hadn't hurt me. He hadn't done anything except toss a bag of food in my room once a day and slam the door shut again.

"Get up."

I slid up the wall I was leaning on, holding the faucet fitting in my fist behind my back. I was plotting how I was going to surprise him by smashing it into his face when he gave me a look that said, *Don't even try.*

"Give me that." He lunged forward faster than I could follow, snatched at my arm, and pried the faucet fitting from my cold fingers. I stared back at him like a sullen child. *Motherfucker.*

He flicked his gaze up and down my body, clearly unhappy. "You didn't clean yourself up. Where are your shoes?"

"You want me to look pretty for you? *Please.*"

He rolled his eyes and took my arm, dragging me out of the room I hadn't left in two weeks, into a nondescript beige and concrete hallway that seemed to stretch out forever.

"Where are we going?" I asked, my voice higher than it should have been.

"To see the boss," he answered. I realized it was one of the first questions he'd answered straight, without a double meaning.

"Who?" I asked. "Caleb?"

He stopped then, tugged my arm so we were facing each other. His dark blue eyes were surrounded by tiny flecks of gold that seemed to burn into my flesh.

We were alone in a sea of closed doors that all appeared identical. I wondered how many other girls were waiting behind those doors, like me.

"If you keep quiet, it won't be as bad," he said in a voice barely above a whisper. "Don't try your smart-ass tactics on him. He will hurt you very badly, do you understand?"

I looked up at him in utter confusion. "What do you care?" I asked. "You're the one who took me. You don't even *know* me. So tell me, tough guy—what do you care?"

The mask went back on. "I don't," he said fiercely. "I'm the lucky guy who'll have to clean your blood off the floor, that's all."

"Yeah, well," I responded lamely, "If you're really a vampire, I guess you'd like that kind of thing."

He laughed and shook his head. "You're really something, you know?"

I scowled at him as we continued to walk.

At the end of the hallway there was a door that was different to all the rest. This one opened easily with a regular doorknob, and wasn't locked behind us. I made a mental note of that.

"Don't bother," he said. "You're not getting out of here."

"What are you, a goddamn mind reader?" I wasn't sure if I wanted to know the answer.

"Let's just say I know how teenage girls think."

"That's not disturbing at all." I deadpanned.

We stepped into the room; a large, cavernous cellar lined with long, skinny racks full of wine bottles. The red wine bottles looked like they could have been full of blood. I didn't want to think about that, though. We walked through the wine stacks when I got an idea. I sure as fuck didn't want to meet this Caleb dude and get murdered, so it was time to do something drastic.

"Ow!" I groaned, doubling over, using my free hand to steady myself on a waist-high rack of bottles.

"What's wrong?" Impatience and concern mixed into one. Ryan released my other hand and I pressed it to my stomach, my hand cold, almost missing the heat in his touch. *Almost.*

"It hurts," I gasped, wincing and gesturing to my midsection. "Oh, god!"

My fingers closed around the neck of a wine bottle covered in dust. In one snap of my wrist, I brought the bottle up in a wide arc, where it connected with Ryan's temple.

Only it didn't. It stopped just shy of his face, an iron claw latching onto my wrist. "Put it back," he said through gritted teeth, gesturing to the rack with an angry nod. I loosened my grip and the bottle slipped from my fingers, the floor rushing up to smash it to pieces.

And he caught it, faster than my eyes could comprehend. The bastard *caught it in midair.*

"Didn't your mother ever tell you about the boy who cried wolf?" His eyes drilled into mine.

"Didn't your mother ever tell you she wished she'd aborted you?" I shot back at him.

He just smiled that cold, unaffected smile. "You know, I like you. I might just keep you after Caleb's finished." For someone who said they liked me, he sure didn't seem to be liking this. Whatever this was. His jaw strained under the pressure of his clenched teeth, and I wondered how much further I'd need to push him before he snapped… or just snapped my neck.

"I hate you," I spat. "I'll kill you, I swear to God."

"Shut. Up."

Ryan placed the undamaged bottle back in its spot and grabbed both of my wrists from behind, frogmarching me forward like a handcuffed inmate.

The air turned colder, if that was even possible. I shivered in my dirty jeans and flimsy camisole. It was ridiculous—I didn't want to see what was on the other side of these shelves. I would have gladly held on to Ryan's leg and begged him to take me back to my room and lock me in there, if I thought he'd listen With each bare foot I placed in front of the other, the feeling of disquiet that banded around my chest got louder and tighter, until I could barely breathe. A steady thrumming noise invaded my head, getting louder and more intense the further I got into the room, and I frowned.

We stepped out of the rows of shelves, not to the gruesome sight I had expected, but into a space with an overstuffed black leather couch and two matching recliners, a coffee table on a Turkish rug in the middle of it all. It looked like a living room, not a torture chamber. Only, on the coffee table there was a large mason jar, lid screwed on tight, with what appeared to be a human heart sitting inside.

I swallowed back my truck-stop sandwich and tried not to think about it.

There was a huge bay window at the far end of the room that let light pour into the space. I hadn't seen the sun in so many days, I practically rushed forward out of the shadows.

And facing that bay window, looking away from us, was the man I would soon know as Caleb.

The first vampire that had ever been created.

His name, he later told me, meant 'The Chosen One', because a demon had chosen *him* alone to carry the vampire virus into humanity.

I held my breath in terror as he turned from the window, looked into my eyes, and smiled. In every other respect he looked like a normal man. But his dark eyes—a deep, chestnut brown ringed with flecks of orange, just like the faint gold flecks around Ryan's eyes, only much brighter—the eyes were what set him apart. They were beautiful and terrifying all at once. He blinked, and those same luminous eyes turned pure black, like his pupils had swallowed all of the light in the world.

When they turned solid black, I gasped. I tried to back up, but all I did was press up against Ryan's chest. I debated turning to run, but I knew I wouldn't make it an inch before they pounced on me.

I'd only ever felt that way once in my life. Hiking in the woods, I'd seen a mountain lion. The casual way it sized me up, the urge inside me to flee, the way I had to force myself to stand my ground—because you couldn't let yourself flee and trigger the lion's instinct to chase you down and devour you—and soon enough, the lion lost interest in me altogether.

I didn't hike alone again after that.

Standing between Ryan and Caleb, the man who had snatched

me in the night and the man who had sent him, it wasn't any easier to quash that flee instinct. The voice inside me screamed. She wanted to run. She wanted to fight. Being surrounded by lions, though—that quelled the urge. Because where would I go? Straight into their waiting embrace.

I stood my ground. It killed me inside to resist the impulse to flee.

"Mia" he said pleasantly, allowing his true age to seep into the echo of his words. "I'm Caleb. It's so nice to finally meet you."

The pounding. It reverberated inside my skull, reaching fever pitch, and I felt sweat starting to collect at my temples. *What the hell was that noise?*

Caleb stepped forward and held out a hand in greeting. Those eyes, *Jesus*, they were so black and so big, you could lose a lifetime inside of them and not even notice. And it wasn't just the eyes that were terrifying. I had noticed a movement out of the corner of my eye and turned instinctively towards it, only for my eyes to land upon the heart in the jar.

It was moving. *It was beating.* It was the pounding noise that was getting louder with each passing minute.

I put a hand to my mouth and stifled a scream.

Ryan dug a finger into my back and I shot my hand out instinctively, where Caleb grasped it much too gently—with affection, even. His hand was hot, much hotter than mine or even Ryan's. It was large and smooth and reminded me of my father's hands. I wondered if his hands had been the ones to rip that beating heart from the chest of whomever it belonged to.

It was beating. How was it beating? *How was it fucking beating?*

The black eyes. The hot hands. The blood. The heart that moved of it's own accord. Suddenly vampires didn't seem like something make-believe. Vampires sounded very, very much like what was going on right now.

Caleb tilted his head to the side, taking in my face, my body, and seemed to like what he saw. A slow grin spread across his tanned face, showing regular, straight teeth. His canines looked pretty sharp, but certainly nothing like what I had seen in horror movies. And yet, I had never been so terrified in my entire life. The eyes. I wanted him to go back to his regular eyes. You know, the ones that had whites and a pupil, instead of a solid film of black.

"Sit."

Ryan tugged me to the side, pressing me into one of the overstuffed single recliners. Thank God for small mercies—I didn't want anyone sitting next to me. Caleb perched on the coffee table directly in front of me. *Man, have you ever heard of personal space?*

"Your eyes," I said involuntarily. I was about to lose my shit and start screaming until somebody knocked me out.

He smiled, blinked, and just like that his eyes went back to normal. I sagged a little, relieved.

"You can go now," he addressed Ryan, without tearing his gaze from me.

My heart sank as I heard Ryan's footsteps fade into the distance, then the thud of the door. He might be an asshole, but somehow, I had a feeling he wasn't nearly as bad as Caleb.

I studied Caleb's face with a mixture of revulsion and wonder. He appeared to be in his late thirties, with smooth, tanned skin that stretched over attractively angular features and a wide, arrogant mouth that seemed to delight at my terror. A face that was old in experience, but still retained the patina of youth. All topped off with a mop of dark brown curls that added an ironic, boyish charm to his terrifying demeanour.

"Where are we?" I asked when I could bear the silence no longer.

"We are in my house."

"Where is your house?"

He gestured to the open window. "Take a look for yourself."

I took the chance to put distance between us, edging out from his gaze and tentatively stepping towards the window.

It was breathtaking—like someone had painted a picture of paradise and stuck it to the window frame. We were at least two floors above the ground, overlooking lush, green forest. In the background, three snow-capped mountains rose from the earth. Between the forest and the building I stood in, a massive, cerulean blue lake stretched out further than my eyes could follow.

My breath caught in my throat as a voice sounded out directly behind me.

"It's a beautiful place."

I spun around to find Caleb had soundlessly moved across the polished concrete floor, and now stood inches from me. I cowered, pressing my back against the thick glass that separated me from my freedom.

Now, I have to add that up until this point, I had never really believed in anything supernatural. I didn't believe in ghosts or magic, and I definitely didn't believe in vampires. My closest association to the fanged creatures was an unhealthy obsession with watching *The Vampire Diaries* as a fifteen-year-old.

"Vampires aren't real," I blurted out.

He didn't say a word, just stared into my soul with those endless black eyes, and that was the moment that I realized all of the scary creatures under the bed really did exist. This guy was not just a regular human psychopath, as I had previously guessed. He really was *a vampire.*

"Shit," I muttered. He laughed.

"How long will you keep me?" I asked suddenly.

He didn't have to think about it. "Forever."

I believed him.

SEVEN

THE NEXT MORNING I CAVED IN. I WAS DIRTY. THERE WAS DRIED blood on my shirt. And I was pretty sure I was starting to smell *really bad.*

I snatched the faucet handle from Ryan's outstretched palm and stalked into the rotting bathroom, slamming the door behind me. The faucet handle was difficult to screw on over the thick rust that had built up, but I managed. Pretty soon drabs of brown, dirty water glugged out of the showerhead into the filthy tub. I took off my two-week-old shirt and turned it inside out, using it to loosen some of the caked dirt and dust from the porcelain. When I had cleared a patch big enough to accommodate my feet, I balled the disgusting shirt up and threw it into the corner of the room.

The water was hot and luxurious and slid down my body like liquid velvet. There was no shampoo, so I used the bar of soap to wash my body, then lathered suds into my stiff, bloodied hair. I was exhausted. I had been plagued with a killer headache since I woke up from my uncomfortable sleep on the floor, and I'd had nightmares about the beating heart in the jar all night long.

I thought about home, just like I had been every day and night as I paced my own personal hell. I thought about Jared, about Evie. I even missed my mom. I would have done anything to get back to them. I thought back to every animal attack I'd ever heard of, every abduction, every person who'd given me the creeps. I was starting to realize that the world I had been a lifelong member of didn't actually exist.

Then cold water cut in, freezing my nerves and making me cry out. "Jesus!"

I shut the water off as quickly as I could and dried myself with the towel I'd so generously been given, then slipped into clean clothes. The black t–shirt and jeans were mine, probably taken directly from my car after I'd been knocked out. I wrapped the towel around my wet hair, feeling calmer and a little bit more like myself than I had in days.

I grabbed my silver ballet flats, the ones covered in snow and mud that I had discarded the night I awoke in vampire hell, and tried my best to clean them up with damp toilet paper. It was a small comfort having shoes on my feet again. The morning felt almost … normal.

I was snapped out of my somewhat serene state by a loud crash in the adjoining room.

I could not have imagined the hell that awaited me on the other side of the door.

I yanked the bathroom door open, rushing into the room Kate and I shared. Kate was crumpled in the corner—nothing new there—but she wasn't alone. *Caleb* was there, clutching her narrow shoulders, dragging her back up to her feet.

"Let her go!" I yelled, pummelling his back with punches that did absolutely nothing. Someone grabbed me from behind and bent my arm back until it was ready to snap like kindling. "Ahh!" I screamed as my shoulder joint crunched out of its socket.

"Shut up," someone breathed into my ear. *Ryan.* I should have known.

I wriggled out of his grip and leaned against the wall, hugging my useless limb to my chest. I snuck a glance at my paralyzed arm. It was too long to belong to me, hanging by stretched tendons. I had the sudden urge to throw up again. And it hurt like a bastard. Waves of pain slammed into me.

I stared on in pain and despair as Caleb put his mouth to Kate's ear. He whispered things too low for me to hear, but his black gaze and twisted grin were clearly directed at me. I looked away, trying not to feel the terror that was encircling me like a bunch of snakes tightening around my useless limbs, trying not to fall into those bottomless eyes that promised an eternity of torment.

Kate's child-like screams tore at my heart until it threatened to break in two. I started to hyperventilate.

"No, no, no!" she protested. "You promised you wouldn't!"

Promised he wouldn't *what*? Kill her? But hadn't she wanted to die?

"Quiet!" he hissed forcefully, and she stopped whimpering all at once.

The vampire smiled. "That's a good girl," he said. He pressed his thumbnail into the creamy flesh at her collarbone. Kate's eyes went wide in horror as her skin broke apart under the pressure, ruby-red blood rising up from the puncture. I watched helplessly as she tried to push him away.

I wanted to yell, "Stop!" But it was useless. I held my breath, squeezing my eyes shut, my last vision a horrific tableau of the vampire sucking greedily at the girl's shoulder. I held my good hand to my ear and turned my face to the wall, but I couldn't block out the noise entirely—the sucking, slurping noise of warm tomato soup being hungrily drawn through a straw. Poor Kate was the straw, and her blood was the soup.

I resisted the urge to curl up in a ball, to try and run away, to scream. I was just there, frozen and pathetic and unable to do a damned thing to help.

Eventually, the noise ceased. I opened my eyes to see Kate dead, drained of blood, and Caleb rising from her lifeless form. He wiped his mouth and turned to me, smirking. A low wail grew louder and louder and it took me a minute to realize that it was coming from me, that I was screaming. I abruptly shut my mouth, and the noise stopped.

I was shaking so violently, my knees threatened to buckle underneath me. Anger *blossomed* inside my chest. Nobody had the right to take someone's blood—someone's life—like this.

"Don't you dare!" I cried as he came closer. "I'll scream. I'll hurt you." As if I could.

He stopped, a peculiar look on his face. He smiled, blood still smeared on his teeth.

"What did you say to her?" I demanded.

"I said –" he spoke in a voice that was older than time, six little words that made tears spring to my eyes "—do you want to die today?"

But it was a lie, he hadn't asked her that. He was asking me, did I want to die today?

A burning hand rested heavily on my throat, so hot I wondered if it would melt my skin. He was clearly waiting for an answer from me.

I shook my head NO. The burning hand squeezed harder, the black eyes grew wider, imploring a response. "I didn't hear you."

"NO!"

He loosened his fingers and let his arm drop slowly from my throat.

"Don't worry," he said cruelly. "You will soon enough." He looked down at Kate's lifeless body with those demon-black eyes. "She did."

I stumbled and sank to the floor next to Kate, nursing my arm in my lap. There was blood *everywhere*, so much more than one person could ever forget. I held my hand in front of my face, the one I could still use. I couldn't stop shaking, and I didn't think I ever would.

I said nothing as Ryan followed the older vampire out of the room. The door slammed, and I heard bolts sliding shut on the other side of the wall.

And then, it was just me and the dead girl on the floor.

I cried until salty tears burned my cheeks, and watched that door, and I was hurting so intensely I couldn't even muster up some sympathetic thoughts for the dead girl who lay less than three feet from me.

I wanted so badly to leave my body right then. I wanted to fly away home, to be with Evie and Jared and my mom. I'd even hug my idiot stepfather. But I couldn't leave. I could never leave. So I did the next best thing. I closed my eyes and remembered a time before I was taken, a time before everything went to Hell.

EIGHT

I LIVED PRACTICALLY MY WHOLE LIFE WITH THE BOY I WOULD fall in love with right under my nose, both of us blissfully unaware of what magic—and horror—would occur as a result of our union. When we were in kindergarten together, we fought like hell over whose turn it was to take the class hamster home over the summer. When we were fifteen he and his idiot friends crashed Evie's birthday party, stole all of our carefully stashed beer and smashed her front window. And in sophomore year, I took great delight in defacing his yearbook photo in the library's only copy.

Was it love, even then? I'm not so sure. But I do know that the summer before senior year, Evie and I took jobs at a local kids' Summer Camp to earn some cash. We were saving for the amazing condo we were going to rent together when we both got accepted into the same college—me into photography, Evie into print journalism. After college, Evie was going to move to Paris and write for Vogue, and I was going to travel the world, take a whole bunch of photos, become the next famous photographer, and then live in a warehouse loft conversion in New York. Plus, we were both going to use our athletic talents to our advantage, using track and swimming scholarships to help us make the big time. Jared was poised for great things, too; he was going to study medicine and become a surgeon. His parents weren't rich so he was working as a lifeguard at the local summer camp, trying to earn a few bucks to bankroll his medical degree.

The three of us had always ended up at the same school—first grade school, then junior high, and finally Blair Academy. But the academy was a big place, and after sophomore year we never really hung out in the same circles as Jared. Jared studied, swam and played football, I ran track and went to too many parties, and Evie studied too much, partied too much, was on the swim team and still managed to top every class she was in.

So, back to our cushy little summer jobs. Evie and I were both on the swim staff for the summer. We had to teach swim classes in the mornings, supervise the kids at lunch, and then do lifeguard duty in the afternoons. On the Saturday after our classes had finished for the year, Evie and I drove to the camp to take our lifeguard and swim instructor tests and get our first aid cards updated.

I sat in the passenger seat while Evie drove my car, a pretty common scenario for us. Her ancient VW was about to fall apart and I swear the only thing keeping it together was sticky brown rust, while I was still driving the car my dad had bought for me a month before he died. A black Honda Element that nobody would ever be able to convince me to sell.

Evie was at the wheel while I frantically read through the first aid guide in case we got tested. "Do you remember any of this?" I looked up in time to see a familiar pink donut reaching into the sky. "Stop, stop!"

She slammed the brakes on, just making the turn into the Dunkin' Donuts across from Jefferson Lake. She parked and we got out, the cool morning air forming goose bumps on my bare legs.

I tugged at my frayed denim shorts, trying to make them cover as much skin as possible. I detested the cold, even when it was only moderately cool on a summer's day that would probably reach the nineties before sundown.

We ordered flavored coffees—French vanilla for me, caramel for Evie—and sat in a plastic pink booth while we waited.

"I hope there are at least some hot guys there," I remarked. My last relationship had ended three months before, and apart from a few mediocre make-out sessions at parties, I was starting to get a little bored. It was time to move on and find a new boy. Our coffees were called and we grabbed them, wandering across the road to the lake.

Since Jefferson Lake was fifty acres across, all the smaller neighboring camps sent their new swim staff to testing day at our larger camp. All up there were probably a hundred or so new swim staff milling around, dressed in bathing suits, goggles perched on foreheads, and the smell of sunscreen and coffee draped across the chilly morning. Evie and I dropped our stuff at the bleachers and wandered over to the lake in just our bathing suits, towels wrapped around our waists and coffee cups warming our palms.

A girl dressed in a lifeguard uniform with SUPERVISOR emblazoned on the breast pocket was calling out names in alphabetical order.

"Cheryl Anderson."

"Miles Barker."

"Mia Blake."

I handed my coffee and towel to Evie, whose last name—Montgomery—meant that she wouldn't be called for a while. I was familiar with the drill from the year before—eight people called up at a time to swim their twenty laps before diving for the weighted buoy at the bottom of the lake.

Taking my place at the third lane, I turned to my right to see the other five swimmers in my round wander up to their lanes. The guy next to me was facing the other way, but I was sure I wanted to do a lot more looking at him regardless of what his face looked like. His body was magnificent—tanned and firm in *all* the right places.

I absent-mindedly dipped my right foot into the water and squealed. "THAT'S FU—THAT'S FREEZING!" I yelped, yanking my leg away. "How are we supposed to swim in there?"

The supervisor didn't look impressed. "You'll be saving children from drowning in there come Monday. You'll get used to it."

I fought the urge to roll my eyes. I wanted to tell *her* to jump in the water, but I bit my tongue and focused on the task at hand. Pretty soon we were being told to stay next to the water and wait until time was called. Somebody had thought to cordon off eight lanes with rope, which was handy. I sat down at the edge and waited. I looked to my right again and hot guy in lane four flashed me a dazzling smile that made me forget all about swimming tests and cold water. Holy mother of all things sexy, he was *fine*. The body sure did match the face, with big eyes the colour of bamboo, a mess of sandy blond hair, and dimples on both cheeks. Oh, and a V that started at his torso and disappeared into a pair of swimming shorts that left little to the imagination. I realized my eyes were lingering a little too long on his lower half and slid my gaze back up to his face. Recognition sparked inside the cotton-wool of my early-morning brain. *I know him!*

I raised my eyebrows, confused. "Jared?"

He smiled again, looking extremely devilish. It had been at least two years since I had had an actual conversation with him, and it was probably about something really immature like tee-peeing the teachers' cars.

"Mia. What camp are you working?" Oh, boy. His voice had gotten deeper. *Damn.*

"J-Jefferson day camp" I stuttered. "You?"

Before he could answer, the whistle blew and seven bodies dove into the lake.

"Crap," I muttered, standing up and executing one of the worst dives ever. I ended up in a half-dive, half-belly flop, and I could just imagine the peals of laughter above me in the bleachers. As I hit the water, the icy temperature knocked my breath from my lungs and time stood still while I floated, motionless, and tried to remember how to swim.

As my head broke the surface, I gasped in a breath and saw that most of the other swimmers were at least half a lap ahead of me already. I groaned inwardly and started swimming, mentally counting each lap in my head. Front crawl seemed to be the best way for me to avoid freezing to death and also offered the fastest path, meaning I could finish and get back to my French Vanilla Latte as soon as possible.

Pretty soon I stopped worrying about the cold, pushed on, and wondered when it had been that Jared Cohen had started looking less like an underdeveloped twelve-year-old and more like Ryan Kwanten. It was enough to make my cheeks burn, which was great, since the rest of me was dragging along like a brick of ice.

I got to the last few laps when a cramp started to squeeze at my lower left calf muscle. It was pretty minor at first. *Sixteen laps down, four to go.* Then, the cramp spread to my foot and I wanted to squeal. I did those last few laps messily, with terrible technique, and started to moan as I hoisted myself out of the pool and onto the slightly warmer pine decking. I ripped my goggles off and threw them to the side, frantically massaging my frozen muscles with my fingers.

"Cramp?"

I looked up from my spot on the ground to see Jared standing above me, his tanned chest covered in hundreds of drops of water that glistened in the morning sun.

I bit my lip and forced myself to look at his face. "Yeah," I groaned. *Thanks for the distraction, though.*

"Here," he said, kneeling down beside me. He pushed my hands away and started massaging my clenched calf muscle with big, smooth fingers. I bit back an involuntary sigh and felt my cheeks redden at the thought of where else I'd like those fingers. Of course, I didn't tell him to stop. I snuck a glance at Evie, who was oblivious to the world and listening to her iPod in the bleachers. I kind of wished she would bring my coffee down to the pool deck. Then again, I kind of hoped she wouldn't interrupt this highly-arousing massage I was getting in the middle of about two hundred of my fellow employees.

"You're not cold," I remarked as Jared's warm fingers worked their magic. "What'd you do, down a quart of scotch before you went in?" I imagined kissing him, finding the taste of whisky on his lips. I'm not going to lie—I didn't even try to distract myself. I was experiencing the female equivalent of a raging hard-on over this guy.

Jared laughed, even though I thought my attempt at a joke was pretty pathetic and definitely not up to my usual smart–ass standards.

And his smile was amazing.

And I fell just a little bit in love with the kid who had stuck craft glue in my hair in first grade.

"I'm used to it," he said. "Swim team and all. Evie and I swim outdoors almost every morning during swim season."

"Oh, I didn't know that," I replied. *From now on,* I thought, *I'm going to be coffee–bitch for the swim team every morning. And I'll sit in the nice warm bleachers and sip my latte while I watch those abs of steel and that cute –*

"All better?" he asked.

"Almost," I lied. It didn't hurt anymore. But he didn't know that, did he?

He smiled again and kept his hands on my perfectly uncramped leg. "You know, Daniel Mansell's having a party tonight. You should come."

"Yeah, maybe." I shrugged casually. "I'll see what Evie's doing."

He stood and offered me his hand. "He's got a pool. A heated one, don't worry."

He flashed those incredible teeth at me once more and wandered off to do his buoy dive on the other side of the pool.

I could barely wait until Evie had finished her laps and we were back at the bleachers to ask her about her swim team partner.

"Why didn't you tell me hair-puller had turned into such a hottie?"

She smiled knowingly. "I told you to come along to swim practice, but you didn't listen."

"We're going to that party tonight," I said, grinning from ear to ear. I made a mental note to myself to raid my mother's alcohol stash and find some whisky so I could take full advantage of one Jared Cohen.

Where did you meet your first love? I met mine when I was five years old, on the playground, when he yanked on my hair. And when I was seventeen, I fell in love with him at a party on the first night of summer, and wondered why the universe had kept us apart for all those years.

The first time I kissed Jared Cohen, it was like little fireflies had landed all over my body, and butterflies swam in my belly. That night we didn't do anything more than talk and land soft, gentle kisses on each other, and it was the most perfect night of my simple little life. If I had known what lay ahead, what we would become, what would happen to the world because of the virus that poisoned our love, would I still have let myself fall in love with him?

I could say no, but we would both know that it was a lie.

NINE

"HEY."

I woke up from a heavy sleep, startled by the voice in the room.

"Oh," I said, struggling to sit up as fresh pain shot up my dislocated arm. "It's you. Here to break the other one?"

Ryan smiled coldly. "I'm hungry. Thought I'd hit you up for a pint."

Well, I didn't know what to say to *that.*

He snickered. "Your face!" He slapped his thigh and laughed some more while I glared at him. "Well, be afraid. Someone is going to be eating you, little girl. But not me."

"Eat shit, asshole," I said quietly. "That's what you should be eating."

I put on my best blank face and stared at the wall opposite me. I was tired of games, and my shoulder was hurting too much for me to maintain much of a conversation anyway.

"Here." He crouched down in front of me and pointed at my

arm. "I've come to fix that."

I didn't move.

"Come on," he said, and gestured for me to scoot forward. I did, reluctantly, and braced myself for a lot of pain as my bones were seconds away from more grating on each other. Ryan put one hand on the front of my shoulder, and the other on my back. I held my breath and squeezed my eyes shut.

"Okay, on the count of three. Ready?"

I nodded mutely.

"One –" A white-hot poker stabbed into my shoulder as he reset it.

"*JESUS!*" I screamed. I looked at him, shaking my head. "What happened to three?!"

"It's like a Band-Aid. You shouldn't hesitate."

I had been dreaming about Jared before he came in, but before that I'd been wondering something.

"Can I ask you a question?" I enquired through gritted teeth.

Ryan shrugged, offering me a hand up. "If I say no, will you ask me anyway?"

I accepted his hand, and he hauled me up to my shaky feet. I stared at his flat brown eyes and his ridiculous smirk and shuddered inwardly.

"She wanted to die," I said, pointing at the body in the corner that had finally stopped bleeding. "But she kept saying no, no, no. What did he really say to her to scare her before he killed her? Did he do something else to her? Why today?"

Ryan raised his eyebrows petulantly. "You just asked three questions. Do you want to know why he killed her, why today was a good day to kill her, or what else we did to her?"

"We?"

"Well, I do have to eat," he replied, grinning wickedly.

"You're disgusting" I said, rolling my eyes. "She was a kid, for God's sake."

"I've had younger."

"You're a fucking pervert, you know that?"

He furrowed his brows, as if he was not only genuinely hurt by my remark, but utterly confused by it. "It's nothing sexual," he replied defensively. "I have to feed, or I die. Do you think about Daisy the cow before you chow down on a piece of filet mignon?"

"Do I LOOK like Daisy the cow to you?!" I shot back, my voice steadily rising.

"No," he replied flicking his gaze from my face down to my chest and back again. "With you, it would most certainly be sexual."

Well. I didn't know what to say to that. I just shook my head incredulously and felt my cheeks burn with equal parts anger and embarrassment.

"Somebody raped her, asshole," I said softly. "It's not a joke. She is—was—a person. Big difference."

Ryan pressed his lips together tightly. "Nobody is getting raped."

"Why would I believe anything you say!?" I demanded, pushing him away furiously. "Go fuck yourself!"

"Forget about that," he hissed, grabbing my wrist. "Caleb's going to call for you in the next few hours. I want you to be prepared so … well, so *that* doesn't happen to you." We both continued to stare at the dead girl who had ceased to frighten me, and who was now just a part of the furniture… or lack thereof.

"Why?" I asked. "You're such an asshole to me, I think you'd like it if I died."

"I'm serious," he snapped, grabbing my shoulders and shaking me for good measure.

"My arm!" I shrieked.

"Sorry." He let go of me and appeared to try and calm himself. "Listen, please. Don't upset him, or he *will* kill you. There is another way. If you're good, and you do what he says, then he'll spare you and you can be free one day."

I narrowed my eyes. "What's the catch?"

He glanced at Kate's body, then at me. "Does it matter?"

"Yes!" I insisted.

"Just do what I told you," he said. "Unless you want to end up dead like *this*." He bent down and picked Kate up, throwing her over his shoulder like she was a sack of potatoes.

I narrowed my eyes at him as he left the room. *Yeah, fucking right*, I thought bitterly. *Either way, I'm not walking out of here.*

For as long as I can remember, the sight of blood and the thought of any kind of unnecessary pain has grossed me out. So as soon as I was frogmarched back into Caleb's den/office/torture chamber, I wanted to throw up. The leather couches and coffee table had been pushed into the corner of the room, and in front of the huge bay window was a metal hospital gurney that I was half pushed, half thrown onto by Ryan. There were leather straps for my wrists and ankles and I realized I was about to be strapped down. Panicking, I drew my fist back and hit Ryan as hard as I could in the jaw. I was surprised when his head snapped back from the force of my blow. Clearly, I was getting better at my right hook.

Two other guys who'd followed us into the room sprang into action, holding my arms as I kicked and screamed, jerking around like a slippery eel. I felt a sharp prick in my forearm and groaned as my head spun and my limbs went heavy and loose.

"You guys never play fair," I mumbled, slumping back on the cold metal, trying to remember how to move my mouth to form words. Whatever they'd just given me hadn't affected my thinking at all, but physically I felt like I weighed a hundred tons. Even moving my fingers was so much effort, it hurt.

Things were happening very efficiently around me. I struggled in vain as one of them wrapped a makeshift tourniquet—a gray scarf—around my right arm and started tapping for a vein.

"What are you doing?" I asked the room. "*What* are you *doing to me*?!"

Nobody answered. I cried out as Ford stuck me in the arm with an IV line, missed the vein, and did it again. *Fucking butcher,* I thought angrily. My veins were bright blue and purple and right on the surface of my goddamn arms—a nurse's dream, I'd been told before. This guy was a hack.

My heart must have been hammering along at a million miles an hour. As soon as Ford got the needle in my arm, bright red blood sprayed out of the plastic tubing on the end, splattering me, him and the floor. I stared at the red stuff, horrified. Was it like dangling a piece of meat in front of a hungry dog? Or four hungry dogs, in my case? I thought about Daisy the cow and shuddered.

I looked to Ryan for—what? Familiarity? I knew I wasn't going to get any help from him, but somehow his presence made things less scary. Which was completely fucking insane thinking on my part. The guy had almost killed me, like, five times now.

But he was gone, and in his place was Caleb with those freaky eyes again. I felt my eyes grow wide as he came closer. I tore my gaze from him and turned my attention back to my blood, and how it was spraying everywhere.

"You're being wasteful!" Caleb's voice boomed.

Ford hurriedly released the scarf that was wrapped around my bicep, and my blood stopped spraying across the room. *Thank god for small miracles.*

The other guy—whose name I hadn't caught yet—wheeled a stainless steel IV stand over to my butchered arm and connected a length of clear plastic tubing to the straw that jutted out of the inside of my elbow. The line began to fill instantly, my blood curling its way like a callisthenic ribbon to its new home. I followed its path with desperate eyes and gagged when I saw its final destination. Sitting atop an old wine barrel was a line of wine bottles, each sculpted from clear glass and labeled only with my name and the letters RC.

RC? Ryan's initials, maybe?

I didn't really care about the writing, only that the first bottle (which looked as if it could hold nearly a liter) was almost full already. When it reached the top, the unnamed guy pinched the plastic tubing, stopping the flow of my blood.

My head spun. I watched in horror as Caleb stepped forward with an enormous red wine goblet in one hand. With the other hand he picked up the bottle and poured *my blood* into his glass, swirling it around the edges and watching it stick to the sides.

"Look at that!" he marvelled, drinking half the glass down in one, open-throated gulp. "The French call them tears." He motioned to the oily streaks of blood that clung to the inside of the glass, and I guessed that he was talking in wine terms.

A wave of dizziness hit me, and I looked back to the wine bottles to see a second one was being filled with my blood. Two bottles would equal one-and-a-half-liters—any more than that and I suspected I might die. My mouth went dry and I started to shake. I was going into shock.

"Too much," I mouthed, staring at the blood-filled tube with a mixture of revulsion and wonder. "You're taking too much."

Caleb laughed, his enormous wine glass freshly refilled. I sucked in as much air as I could, hyperventilating, and probably only bleeding faster because of it. *How convenient for him.*

Unexpectedly, the flow of blood stopped, just as quickly as it had started. I felt rough hands yank the tubing from my arm and hold something soft against my skin, staunching the bleeding. My head lolled forwards so that my chin hit my chest, and real tears dripped down my face.

"Delicious," Caleb pronounced, and I couldn't help but look. He was drinking more blood, from the enormous wine goblet. He poured it down his throat without pausing, his Adam's apple bobbing with each gulp, and in a matter of seconds the glass was empty. He took two incredibly quick strides and erased the space between us, coming so close that I could smell the coppery scent of my blood in his mouth.

I looked past him, focusing on the view outside. How badly I wanted to fly away, over those lush trees and clear lake, to anywhere. Home. That's where I wanted to be. I thought of my dorm room, and my bedroom, and cruising in my car with Jared and Evie, and imagined a different morning where I could kill every vampire who shared that room with me.

"Beautiful, isn't it?" Metallic words touched my face, made their way into my nasal cavity. I gagged again and leant over the side of the trolley, vomiting on the polished ground. I choked and retched as bile filled my throat and my nostrils.

My vomit didn't seem to faze Caleb in the slightest. A glass of water materialized in his hand, as if by magic, and he offered it to me.

"I'm kind of fucking tied up here!" I snapped. "Not to mention drugged and bleeding."

He looked amused, a smirk forming at the corners of his mouth. He undid the leather restraint on my non–tapped arm silently and quickly, then placed the glass of water in my shaking hand. I took a sip, swishing the water around in my gross–tasting mouth.

"I need to go to the bathroom," I announced.

"Can you walk?"

I nodded, taking little sips of the water. I had no idea if I could walk, but I could at least try. Whatever they'd injected me with earlier had worn off incredibly fast, and my dizziness was starting to dissipate a little. I waited with excruciating patience as he undid my other wrist restraint and then started on my ankle straps. The second my ankles were both free, I wriggled backwards on the cold bed and rolled off the side, landing on my toes. I took up a squatting position on the concrete floor, and smashed the water glass as hard as I could against the ground. It shattered, leaving me with wet feet and holding one big shard of jagged glass against four vampires.

They all started laughing. Assholes.

Caleb looked down at me with affection a father might show

for his daughter plastered across his godforsaken face, and even *he* managed a laugh.

"Ryan," he said, "What have you been telling this girl?"

Ryan appeared next to him, a thin smile plastered on his face that did not reach his worried eyes. "I've told her to behave herself," he said, irritation in his tone. "Obviously, she didn't listen."

"You never did have my power of persuasion, my boy."

"No, Sir, I didn't."

"Get up," Caleb commanded.

"Go fuck yourself," I snapped back.

He appeared taken aback, as if shocked that I hadn't obeyed him immediately. He came closer and I rose to my feet, brandishing the shard of glass in front of me like a dagger.

"You're going to regret this," he said, barely containing his anger. I raised my glass dagger higher.

"Do what he says, Mia." Ryan's voice cut through the tense exchange.

Caleb turned and gave Ryan a withering look, and that's when I struck. I charged forward, my target Caleb's neck, and used all of my forward momentum to bury the piece of glass straight into the side of his neck. He stared at me, incredulous, and touched his wound with long fingers.

Now, let me say: that piece of glass was huge. It was, like, five inches long and I buried it pretty deep. I smiled at first, triumphant that I had kicked some vampire ass. He coughed once, twice, and pulled at the glass, gently sliding it out of his neck. He tossed the glass on the ground with such casual indifference I was dumbfounded.

"Ouch," he said, as Ryan and Ford grabbed my arms and effectively pinned me where I stood.

I looked at his completely healed neck and felt my mouth fall open.

"You're a feisty girl," he said.

"Thank you," I replied.

"I *eat* feisty girls like you for breakfast."

I rolled my eyes. I had nothing left except the power to be a smart mouth, and I was damned if I was going to go down without fighting with everything I had left in me.

I lifted my chin stubbornly and stared into those milky eyes.

"Take her," he ordered the others. "Finish the process."

Ryan and Ford began dragging me out of the room. I winced as I tried to avoid the broken glass and failed.

"The process?" I cried as wet shards stabbed into my feet. "What's the process?"

"Shut up," Ford ordered.

"You just signed your own death warrant," Ryan hissed in my ear. "You *stupid* girl."

TEN

So I had thought the whole siphoning my blood thing was the worst, scariest thing I'd ever had to go through. Mostly because I had really believed they were going to take all of my blood until I passed out or died.

I soon found out that there was something much worse.

Ryan and Ford had taken me back to my room and tied me up with the thick rope that dangled from the ceiling—the exact same position I'd been stuck in when I first arrived. Only this time there was no Kate to help me down, and I was tired and drunk with blood loss and just absolutely out of ideas. My shoulder was still recovering from being dislocated only hours before, and I screamed when my arm was forced up and tied in place.

The room I had been confined to was impossibly full with four people (or three vampires and a teenage girl) in it. Nameless-guy wheeled in a steel trolley covered in surgical equipment, and I looked away, not caring to imagine what horrific things were potentially about to happen.

"Did you guys raid the props department of *Grey's Anatomy* or something?"

Nobody answered me.

"What's that?" I asked, looking at the huge motherfucking needle Ryan was handing to someone behind me. I had been ignored all the way back to my room, so I wasn't surprised when nobody answered. But still, I panicked, because I couldn't see the needle anymore.

I screamed in absolute, horrific, agonizing pain as someone took that fat needle and *jammed* it into the back of my head. Something that felt like molten lava began to spread out around the base of my neck, up past my ears and right into my skull. Now that they had taken something out, they were putting something in. It felt like acid eating away at my brain.

"What are you doing to me?" I cried out.

"Just try to relax," Ryan said, in a voice that sounded less kind than his face looked.

"Please," I begged, hating myself for being weak. "Just tell me what you're doing!"

"There's a needle tapped into the base of your skull," Ryan explained.

"Jesus," I moaned, "Why?"

I got no answer. Ryan stood in front of me and watched as someone behind me injected three more lots of the burning stuff into the tap in my skull. Each time I screamed.

"Tell us your name," Ryan asked, in a voice that suggested he had done this many times before.

"Fuck. You." I replied.

"Go again," he said to whoever was behind me.

I gasped and held my breath, waiting for the burning pain to pass.

"What's your name?" Ryan asked again, and dread filled my stomach like cubes of frozen ice. He was prodding me with a knife.

A big, sharp hunting knife.

"Mia," I whispered.

"Louder!" he demanded, pressing the blade against my ribcage.

"Mia Blake!" I yelled at him, choking after the sudden exertion.

"Give her more," he said tonelessly.

Each time I repeated my name, the needle went back in, and the burning fire spread through my skull and across my veins hotter every time.

"What's your name?" Ryan asked. I stared at the floor.

"Hey!" he jerked the chains, sending pain shooting through my shoulder. I choked. "I can't remember," I wheezed. I had guessed the game we were playing. Had I guessed right?

Ryan frowned. "Are you sure you don't remember your name?" I nodded, panting despite the cold chill in the room. *It must be night time,* I thought. *I am going to die tonight.*

I watched as Ford pushed Ryan aside. In his hand, he held a gun. Ryan—looking rather reluctant—swapped places, and I guessed that it was his turn to play nurse with the needle. Ford pressed the barrel of the gun up under my chin and sneered.

"If you don't tell me your name, I'm going to find *Jared* and rip his heart out," he hissed, squeezing my throat with his free hand.

"Don't you hurt him!" I spluttered. "Stay away from him!"

"Liar," he muttered, striking my face with the side of his gun. I felt a crunch as my cheekbone all but shattered, and I momentarily lost vision in my left eye. *I'm going to die here, alone.*

I don't want to die.

He tugged on the chains and my shoulder grated painfully. "I didn't hear that name?" he prompted as metal bit into my flesh.

"Mia," I gasped, "you motherfucker."

My anger didn't faze him in the slightest. On the contrary, it amused him.

"Swearing doesn't suit you, babe," he said, and nodded to Ryan. I winced in anticipation as he pushed the plunger again, sending the burning liquid into my veins.

"Mother. Fucker!" I repeated as the stuff coursed through me. The agonizing pain was enough to make me cry, and since I no longer cared about maintaining my pride, I gave in to the desire, scrunching my face up and letting the tears flow.

"Name?"

"Bite me," I mumbled.

"I would *love* to bite you," Ford replied, sounding bored. "But you don't belong to me, baby. You belong to Caleb."

I gritted my teeth as another wave of fire and ice entered my veins, and the familiar roaring sound in my head drowned everything else out. A pair of teeth nibbled at my ear, and a voice that sounded like honey whispered to me to *let it all go*. The suggestion only made me fight harder.

It went on for what seemed like hours. Each time the liquid passed through me, it felt like everything I had ever known was being washed away into nothingness. It was almost as if it would be easier if I just let it all fade away, forgot who I was, become a shadow. But something deep inside my gut clenched each time I felt like letting go, and it wouldn't let everything fade to gray. I lost count at twenty. Twenty injections and more. I no longer had the energy to say my own name aloud, so I repeated it to myself instead. *Mia Blake. Jared Cohen. Evie Montgomery. Blairstown, New Jersey.* I was starting to lose touch with reality, but I clung to my memories fiercely. I had heard of drugs that wiped memories before, and I was terrified the painful liquid was eating away at my soul like battery acid on bare flesh.

After what seemed like an eternity, they stopped. I barely registered what was happening, other than the sound of the syringe dropping onto the stainless steel trolley, where it clanged and rolled to a stop. The three vampires spoke in hushed voices.

"Too much?"

"Show the boss."

"Stubborn bitch."

I heard a door open, and breathed a sigh of relief at the temporary reprieve. It slammed shut, and I closed my exhausted eyes. But I was not alone.

Ryan stood before me, his smooth face pinched with—worry?

"Please," I said before I could stop the words. I hated pleading, it made me look even weaker. But I couldn't take one more shot of the burning stuff. I just couldn't do it, and he knew it.

He brushed a stray hair from my face, tucking it behind my chewed ear. "What are you?" he mused, and my heart thudded wildly. "Why won't this work on you? It should have killed you by now."

"I know you don't believe me," he murmured, his brown eyes full of something. Pity? Regret? "But just—just hang in there, okay? It'll all be over soon."

Hang in there. Ha.

I felt pressure, a tugging at my wrists, and all of a sudden, I was falling through the air. I cried out as my knees slammed onto the unforgiving floor. I was cold, so cold despite the relatively warm temperature of the room. I crawled over to the pile of blankets Kate had once inhabited, shivering violently. I rummaged through the pile in a stupor, hardly seeing what I was doing, when my fingers closed around something hard and rough. I tentatively pulled and the object came free from the pile of material—a splintered piece of wood, sharpened at one end and possibly broken off the plywood board that covered the window.

A stake.

Excitedly, I felt through the blankets for more weapons. I found one more crudely fashioned stake and a dark green hoodie that might have belonged to Kate. I wrapped the stakes tightly in one of the blankets and clutched it to me as I lay down on the cool limestone floor. I rolled into a ball on my side and touched the back of my neck gingerly, feeling a hard lump where the tap had been. I had no recollection of it being taken out, and for that I was grateful. I closed my wet eyes, unable to stay conscious for even a minute longer.

And this time, when the darkness closed in, I surrendered willingly.

ELEVEN

More time passed. I had no concept of how long, but I guessed it felt longer than it really was. Every time I felt like giving up, like surrendering myself, like forgetting, I searched myself for every piece of anger I could muster up, and I held onto it all like a hot ball of hate to fling at my kidnappers.

And in amongst all of that seething rage, I dreamed of Jared. I dreamed of my mother.

Hours (days?) passed, and I heard a key *thunk* in the door. My stomach rumbled as I heaved myself off the floor and onto my feet. I hated being vulnerable on the floor, so even though I could barely stand, I chose to be stubborn and leaned against the wall.

Caleb appeared in the doorway. I was surprised; I'd only seen him in the room once in all this time, and that was when he was murdering my roomie. He shut the door firmly behind him, and surveyed me curiously.

"How do you feel today?" he asked, without a trace of the anger or the black eyes I'd witnessed the day before. A hundred possible caustic comments presented themselves, but I didn't answer him. He took three steps and was close enough for me to reach out and punch him. So I did. But my fist was clumsy and barely connected with his face. I think it hurt my hand more than it hurt him.

So you could say that I had it coming when he drew his fist back and slammed it into my cheek, so hard that I swear he almost took my head off.

He smiled as I groaned and clutched my face. "Today is an angry day," he observed, with obvious amusement. "I like those *so much better* than crying days."

"I'm a person!" I yelled, glaring at him. "Do you get that? I'm not just a personal blood supply for you!"

His response shocked me. "I know," he said matter-of-factly. "And if it makes a difference, I am sorry for what's happened to you. For what will happen."

I straightened in surprise and looked him in his freaky eyes as he started to pace the length of my tiny dungeon room. "If you're really sorry you'll let me go. Please. *Just let me go home.*"

He laughed. "You know I can't do that. If I let you go home, you would ruin everything I've started here. All my hard work, gone, because of one silly girl?"

"I promise I won't tell anyone," I begged.

"I let a girl go once. She ran straight home and told everyone about the vampires. The hunters came for us in their hundreds. They gunned us down until we were almost extinct." His eyes grew dark. "If you ever go home, I'll be right there, little girl. I'll be killing your big strong boyfriend *Jared* before he can even take a breath. Then I'll eat your mother, and the little blonde girl, too."

"Then kill me!" I said angrily. "Because you can't make me forget who I am!"

"It will be over for you soon enough," he replied indifferently, pausing his pacing in front of me. He reached into his shirt pocket and produced a pressed white handkerchief, offering it to me. "Here.

Clean yourself up."

I looked at the napkin in disgust and gathered all of the blood and saliva in my mouth, spitting it as forcefully as I could at him. It landed on his cheek and made a red trail down his face.

I immediately realized what a colossal mistake that was. I had just spit a mouthful of blood *at a vampire.*

Suddenly, it felt like all of the air had been sucked out of the room, and I backed up against the wall with my hands held out in front of me.

"Wait -" I cried out–

"You shouldn't have done that," he growled, as he pinned me against the wall. I screamed as teeth ripped into my neck and my blood was hungrily, ragefully taken by force.

I had never really believed in the concept of people having a soul until the first time a vampire bit me. I hadn't really thought about it at all, to be honest. When my dad died, that was it, as far as I was concerned. No afterlife. No heaven or hell. Just birth, life, and death. Ashes to ashes, dust to dust. But when Caleb started to take my blood, he was taking something else along with it. It's hard to put into words, but it was like he was dragging pieces of my soul out along with my blood. Taking every ounce of energy within me, so that I was frozen, unable to speak or breathe or even think whole thoughts. Invisible fingers probed inside my chest, constricted my throat, twisted the chunk of meat inside my skull until it buzzed and screamed in agony.

I stopped fighting back almost immediately. I mean, it had only been a couple of days since dramatic–blood–loss–episode number one, and I very much doubted my body was anywhere near better when Caleb bit me. Besides, the word 'bit' sounds too nice, too neat. In reality, it was like a rabid dog had latched onto that hollow where neck and shoulder meet and proceeded to rip into my flesh.

I wanted to throw up, but I was frozen. He sucked greedily, again and again. The black dots that floated in front of my eyes said

Too much. I was on the verge of blacking out when I was tossed to the floor like a rag doll.

I scurried backwards on my hands and heels, one hand pressed to my bleeding neck. I tilted my gaze so that I was looking up into the face of my attacker, my blood smeared across his face.

"When are you going to kill me?" I whispered to him.

He stared at me like one might stare at a cockroach twitching on the floor.

"Ryan!" he barked. Ryan appeared at his side. He must have been waiting in the hallway. His face remained blank.

"Sir?"

"Take this one back to your room." He gave me another withering glare. "Let her sleep this off. Transfuse her, let her recover before we attempt the Turn. And Ryan?"

"Yes, sir?"

"Strap this bitch down. I don't want to take any chances."

"Of course."

And with that, Caleb left. Ryan wordlessly hoisted me up, throwing my sore arm over his shoulders. I moaned.

"Sorry," he muttered, gently disentangling himself from that side of my body and using my good arm instead.

"Wait!" I said. I grabbed my bundled up blanket, knowing that there was a crudely fashioned stake from the broken window frame hidden in its folds. I clutched it to my chest as we left the room, not really knowing why I'd taken it, but feeling like it might be the last hope I had left.

Draped over Ryan's shoulder, I stumbled blindly next to him as we made our way up the hallway, in the opposite direction of Caleb's lair. It took ages to get to Ryan's room, especially when we had to navigate stairwells, lifts and even more impossibly long hallways. I had thought I'd had no idea where I was before, but now I was completely and utterly lost. We went up several flights of stairs, so I guessed we were somewhere high. Finally, though, we reached a large wooden door at the end of a long limestone corridor. Ryan disentangled himself from me, and I leaned on the cool wall for support. In theory, I could have run—I was completely unrestrained and Ryan was fumbling with a brass key—but I had nothing left inside of me. No energy, no fight, not even any hope except that the end was approaching quickly, and so I didn't resist when Ryan took my wrist in his hand and led me through the open door.

I didn't notice much of the room in my state of exhaustion. I just remember the feeling of a cool, damp breeze on my skin, despite the fact that we were deep inside Caleb's building and there were no windows in view.

My head wobbled on my shoulders as I was led through a minimally decorated living room, then through a kitchen that was all stainless steel and dark marble. I stopped in my zombified state, looking around the kitchen in drunken wonder.

"You eat?" I asked, staring blankly at a package of bright red tomatoes on the counter.

Ryan smiled (what a change from yelling and putting taps in my brain) and nodded. "Yes, I eat."

"But you're a vampire," I insisted groggily, rubbing my eyes like a little kid.

That made him laugh, but this time, there was no trace of malevolence lingering in his voice. He just sounded like a regular guy. "*Now* you believe in vampires?" he asked.

"I just almost got my throat ripped out," I said morosely. "I'm a believer."

"Come on." He tugged my wrist and I followed in a bloodless stupor. We entered a small bedroom that actually looked to be the same dimensions and shape as my dungeon—even the door for the attached ensuite was in the same place, but this room had chocolate colored walls, an oak dresser and a matching four poster oak bed that seemed to take up every inch of spare space. Next to the bed was an IV pole hung with a bag of blood, condensation gleaming on the plastic packaging. When I saw it I froze, remembering the torture device I'd been hooked up to.

He must have felt me stiffen, and he immediately guessed what I was staring at.

"It's okay," he said quickly. "It's just to make you feel better."

"Better?" I said incredulously. "Aren't you just going to kill me?"

We shared an uncomfortable silence as he tried to answer my question.

"Look," he said, exasperated. "I don't know you. I don't know why you're here or what's going to happen."

"He's going to kill me," I said flatly.

"Nobody is going to kill you," he said firmly. "Honestly, I don't lie. There's no point me giving you false hope."

"He won't let me go," I insisted.

He looked at the floor. "No, probably not."

"I wish he would just kill me, then," I whispered.

He laid me gently on his bed, carefully avoiding my neck, and arranged the blankets around me. I held tightly onto the blanket I'd carried with me, the one that contained my crudely fashioned wooden stake—and my last shot at freedom.

"I need to put this IV in," he said apologetically. I looked away, barely registering the tiny prick as the needle entered a fresh vein in my arm.

"Sleep now," he said, still with that persuasive tone, but gentler. I obeyed, settling back on the pillow, firmly clutching my blanket. Ryan sat in a plush leather chair beside the bed, fidgeting with the IV blood bag, and then the plastic tubing, until there was nothing left to fuss with.

I lay there for what seemed like ages, waiting for Ryan to relax beside me. Finally, I couldn't wait any longer. I shifted and felt him tense beside me immediately. Shit. This could take me a while. I thought of all the things a normal sleeping person would do. I sighed, I rolled over, I shifted, I even threw in a couple of snores for effect. My right hand reached into my blanket and curled around a splintered piece of wood I had fashioned into a crude stake by rubbing it along the concrete floor in my cell. It was now or never.

I cracked open one eye and saw Ryan, engrossed in Stephen King's *'Salem's Lot*. How fitting. I would have made a dig about a vampire reading a Stephen King book, but since I was about to kill him, it would have to wait until he was staked.

I drew a deep breath, opened both eyes, sat bolt upright in bed and struck out with my stake.

I don't know who was more surprised—me or him. Him, at the fact that he had just been taken down by a girl, or me, that I had managed to get the stake into his chest without getting murdered.

He gasped, looking down at his chest. "You … *Bitch*," he said angrily, clearly still dazzled by my wicked ninja skills. I had hurt him, sure, but I didn't think the stake was in far enough or at the right angle to kill him. Which meant *time to fucking run*. He opened his mouth to yell out, but a pathetic little cough came out instead.

I threw the covers off and stood clumsily, backing towards the door. The IV was still nestled in the crook of my arm. Not for long. I winced in anticipation and ripped the thing out of my arm, groaning at the sharp pain. My arm started dripping blood. Great. *Focus, Mia*. I looked back to Ryan. It was disgustingly satisfying to watch him writhe in pain as he tried to pull the stake out of his chest. I couldn't believe I had missed his damned heart at such close range.

I opened the door, giving him one last glance. He kept gasping and thrashing about, but there was no time to knock him out or gag him. Or kill him, which was what he deserved. I had to leave. I hurried through the kitchen and lounge room, banging into cupboards and dragging myself along walls until I reached the door. Gingerly, I opened it, and stepped out of the apartment. I closed the door quietly, not liking the way I could hear Ryan's muffled choking. Thankfully, the hallway appeared deserted. I moved fast, tiptoeing down the corridor towards what I hoped was a way outside.

The hallway stretched for miles in both directions, and each time I reached an intersecting hallway, I took the brighter looking direction. The vampires seemed to avoid sunlight, and I figured the sunnier it was, the less chance I would have of running into one.

Unfortunately for me though, logic didn't prevail. Through the maze of corridors, it only took a few moments before a vampire was walking down the hall, coming straight for me.

Shit! I wavered for a moment. I was now completely lost, and in no hurry to retrace my steps and try escaping in another direction. I could hide somewhere and wait for the guy to go, but Ryan was probably healed by now, and on his way to catch me and drag me back to my cell. I had to keep moving. I continued towards him as casually as possible, and then took the first intersecting corridor that presented itself.

"Hey!" he yelled straight away, and I froze. *Don't stop. Just get away.* Vampires moved fast though, and by the time I started moving again, he was right with me. I turned to face him, and smiled nonchalantly. Fuck. "Hey, yourself!" I replied cheerily.

He eyed me warily, coming closer. "You're the girl from New Jersey, right?"

I laughed breezily. *Shit Shit Shit.*

"I don't know," I shrugged. I was supposed to have forgotten where I was from, after all.

The guy might have been undead, but thankfully he didn't appear to be very smart.

"Hey, what's that in your pocket?"

"Huh?" *Damn it.* He had seen the stake. He rushed at me, just in time for me to fish the stake out of my waistband and hold it in front of me *and* for Ryan to come around the corner. I couldn't tell who was more pissed, and I didn't want to hang around to ask. The dumb guy charged me, and I pointed the sharp part of the stake outwards. As he approached I thrust out with it, sidestepping him at the same time. Incredibly, he missed me and the stake altogether and smashed into the stained glass window directly behind me. No, he smashed *through* the window and kept going. I jumped, wincing as I heard him hit the ground. It sounded like we were pretty high up, judging by the timing of his fall and the ensuing splat.

Ryan blinked in disbelief, his bloodied shirt flapping in the new breeze created by the open window. I must have done some decent damage, because there was blood all over his shirt, soaking his jeans, and trailing behind him on the floor in neat little drops. I wished the wood splinters in his chest would become infected and cause him a long, traumatic death.

One could hope.

Ryan glared at me, and I smiled sweetly in response. Sunlight flooded into the hallway through the broken window, hurting my raw eyes. I hadn't seen much more than a crack of sun through boarded–up windows in weeks. Instinctively I stepped backwards and up, hoisting myself onto the narrow window ledge that led outside, where dumb vamp had eaten concrete.

My elation turned to despair as Ryan came closer, effectively blocking off the other hallway in both directions. It left me trapped on the ledge with no place to go except back into the arms of my captor.

I stole a glance outside and was slammed by a wave of vertigo. Shit! I was at least four floors up, not one or two as I had foolishly hoped. And not only was there nothing soft to jump onto, there was also nothing to shimmy down but smooth limestone wall. I couldn't even hope to land on Dumb Vamp to cushion a fall. He was already gone. Superhuman strength and all that, I suppose.

I was stuck.

"Come on" Ryan beckoned, coming at me with hands outstretched. "You've got nowhere to go."

I glanced from him to the ground below. He was wrong. I did have somewhere to go. And I had no hope left inside me that I would escape, unless I took this beautiful sunlight and broken window and–

"Stay where you are or I'll jump!" I yelled, thrusting my stake at the air in warning. Ryan smirked, coming closer.

"Don't be stupid," Ryan said, as his hand began to close around my wrist. "You won't jump."

Eat shit, motherfucker. I jumped.

TWELVE

There had been no time to think. Trusting my instincts, I had held my arms out and shifted my weight so that one foot left the safety of the stone windowsill and pushed away until it touched air. Ryan had reached out and tried to pull me back, but even with his superhuman abilities, he was no match for gravity.

The fall itself was over in an instant. Some people say you black out as soon as you hit bottom after falling, but that's not right. We landed together, awkwardly, the concrete and the weight of Ryan's body shattering me.

For a split second the world ceased to exist—there was only darkness, and my soul floated within that darkness. I thought that I had died from the impact; it had come on so suddenly. But after a few seconds I started to *feel.* And what I was feeling was beyond any pain I had ever experienced in my short time on earth. My head screamed from the impact, but I could barely make a sound. Somehow, that made it worse—being torn apart inside and not being able to make a noise.

I became more aware of where I was, of my surroundings, as the crushing weight on my back rolled off. I sucked in a small breath and coughed up wet stuff. I didn't want to know what it was. Finally, I got enough air in my lungs again, and I screamed and screamed.

The left side of my face, where I had directly impacted the ground, felt like it had cracked open entirely. I could feel my pulse in my temple, and I guessed it was my blood pumping out of my damaged skull; when I tried to lift my head, move my legs to crawl away, nothing happened.

"You stupid girl," a groan came from beside me, and I opened my eyes. I could still see, though my left eye was quickly being swallowed up by the pool of blood that grew underneath me. I tried to move again, but I could only manage a pathetic reach with my bloodied arm. Ryan was beside me, bleeding and injured as well, but it looked like he was healing rapidly. *How nice for him.* He dragged himself to a sitting position and squinted at me in the bright sunlight.

I dragged a shaky breath and whimpered in agony as Ryan took my shoulders and rolled me onto my back. "Sorry," he muttered, letting go of my shattered left shoulder.

Now you're sorry? I couldn't believe what I was hearing.

Ryan looked around the courtyard. Apparently, we were alone for the moment. The IQ–challenged vamp who had sailed through the window had obviously recovered from his fall quickly enough to haul ass.

"I'm going to die," I whispered, closing my eyes in defeat. Once I had accepted the fact, a feeling of peace washed over me, and although I still felt the pain, I also felt relief that I could finally get away from this hell on earth. Now I understood why Kate had wanted Caleb to kill her. Anything was better than being a vampire's thirty–day blood supply.

"Hey, wake up. You're not going to die. I'm going to help you."

I jerked on the ground where I lay, and my eyes flew open. "No,"

I whimpered. "No!"

Ryan shook his head slowly, taking a shard of shattered window and creating a long cut down his arm. "You'll be okay," he said solemnly, taking my bleeding—broken—left arm and pressing his single wound to one of my many.

"No!" I tried to push him away with my good arm.

"I'm trying to help you, Mia." He grabbed my arm, completely immobilizing me.

"I don't want your help!"

"You'll die."

I took one more breath and began to weep. "Please don't do it," I begged him. "Please just let me die."

I began to writhe and gasp as vampire blood trickled into my veins. It made my fall feel like a scraped knee. It was intense. It was unrelenting. It was every star and every sun in every universe burning though my blood like wildfire. I choked on a wail as I felt darkness and white-hot pain invade every cell in my being.

"Make it stop!" I begged deliriously.

After that, I couldn't speak. I was too busy screaming as vampire blood overwhelmed my nervous system. I screamed and screamed, but there was no end. After what seemed like several eternities screaming into the waning sunlight of the afternoon, I blacked out.

THIRTEEN

DRINK.

That was the first thing he said to me.

I opened my eyes. Naked save for a bloodied white sheet, my tender skin covered in sticky red blood. My broken body somehow, *impossibly*, repairing itself.

I felt something warm at my lips. *Blood.*

I tried to turn my head to the side, to see where I was, and groaned in pain. Staying still felt better. I was sticky and bruised. My body was fighting hard to mend all the deep gashes and crushed bones. I lifted an arm and gently felt my eye where I had taken the impact of the unforgiving ground. It was excruciatingly painful to the touch—but it wasn't shattered anymore. It was in one unbroken piece, as if my fall had been a terrible dream. The oddly comforting metallic taste on my lips told me otherwise, though.

I reached out with my hands, touching stiff sheets. I was burning up, but I was shivering, goosebumps lining my arms.

It was so hard to keep my eyes open, but I fought to stay awake. I wasn't dead. I still had something left inside of me. I couldn't give up yet.

A face appeared above me. Something warm and coppery breached my lips.

"Drink," he repeated.

I did.

Time passed—how much, I have no idea—and I stayed in the same spot, and I slept off death.

Later, I heard the words again.

Wake up.

Night time. It could have been days, weeks, months—or just a single hour since I'd last been awake. I had no idea. I felt a little clearer, and I found I could move my head without wanting to scream.

"Get up and take a shower."

I got up. I walked to the bathroom on shaking legs.

Standing under the hot water (how long had it been since I'd had a long, hot, uninterrupted shower?) was bliss. Bliss that soon ended up with a pile of questions. I started to hyperventilate at the sheer impossibility of what was happening. I was trying not to think about it—but who was I kidding? I knew why I was 'magically' all better. And I knew it wasn't Starbucks Gingerbread Lattes that I'd been drinking every time I was woken up by soft words and warm, soothing liquid that slid down my throat like—well, like Gingerbread Lattes at Christmas time. It had been blood. *Vampire* blood.

As I watched the dried blood start to flake off and dissolve into the steamy water, a wave of dizziness hit me. I sank down to a sitting position on the side of the narrow tub, the flimsy shower curtain resting against the film of water on my back.

How could this be possible?

How could I be alive?

I tentatively massaged shampoo into my long, dark brown hair, picking out little pieces of glass and clumps of dried blood and thick knots. One of the pieces of glass gouged the tip of my finger and I flinched. A drop of blood appeared, then another, and I rinsed it underneath the water.

I looked at it again. The cut had completely disappeared.

I held my hand to my mouth to stop myself from crying out. This could *not* be happening.

And I could not believe how, from a snow-filled parking lot five minutes from home, it had ended up like *this*.

A knock at the door made me jump.

"You okay in there?"

"Yes." My wavering voice sounded like a stranger's. How long had it been since I'd spoken?

I shut the water off, swallowing a painful lump in my throat. I may have been 'rescued', but I still felt like I was a prisoner—I'd just switched one cage for another.

And now I was alone with *him*.

Thunder rolled overhead, and I heard rain. The whole room shook in the wind. Blinking wearily, I reached for one of the folded beige towels on the sink and wrapped it around my dripping hair. I wrapped the other towel around my torso, took one last look in the filthy, foggy mirror, straightened my shoulders, and ventured out of the bathroom.

Ryan had taken the bloodstained sheets off the bed while I was showering. They were balled up in the corner of a room that was the size of a postage stamp. A double bed on one side, a small sofa and an ancient-looking TV set bolted to the wall on the other. In between, a door that led to the outside world.

"I got you some clothes to wear." He gestured to the neatly folded pile on the end of the unmade bed. I took them back into the bathroom and quickly slipped them on—a black fitted camisole, dark denim jeans and a pair of bright red Havaianas that were two sizes too big for my feet. No bra or underwear, but the camisole was thick and supportive enough to leave something to the imagination. I refolded the damp towels and closed the bathroom door behind me.

"Someone is on the way to get us."

I nodded.

"Are you—thirsty?"

I walked gingerly to the sink, filled a tumbler with water, and gulped it down.

Then refilled it.

"No," I said.

"Hungry?"

"Nope."

I sat on the edge of the bed, then got up and looked out of the window. We were on the ground floor of what looked like a horseshoe-shaped arrangement of motel rooms. The plastic sign out front read *La Guena Mexica*.

Where the hell are we?

"Mexico."

I dropped the glass, startled. It bounced on the thin carpet but didn't smash, water sloshing onto my feet and the ground.

"I'm sorry, I didn't mean to scare you."

"How did you –"

He started towards me, but stopped in the middle of the room. I can't say I had the most receptive expression on my face.

"We're linked," he explained softly, pointing to his head, then mine.

"You've got to be fucking kidding me," I scowled at him.

"Think of something," he offered.

I threw out some random thoughts. Cheese. The Eiffel tower. My cat.

"I prefer mozzarella. I've been there many times. I'm more of a dog person."

I sat back, stunned.

"I don't want you to do that anymore," I said. "Don't ever do that again."

"Okay" he said. "I'll try. But it's kind of like a two–way radio. Sometimes I can't help but pick up the signal."

"Well, maybe you should try harder," I replied.

I heard a faint *thumpthumpthump* and looked around to see where it was coming from. Sure enough, my eyes landed on the large mason jar from Caleb's room, the jar that contained the human heart. The still-beating human heart. It was sitting neatly on the sink, as if it belonged in the room with us. I felt bile rush up in my throat and fought to swallow it back.

Ryan saw my face and grabbed a blanket from the foot of the bed, draping it over the jar.

"I can still hear it," I said quietly. He didn't answer me.

"You want to go grab something to eat? Our lift is still a few hours away."

I looked around helplessly.

"What is it?"

Thanks for not reading my mind. "What are we going to eat?"

"Food?"

"It's just –"

"I can give you more blood if you think you need it. Try listening to your body.

Do you feel like a burger? Or do you feel like something else?"

Ugh. I could guess what the something else was. The same something that had been fed to me as I fought off death. My stomach rumbled loudly. "Burger," I decided.

He opened the door with one hand, and passed me a pair of

dark sunglasses and a baseball cap with the other. "Here. Put these on. It's pretty bright out there."

And I stepped willingly into the day, a walking dead girl with an ache in my belly and trepidation in my heart.

FOURTEEN

THE DINER WAS ONLY A FEW HUNDRED METERS AWAY FROM THE motel room, so the rain didn't affect us too much. I ordered onion rings, a large bacon cheeseburger with the lot, and curly fries. My vampire friend (what was I thinking? My psychopath kidnapper) ordered a small plate of nachos. I suddenly felt self–conscious.

"It's okay," he said. "I'm old, I don't—I can't—eat a lot at once."

"How old?" I asked. "What do you eat? Where are we going?"

He just stared at me.

I chewed on an onion ring and swallowed thickly. My throat was still on fire, my cheeks red–hot with a burning fever. A flash of falling through a stained glass window came to me, and I shifted uneasily.

"Why'd you do it?" I asked.

"Do what?"

"Save me. Make sure I didn't die."

He studied me for a long time, a peculiar look on his face. "I honestly don't really know. I'm just making this up as I go along, Mia."

I baulked at his casual tone.

"Don't say my name like we're friends," I said stiffly. "This is your fault, all of this. You *took* me. You chased me and made me jump out of that window. Don't say my name."

"Okay, then," he replied, a trace of a smirk haunting his mouth. "I'm making this up as I go, *honey.*"

I glared at him. "I want to go home."

Ryan nodded, taking a sip of his coffee. "Soon."

"How soon?"

"I just need to figure out the details."

"What details?"

He was grave. "I need to make sure you … can survive on your own."

I snorted. "Are you kidding me?"

"Well, are we going to talk about the elephant in the room, or just avoid it and change the subject all the time?"

I eyed him warily. "So talk."

He sighed. "You're one of us, now. You're a *vampire*. I know you're having a hard time believing that, but it's true."

"How am I supposed to believe that when I don't believe in fairy tales and monsters and glittery fucking vampires?"

Ryan laughed. "Honey, we don't sparkle. We bite."

I huffed. "You'd make a lousy salesman."

"Immortality tends to sell itself." He smirked. I rolled my eyes and chewed on a French fry. "Can't you just tell me what I need to know so I can leave?"

He raised an eyebrow. "It takes a bit more than a crash course and a few hours to teach you what you need to know."

I stared at him. "How am I supposed to know what to believe? As far as I'm concerned, this is your fault. And I wish I had stabbed you in the heart."

He extended his hand across his uneaten nachos. "Give me your hand."

I didn't.

"Oh, come on, I won't hurt you," he said impatiently. "It's not a trick. Here."

I reluctantly rested my palm on his. "Now what?"

"Just relax. Close your eyes and open your mind. Let me show you."

"I can't see anything," I complained. But no sooner had I finished my sentence, that something slammed into my head like a ton of bricks and I had to grip the table with my spare hand to keep from falling off my chair.

Suddenly, I could see everything I wanted to know, or almost everything. I saw the small village in Italy where Ryan was born. I saw how he had been Turned into a vampire by Caleb one night in Venice, how he had left his homeland and travelled with his new-found vampire family to Spain. I felt the searing rage that his newborn bloodlust entailed, saw the faces of those he killed. I tasted their blood and the energy it contained in the back of my throat. There was a massive palace where he lived with many other vampires, led by Caleb. Hundreds of years later, I saw the beautiful blonde Spanish princess he fell in love with. I saw her Turned into a vampire, how something had gone wrong, how she had almost been killed. I saw a girl who had been beaten and drained almost to death, a girl who had changed his loyalties and made him abandon the only life he had ever known, and I realized with a shudder that that girl was me.

I tore my hand away, struggling to catch my breath.

I tried to think of something to say. "Are you really that old?" I managed finally.

Ryan smiled and nodded, taking a bite of his nachos like the psychic-link thing hadn't just taken all the energy out of him. Me, I was exhausted from the mental novel I'd just been subjected to.

"You regret it," I said. "I believe that. But how am I supposed to trust you that this isn't just another game? I mean, you've moved me from one jail cell to another, but I'm still your prisoner."

"I understand you're wary."

"That's an understatement, don't you think?"

His cell beeped. He stared at the screen for a moment.

"Our ride's here soon," he said. "Better wait in the room. We don't want to blow our cover before we even get out of the country."

"Wait, where are we going?" I eyed him warily over bottles of ketchup and mustard.

"Home." He stood up and threw a twenty down on the table.

"Where is home?" I didn't move from my seat.

He sighed. "Not New Jersey."

I cleared my throat. "I need to go to the bathroom."

He eyed me suspiciously. "Last time you said that, you stabbed someone."

I raised my eyebrows. "Seriously?'

"You can go back at the room."

I shook my head. "I'm about to burst. I'll just be a minute."

He shrugged. "Okay, whatever. Hurry up."

I stood and made a beeline for the bathroom, feeling heat at my back. "You're coming to watch?" I guessed, disappointed.

"I'll wait outside the door. Pee fast."

I entered the bathroom, the door swinging shut behind me. There were two stalls and a rusting basin bolted to the cinderblock wall. I immediately entered the furthest stall and locked the door behind me. It was like my luck had suddenly turned for the better. A giant window, as wide as the stall and two feet tall, hung over the toilet. I put the lid of the toilet down and stepped up as quietly as I could onto the plastic, levering the window open with such ease, it could have been a set-up. Without looking back, I shimmied feet-first through the window and landed with a satisfying crunch onto the gravel ground outside. I was in the parking lot of the diner, the motel at my right and the busy highway a couple hundred feet away.

The rain had stopped, making things even easier.

"Well, fancy seeing you here," a voice drawled, and I swore under my breath as Ryan sauntered around the corner, a smug smile plastered across his face.

I searched around for a weapon, anything I could strike him with. Bingo. A rusted tire iron lay half buried in the gravel near my feet, thorny weeds growing around it like chains. I leaned down and pulled it free, brandishing it like a sword in front of me. Ryan charged me as I brought the tire iron up in a wide arc, slamming it against the side of his head. Dark blood exploded from his cheek and he crashed face first into the loose road base. I slammed it into the back of his head again and again, as he tried to crawl away.

"I'm trying to help you!" he yelled as his mouth hit gravel. "Stop it!"

I laid one final, spectacular blow on the back of his skull and dropped the tire iron, making a run for the highway. He might have been an old and awesome vampire, but I was a state track runner, and I was fast.

Not fast enough. I felt a hand latch around my ankle and I landed awkwardly on my ass so hard, the shock went all the way through my tailbone and up to my head. I scurried backwards on my hands and heels, when Ryan landed on me from where he stood, effectively pinning me to the ground. I thrashed about, nails gouging at flesh and feet kicking blindly.

"Stop."

"You tricked me," I said sullenly, panting.

"It was a test," Ryan said, hauling me to my feet and pressing me against the wall. "You failed. Or passed. You did exactly what I thought you would do. You're predictable."

"You're an asshole," I said, humiliated. He had played me again.

"Listen," he said urgently, his fingers biting into my shoulders. "I can never go back there, do you understand? Centuries of loyal service, of being at the top of the chain, all gone. My friends? All gone. My house? Gone. I got you out of there because I didn't want you to die like that."

"How would you prefer me to die?" I shot back, shoving him in the chest. He relaxed his fingers but didn't let go of me.

"I don't want you to die at all," he rephrased. "I want to help you. I was going to help you escape *before* you jumped out of the window, you stupid girl."

His look was so genuine, his frustration so heartfelt, that I couldn't help but trust him a little bit. Not much, but enough to stop struggling.

"Why me? Why not Kate? Or any of the other people you've helped him kill?"

Ryan seemed to deflate a little, looking to the highway for inspiration.

"I guess … I'm tired," he said finally. "I don't know why it was you. Maybe because—because once someone forgets their human life, it gets easier. But you, you wouldn't forget, and I've never seen that before."

My eyes started to burn. "I want to go home," I said stubbornly.

"Jesus Christ, you're like a broken record!" Ryan said, letting me go. "Fine. Go. Hitch a ride with the next trucker. I guarantee you, you'll be dead before nightfall."

I stood there dumbly, having just been given my freedom and maybe not wanting it any more. I swore under my breath and looked out to the cars going by, ordinary people oblivious to my plight.

"You're the one who started this," I accused, turning on him. "*You* are the sick bastard who followed me to my car and beat the living shit out of me, more than once. There is something fundamentally wrong with you, do you get that? You are a bad person. You're a fucking psychopath!"

Ryan studied me for a moment. "There *is* something very wrong with me," he agreed. "Over the years, I've let the darkness inside me rule my life. I've killed countless people just like you."

"Way to make a girl feel safe. I'm done here." I stormed towards the highway, resisting the invisible ribbon that pulled me towards Ryan like a magnet.

You made me want to be a better person, he said in my head, and I stopped dead in my tracks.

Wanting it isn't good enough, I replied.

You're the reason I'm leaving that life behind. I want to help you. It was a pleading, more than anything else.

I didn't know what to say to that.

What about everything that I have? I demanded. *What about MY life?*

Three months, he pleaded. *Three months for me to teach you what you need to know. To make sure you don't kill someone if you get hungry. To make sure you can hide what you are. Three months for me to make sure Caleb isn't a problem for either of us. Then you go home to your boyfriend and your family and your life and forget all about me.*

I turned to face him, and his sad kid face tore at my heart. I'd always trusted my gut instinct, and it had never let me down. The only time I had ever ignored it, I had been kidnapped. My head told me to run. My gut told me he was right, that I should stay.

Three months is a long time, I said across the lot.

Not when you have eternity, he replied.

I thought about it. About how weird everything felt. About how good the blood had tasted when he fed me as I slept. About how I had no fucking clue how to get more of it if I needed it. About how I might hurt somebody without meaning to.

Two months, I countered reluctantly.

The bastard just *smiled*.

I stared out to the highway, trying to figure out why the hell I had agreed to stay, when my skin started to burn.

I yelped, pressing my hands to my hot face. I shied away from the sun's overpowering rays, covering my face with my arms. I felt a hand on my wrist as Ryan pulled me towards shelter.

"What's happening to me?" I gasped.

A firm grip steered me towards the motel room. We stopped for a moment in the shade created by the veranda that was attached to the diner entrance.

"It's just the sun. New vampires are very sensitive."

"Well, shit!" I said. "Am I going to burst into flames?" The mental image was horrific.

"No. That's a ridiculous myth propagated by television shows and novels. But," he paused for dramatic effect, "You'll probably feel like you are burning alive."

"*Awesome*," I muttered.

FIFTEEN

TEN MINUTES LATER, I WAS SITTING ON THE EDGE OF THE bathtub in our motel bathroom, gritting my teeth as Ryan laid strips of cold, wet gauze across my face and neck. The sprint across the parking lot had been nightmarish—though I had tried to cover my face with my shirt, it hadn't been very effective. The sun is pretty good at burning newborn vampire flesh, something I've since seen first-hand.

My arms were raw and a couple of blisters had already popped up. In comparison to how fast my cut finger had healed in the shower, this seemed contradictory. Heal immediately from one thing but fall prey to something as innocent as the sun?

"Can I ever go in the sun again?" I asked anxiously.

He wrapped a wet towel around my right arm. "Of course. It's just an initial reaction. Once you build up a tolerance, you'll be fine."

"So I have to feel like this for how long?"

He stopped fussing with my arm and sat on the edge of the bathtub beside me. "That depends. If you take my blood, you'll heal pretty much straightaway. And you'll have less problem the next time you go out in the sun. My tolerance will help you."

"And if I don't drink your blood?"

He stood and went over to the sink. "A couple of weeks, maybe more. And if you go back in the sun during that time, you'll be even worse. The sun's about the only thing that can scar a vampire's flesh. More than, say, a broken wine bottle to the head or a stake to the chest." A warm, metallic scent wafted across to me. It didn't smell all that bad, to be honest. It smelled good. Which was, in itself, A Very Bad Thing.

I groaned. "Okay."

He smirked.

"Well," he said, "don't be so appreciative."

"I would have stayed in here," I complained. "You're the one who took me out in the fucking sun."

He presented me with a small glass tumbler, filled with fresh, warm blood. I stared at it apprehensively, slightly disturbed by the fact that not two minutes ago it was pumping around Ryan's circulatory system.

I pinched my nose shut and threw the blood down my throat like it was tequila, gulping and gasping and trying not to throw up. I took one of the sugar packets that I'd jammed into my pocket at the diner and ripped the top off, pouring it over my tongue.

"I wanted to see what your tolerance was like. And I'm also the one who saved your fucking life a few days ago, remember?"

"You're also the one who fucking kidnapped me," I shot back, but between the words *kidnapped* and *me*, tires squealed close by and Ryan's gaze switched to the window.

I felt the color drain from my face, and a voice inside my head told me to *stay silent and still*. I did.

Ryan looked at me, putting a finger to his lips as he handed me a stuffed calico bag about the size of a deck of cards. It smelled like lavender and cat pee. He motioned for me to keep holding it, and he did likewise with an identical bag.

Footsteps echoed like machine gun bullets across the parking lot. I realized that if I concentrated hard enough, I could figure out approximately where people were in the parking lot. I could even hear how many cars were out there and the heartbeats of the people who were presumably searching for us. I could also hear my heartbeat. It was fast, and it was afraid. I looked at the empty tumbler I'd just drank from, an oily red smear still coating it, and wondered.

We sat there as the minutes dragged on. Finally, the footsteps seemed to retreat and the sound of skidding tires marked a hasty exit. It frightened me that someone was trying so hard to find me—us—and I didn't want to imagine what would happen if I was captured again. I very much doubt I would be taken back alive, especially now that I was a vampire and presumably useless for Caleb's torturous bloodletting experiments.

Finally, Ryan took a breath and seemed to relax marginally. "Are you okay?" he asked.

"I'm fine. Did you just hold your breath that whole time?"

"I don't know. I wasn't thinking about it. I guess so."

"Wow."

"Vampires get most nutrients and oxygen from drinking blood. Breathing is just a habit at my age."

"Riiiight. So … what's your plan? How are we getting out of here?"

Ryan glanced at me, apparently amused. "We'll wait. Our ride is here very soon, and she can protect you better than just me and a couple of hex bags."

I eyed him warily. "You're such a bad ass, why can't we just steal a car and drive ourselves to wherever it is we're going?"

"I might be a 'bad ass,'" he used his fingers to make rabbit ears, "but I'm no magic user. These hex bags will help us hide in here for a few hours, but if we leave now, we'll be followed."

I tensed up, panicking. "I don't want to go back there."

"You won't! Just stay calm, don't freak out."

"I already am freaking out." My heart was thumping so loud I could barely think.

"I'm aware of that, thanks."

"Get out of my head! Again!"

"It's a little hard not to hear what you're thinking. You're like a goddamn emergency beacon, shouting out our coordinates."

"And you're a goddamn psychopath! Magic will help us get out of here? I think this is just one, big prank you assholes are playing on me before you kill me."

Ryan's cell vibrated on the bathroom counter, and the screen lit up. He snatched it up and studied the screen. "Not long now," he said in a voice that didn't sound at all reassuring.

"She should have helicoptered in," I deadpanned. "Would have been quicker."

Ryan nodded. "She did want to bring the Apache. I told her it'd attract too much attention."

"Well, good for you." I looked around the tiny bathroom and longed for some wide open space. I studied the skin on my arms and realized it was almost completely healed. No blisters, and only a slight reddish tinge that was getting fainter by the minute.

"Hey, it worked."

Ryan took my hand and studied my arm. "You're a fast healer," he said.

I told him about how I had cut my finger in the shower. "Will everything heal that fast?"

He shook his head. "I have a lot to explain, and I'll try my best to do that on the way home. For now, yes you will heal fast, but you're not invincible. A lot of new vampires get too cocky, think they're indestructible, and they get themselves killed pretty fast."

"What's going to get me killed?" I asked softly. "Apart from those guys outside."

"Well, fire's really dangerous for vampires. It will kill you just as soon as a regular person. Bullets aren't so bad, as long as you don't get hit in a major artery. There are a few plants that are poisonous to vampires. None that you'll find anywhere around here."

"Just one more question," I said. "How the hell are there such things as vampires? I mean, how did you come about? Was someone bitten by a bat or something?" I scowled. "Will I turn into a bat?"

"That's a long story," he smiled reassuringly. "A bat–free story, though. Let's wait for the car ride for that one."

Ryan's phone buzzed again. "She's here," he said. I followed him out of the bathroom and into the main room. "Grab your stuff, let's go."

I stood in the middle of the room, still clutching the calico 'hex' bag. "Uh ... what stuff?"

He grabbed the pile of bloodied sheets and dumped them into my arms, then gathered up his own duffel bag and that hideous glass jar. "Here. Let's go, quickly. Don't lose that hex bag."

I stumbled out into the intensifying midday sunshine, relieved to feel only a slight irritation on my exposed skin. I wanted to ask how many days we'd been here, but now wasn't the time. Ryan walked briskly to a Ford Explorer that sat idling halfway between the motel room and the diner. I followed, tossing the sheets into the car and taking a seat in the back.

A pretty woman with straight, strawberry blonde hair, huge green eyes and high cheekbones looked me over from her spot behind the wheel. I smiled awkwardly as Ryan dove into the front passenger seat.

"Go!" he urged, slamming his door as the woman spun the wheels and screeched off down the street. I questioned the instinct to put my seatbelt on, thinking it useless now that I was technically dead. Or undead. I made a mental note to get my new–found status cleared up.

We ended up on what looked like a freeway, and after about ten minutes, the woman driving seemed to relax slightly and backed off the gas. Ryan popped the safety back on his revolver and rested it on his lap.

"Mia Blake," he said, gesturing, "meet Ivy. I think you two are going to like each other."

I swallowed dryly. "Thanks for the ride," I said.

She turned and grinned at me, her perfectly straight, white teeth looking more Hollywood than Dracula.

"No problem," she said. "I would have brought the helicopter if I could."

I nodded in disbelief as we made our way to Los Angeles.

SIXTEEN

THREE HOURS AND ONE VERY TENSE BORDER CHECK LATER, WE were pulling up to a palatial Spanish-style mansion in Santa Monica. I only knew it was Santa Monica because of the end destination on the GPS screen that was mounted to the dash in front. I hadn't really been talking for a lot of the trip. I longed to sleep but wanted to make sure I didn't miss anything important.

We drove through a set of gates and into a large, walled lot that seemed to stretch out for miles. There was a circular driveway leading to the split-level residence. The house appeared to be made out of limestone, and was rendered in a burnt red color. A thick green grapevine twirled up a trellis between two gigantic windows and black iron balconies jutted out from the second floor. I took a look at the stairs leading up to the massive double wooden front doors and guessed they were made from marble.

The house probably would have fit in perfectly in Mexico, but here we were, in what looked to be a wealthy part of Los Angeles. I had never been to the West coast, and the heat struck me as soon as I got out of the car. It was a dry, intense heat that made my skin prickle in discomfort.

Ryan appeared beside me. "You feel okay?"

I nodded, suddenly woozy from thirst and the heat. "Where are we?"

"Ivy's place." Ryan placed his hand in the small of my back, guiding me up the stairs. I looked at what he was holding. "Hey!" I said indignantly. "That's my bag!"

Sure enough, he was holding my handbag. I had assumed that I would never see it again, but here it was, taunting me. I hadn't seen it since the night I'd been taken, and looking at it now brought back every awful thing that had happened that night.

I don't want your ring, or your Canal Street knock-off.

I clenched my jaw, my chest swiftly filled with rage. When we got up to the front door, I stopped dead and refused to go past the threshold.

"What's wrong?" Ryan asked, but I could tell he already had some idea what I was thinking.

"I want to go home," I said stubbornly.

Ryan sighed. "You're not a prisoner here. You can do whatever you want. But," he pointed at my swiftly reddening skin, "you're going to regret it if you stay outside."

I stared at him angrily, searching his face for any sign of malice or lies.

"Give me until sundown," he said quickly. "You can rest, we can talk. Then you can make a decision about what you want to do."

I wavered in the doorway. Should I shelter in the little shade there was, somehow get to a phone, and call the police? For the first time, it didn't seem so clear-cut anymore. I was starting to turn a beautiful shade of lobster red when Ivy breezed past me, carrying a duffel bags and dragging a roll-along suitcase that I'd seen before.

"Is that my stuff?" I shrieked, pointing. Ivy handed the bags to Ryan and gestured for him to continue inside the house.

"How did you get my stuff? Did you hurt my mom?"

"Your mom's fine. She packed these bags for you. She thinks you're at an intensive track camp at The University of California."

"Why does she think that?" I demanded, feeling hotter by the second.

"You've been emailing her almost every day," Ryan answered. "Come inside, I'll explain."

"I can't believe this." I shook my head, overwhelmed. My mom thought I was at track camp? No wonder nobody had rescued me. *Nobody even knew I was missing.*

"Look, kid," Ivy said, studying my face intently while she chewed strawberry–flavored gum. I knew it was strawberry because my sense of smell had become so acute in the past few days. I could even tell what brand of gum she had in her mouth. "I know where you've been, I've been there as well. I was taken by the same person you were."

"Him?" I said incredulously, pointing through the door where Ryan had disappeared.

She smiled, shaking her head. "Not him. Caleb." She paused, looking me up and down. "Ryan's not a bad person. He –"

"–is a *terrible* person," I interjected. "I'm not buying, lady."

She pressed her lips together, seemingly amused. "You're not scared of me, are you?"

I narrowed my eyes. "Are you reading my mind or my face now?"

The smile disappeared, replaced by a frown. I stood in front of one incredibly pissed–off vampire, and I had no idea what I'd said to get that reaction from her.

"Get inside," she hissed. I tried to resist, but her words were absolutely magnetic. I shuffled through the door, into the house, and jumped as it was slammed shut behind me.

My eyes adjusted instantly to the dimly lit hallway, which surprised me. I didn't have time to think about my new improved vision, though. I walked down the terracotta–tiled hallway, into a huge, open–plan kitchen and dining area. Through that room, the hallway continued, and I saw Ryan disappear into a doorway on the left. I followed dubiously, making sure to pay as much attention as possible to my surroundings. It looked, for the most part, like a regular house. Which was kind of a relief after the twisted shit I'd seen in the last few weeks.

I poked my head into the room where Ryan had disappeared, to find a large double bedroom. Ryan had set my stuff on the floor in front of a white, canopied, King-sized bed.

"This is your room," he said. "Until you go home."

"Which home are we talking about now?" I asked, barging past him and snatching up my handbag.

"Mia," he said, and I felt dread at hearing my name come out of his mouth. I ignored him, kneeling in front of the bed and dumping the contents of my handbag onto the fluffy white duvet. My iPhone, keys, tampons and a can of mace spilled out in a messy pile. I grabbed the phone triumphantly and pressed the ON button.

"Mia, can you listen for a minute?" I felt him crouching beside me but didn't look. I looked at my blank iPhone screen in frustration and tried pressing the power button again. It was no use. The battery was probably drained by now. I started opening compartments in my handbag, finding tissues, study notes and crumpled up receipts, but no charger.

"Mia?"

I rummaged some more and my fingers brushed against a smooth, almost waxy piece of paper tucked into the side of my bag. I dug it out and stared at life as I had known it before Ryan had taken me. It was a strip of photos from one of those old-school photo booths. On the last day of work at Jefferson Lake, the camp had held a carnival day, complete with pony rides, water slides—and a photo booth. Jared, Evie and I had crammed into the kid-sized compartment and posed for laughs. The first two photos were of all three of us, pulling stupid faces. Then there was a photo of Evie and I, smiling and laughing. The last photo was Jared and I, sharing a corny kiss. I stared in horror at my old life as I tried to hold the shattered pieces of myself together.

Ryan took the phone from me and placed it on the bed in front of us. I didn't care about the stupid phone any more. Even if I did call home, what was I going to say? The truth? It sounded fucking ridiculous. *I got kidnapped by vampires, Mom. How are you?*

"Mia!" Ryan snapped, grabbing my shoulder and shaking me out of my thoughts.

"*What*?" I yelled. Tears filled my eyes but I refused to let them spill over.

He let go of my shoulder and spoke in a softer voice. "I know this is hard for you. There are things happening right now that you can't even begin to understand. Just remember this: You're not dead. It was close—you were almost gone too far for my blood to bring you back. You can see them again," he gestured to the photo strip in my hand, "but first I need to make sure you're safe. The people who were after you in Mexico still want you back."

I glared at him. "Is this supposed to make me happy?" I asked coldly. "Because it doesn't. At all."

He looked genuinely confused. "I saved your life after you jumped out of a *window*. You nearly bled to death. You *should* be happy."

"I never asked you to save me," I snapped, feeling sick for the thousandth time. "I asked you to leave me there to die, remember?"

He shook his head, got up and left the room. I slammed the door behind him with a satisfying crash.

I took a deep breath and looked around my new cage. It sure was pretty, but it was still essentially a cage. The only things missing were a length of chain hanging from the ceiling and a dead girl in the corner.

You know, I like you. I might just keep you after Caleb's finished.

I pressed my palms to my burning cheeks and wondered what the hell could possibly happen next.

SEVENTEEN

After Ryan left, I stared at the door I'd slammed shut on him. My brain felt tired—that nauseating, burning fatigue that takes hold and makes you feel like you're never going to have an ounce of energy as long as you live. I think I was in shock, too—nobody dies and wakes up again without some kind of major issues. I ended up curling into a ball on the bed and crying. I cried and cried until there was nothing left in me, until I was calm and still and quiet.

After a little while, I sat up, wiped my itchy face with clammy hands, and decided to have another go finding a phone charger. I had just finished tearing apart the contents of the suitcase some vampire had neatly packed for me when there was a knock at the door. I looked up, eyebrows raised.

"Yeah?"

The door opened. Ryan had changed into a black fitted t-shirt and denim shorts, his bare feet silent on the polished floorboards of the hallway. If he were just a regular guy, I would have been tongue–tied at his effortless magnetism—the guy practically *oozed* sexuality. But as it was, everything about him just irritated me. He held a white phone charger in his hand and tossed it to me. I caught it mid–air. Seemed my reflexes had gotten better since the Turn.

"Thanks," I said tightly.

He leaned against the doorway, crossing his ankles lazily. "I'm sorry about before."

I shrugged. "Whatever."

He rolled his eyes, further irritating me. "Don't roll your eyes!" I yelled loudly. "I'm not going to forget what happened, *Ryan*." I said his name with such derision that his smile vanished, replaced by what looked like exhaustion. It was the first time I'd seen any real reaction from him, he was normally so composed.

"Plug that in. Your phone should turn on in a few minutes."

"It probably doesn't even work," I said angrily, but I stomped over to the wall and plugged it in anyway. After I attached my phone I returned to the bed, sitting with my arms crossed like a sullen child.

He came into the room, sitting on the bed beside me again. I shifted to the furthest end, as far away from him as possible.

"Did you mean it?" I blurted out suddenly. "That you were going to keep me after Caleb was finished with me?"

His face lit up in understanding. "Oh, you remember that."

"Yes," I hissed. "I do."

"No, I didn't mean that. Mia, I want you to think for a few minutes. Your phone's charging, you can call your family in a minute."

I raised my eyebrows questioningly.

"This is going to be hard for you. Becoming a vampire—it's a huge process."

"It hurt," I said quietly, staring at the floor. "Does it hurt for everyone?"

Ryan frowned, pressing his palms together. I could practically see the cogs turning over in his brain. I could tell he wanted to answer my questions carefully. "Yes," he said finally. "Some don't even survive the Turn. I'm very surprised you did, with the way you fell."

I touched the fine bones structured around my eyes, eyes that could see better than ever before. "I still don't really believe it," I said softly. "I felt my skull smash. I've never seen so much blood. How could I not have died?"

"You did die. For all intents and purposes, your heart stopped beating, you weren't breathing."

"I was dead?" I blinked back fresh tears. "For how long?"

"Mia, I don't think –"

"How. Long?"

Ryan sighed. "A few hours, maybe more. I got you out of there as soon as I could and took you to the motel."

"And?"

"And I fed you my blood. Through an IV at first, to get you back, and then from my wrist."

"So, if I was dead …" I was at a loss for words. "Where did I go?"

He shook his head and spread his palms. "I don't know."

"Don't lie," I said tiredly. I don't know how I could tell with such certainty that he was being untruthful, but I just *knew*.

He cleared his throat. "You were probably on your way to what we call The Underworld. Your soul, I mean. It's where all souls go after they pass. Once you enter The Underworld, you can never leave."

I shook my head. "I believe in stuff like physics and gravity and the big bang theory. I do not believe in Heaven and Hell." I thought of my father, then. How, when I had seen his coffin being wheeled into the crematorium, I had wished so badly that he was going somewhere better, but I knew that he was just dead. Gone. Ceased to exist. If there really was an afterlife … well, it was just too good to be true.

Ryan smiled knowingly. "You don't believe in vampires, either. And yet, here we are."

"Yes, we are. So tell me what I need to know, so I can make my call."

"You're not in prison. You can make more than one call."

Prison is exactly what this is like.

"Whatever. You want my attention, here it is. Talk."

"How do you feel?" he asked.

"Sick," I replied honestly. "Sick and tired. I can see a little better, I guess. That's about all."

"The sickness will pass," he said, not at all convincingly.

"That sounds like a lie," I grumbled. "Not a very good one, I might add."

"Well, the more blood you drink, the better you'll feel."

The thought of drinking blood was simultaneously interesting and nauseating. "Forget the blood," I waved my hand dismissively. "Just give me the short version of Vampire 101."

That made him smile in amusement. Which pissed me off. I wasn't there for his amusement.

"The order to take you that night came from Caleb," Ryan began. "I was in New York doing some recon work –"

"We call it 'stalking' where I come from," I interjected caustically.

"—when I was told to come to you. I took you, yes, but I didn't realize what he had planned for you."

"Huh, what? He bit me, like, one time when I pissed him off. You did a lot worse, buddy." I prepared to launch into a checklist of the injuries he'd given me, but I couldn't be bothered speaking words that would fall on deaf ears.

"I thought I was taking you to be Turned. Usually, that's all he does. Simple, straightforward, easy. I had no idea what he'd been doing while I was on the east coast, you have to believe me."

"That doesn't make it better!" I exploded. "Minus a few torture sessions, I still end up like this! Burning, sick, *alone*. None of that would have changed if he had just Turned me."

"You're not alone" Ryan said gently.

"Fuck you," I replied.

"You don't understand," Ryan pleaded. He was starting to lose his cool, and I realized it was because he was afraid—of me leaving. "Vampires, we're just regular people who were infected with a virus. We used to be able to have children just like everyone else, but now, vampires can't reproduce. The only way to make sure we survive is to Turn humans."

My whole body went still and cold. "Vampires can't have children?"

His eyes were sad. "No."

I stared at him in disbelief. "I can't have a baby?"

He shook his head. "I'm sorry, Mia. The last known baby born to a vampire mother was over four hundred years ago. The virus freezes your reproductive cycle."

I thought of the plans I had had for my future, the dreams. I was going to go to college, get an awesome job somewhere. Then eventually Jared and I would get married, and have tiny babies together. I was in no rush to have kids, but I had always imagined one day I would be a mother. Two kids, a girl and a boy.

And this asshole had just taken all of that away from me.

"I fucking hate you!" I screamed, picking up my phone and hurling it at him, followed by the charger which I ripped out of the wall socket, the lamp from the bedside table, and then the bedside table itself. He dodged each item with ease, but the poor wall behind him didn't fare so well.

I just hurled that solid wood table like it was a bag of cotton candy.

"Mia –"

"Get out!" I yelled, sobbing.

Ivy appeared in the doorway. "What's her deal?" she asked Ryan, watching me rage.

Ryan glared at her. "You're not helping," he scolded.

"Wasn't trying to," she replied, never taking her eyes off me.

"Sam?" she called down the hallway. "Can you come here a minute?"

I stopped throwing shit around the room. "Who's Sam?" I demanded.

"Sam doesn't need to get involved in this, *Ivy*," Ryan said tightly.

"Who's Sam?" I repeated, louder this time.

"I'm Sam," A voice answered me first, and then a tall handsome vampire (I was starting to recognise them on sight) with shaggy brown hair, dark brown eyes and incredibly sleek, muscled arms appeared beside Ivy in the hallway. He looked from me to Ryan, balling his hands into fists. The two had a tense stare–off, until Ivy cleared her throat.

"Sam," she said pointedly. "Ryan has brought Mia here to help her adjust to our way of life. She doesn't really *trust* him though, seeing as he kidnapped and tortured her and made her jump out a window."

"I didn't make her jump," Ryan said weakly.

"Oh, well in that case," Sam answered sarcastically. "What *are* you doing here?"

Ryan started pacing the length of the large bedroom.

"I didn't know who else to trust, okay? Caleb has eyes and ears everywhere—I figured you guys were my only safe option. It's not like he can get into either of your minds."

Sam appeared to relax slightly. Ivy looked bored.

"These people don't even like you?" I said to Ryan incredulously. It had all just clicked for me. These two *hated* Ryan by the sound of things. "Why *are* we here?"

Ryan threw his hands up, frustrated. "This thing that connects you and me? It also connects me to Caleb. I can feel him right now, trying to get into my head and figure out where we are. All of my friends? Are vampires, either made by Caleb or somehow connected to him. So he's pretty much sifting through all of their brains, right now, trying to find us."

"Do you have protection from him?" Ivy asked.

"Only these stupid hex bags." Ryan pulled his from his back pocket and threw it on the bed. "The other reason I came to you. I need a witch to help me stay hidden. You're the best there is."

"You have the heart, too," I said automatically. Ryan glowered at me. *That was supposed to be a secret*, he said silently.

I smiled.

Ivy looked pissed. "You didn't tell me the whole story, Ryan. Let's talk. *Now*." She stormed off in the direction of the kitchen, and Ryan followed closely behind her.

I looked at Sam awkwardly. "So ..." I said. "What do you do? Besides drink blood and kill people."

"I'm a Doctor," he answered, looking confused. "A professor, actually. I work at UCLA. What happened to you?"

I shrugged. "You know. Vampires take you from a parking lot, you wake up in Mexico, they shove little taps into your brain. The standard B-grade horror movie." I fidgeted awkwardly, not sure what to do with my hands.

Sam looked horrified. "You saw Caleb?"

"Oh, yeah." I pointed to the disgusting round bite scar on my neck. "He had the buffet."

Sam stepped closer, studying my neck. "There's nothing there," he said.

"What?" I turned and rushed into the ensuite bathroom. I leaned in as close as possible to the large mirror, studying my neck with my new laser–accurate eyes. Nothing. Not even a scratch. In less than a week, my infected, pus–leaking vampire bite had completely healed without so much as a scar.

Sam stood in the doorway that led from the bedroom to the bathroom, but I could tell he didn't want to come any closer, and that made me wonder. Ryan didn't care about my personal space. I was surprised he cared for me at all, after the things he'd said and done back in Mexico.

"You're a doctor," I said, turning to him. "How did I lose a massive vampire bite?"

Sam frowned. "How long since you Turned?"

"Since I *was* Turned," I corrected him. "You're implying that I did this to myself. Quite the opposite. I expressly asked that this *not* be done." As I heard myself talking, I realized that I sounded like an entitled little bitch, but I was beyond caring.

Sam blinked. "Right. How long since you *were* Turned?"

"I don't know," I answered quietly. "A few days? Less than a week. I don't remember a lot of it."

"Well, the good news is you're not going insane," Sam said, obviously trying to lighten the mood. "Vampirism is caused by a virus. It attaches itself to your DNA, makes its way into every cell in your body, and takes over. Vampires can heal from a wound in a matter of minutes. Have you attacked anyone yet?"

"What?" I looked at him incredulously. "No. Ew! Why?"

He shook his head, seemingly pleased. "It's just … you seem remarkably lucid for a newly infected vampire."

"Remarkably lucid?" I echoed. "All I've done for the past few days is throw up, cry and bleed."

"Thank God for that," Sam replied. "Usually, vampires spend their first few weeks—or months—attacking everyone and everything they can."

I cast a sidelong glance at the broken lamp and overturned bedside table in the corner and tried to appear calm and generally non-violent. "Is that what you did when you were Turned?"

He paled. He looked like an injured puppy dog.

"Sorry," I apologized. "It's none of my business."

He just searched my face, as if looking for the answer to a question I didn't know.

This is awkward.

"That's what all vampires do," he said quietly. "The bloodlust, it's quite horrific."

"Bloodlust?" I echoed. "Like being hungry?"

He stared at me like I was a freak. I shifted uncomfortably under the weight of his eyes.

"Like being a homicidal maniac," he said, "with zero impulse control."

"Oh," was all I could think to say. I tried to imagine Sam as a homicidal maniac with zero impulse control and failed. The guy looked too normal. Ryan, on the other hand …

"Do you want something to eat?" Sam asked, abruptly changing the subject. "I just put a pizza in the oven."

I wanted to ask if the pizza sauce had blood in it, but I stopped myself. This guy seemed nice enough. I figured I should really save all of my snark for Ryan.

"Um … sure," I shrugged, suddenly starving. My last meal had been in Mexico, like, ten hours ago at the diner. All I'd eaten in the car was a half-melted Snickers bar and some salted potato crisps.

"This way," Sam said, taking off down the hallway. I grabbed my favourite Yankees sweater from the pile of clothes I'd emptied onto the floor and followed him out into the kitchen area. Ryan and Ivy were nowhere to be seen, which made me feel better. Sam seemed genuine and pretty normal, whereas Ivy seemed volatile and on edge. And when she had told me to *get inside*, I hadn't been able to resist her, which scared the crap out of me.

How had she made me do something just with words? Was it because she was a witch? Or was it because she was a vampire?

I wasn't even sure I wanted to know.

EIGHTEEN

THE LARGE KITCHEN BOASTED WIDE FRENCH DOORS THAT LED out to a sheltered outdoor lounge and barbecue area, and beyond that, a massive turquoise-colored pool that was shaped like a kidney. I walked through the open doors and was hit by the pleasant smell of pepperoni and cooking dough. Sam stood in front of a red metal pizza oven, with a paddle in his hands. I watched in all my starving awe as he scraped a pizza from the bottom of the oven and slid it onto a plate.

He cut the pizza into eight slices and gestured for me to sit at the long outdoor table. It was smooth on top but the sides were uneven, as if it had been carved from a single tree trunk. I sat across from Sam and took a piece of pizza. "Ow!" A string of molten cheese stuck to my thumb. I decided to let the pizza cool for a minute.

"So, you live here?" I asked.

Sam nodded as he took a bite of pizza, apparently unperturbed by the molten lava cheese that covered it.

"And you and that Ivy chick, you're a thing?"

He laughed with a mouthful of food, I guess because I referred to her as a chick. "Mmm–hmm."

"How long have you been a vampire?" I asked.

"How do you know I'm a vampire?" he replied.

I wrinkled my nose. "I'm not sure," I answered. "I just do."

"Sixteen years," he said, going for a second slice. "Since the summer of '97."

"Sounds like a song," I said, taking a tentative bite of pizza. It was good. Gooey and cheesy, with just the right amount of pepperoni on top. My stomach growled loudly.

"Almost. That's the 'Summer of '69.'"

I guessed he looked a little older than me, twenty maybe, and counted back in my head. "So, you're like ... thirty—something now?" He was the best looking thirty-something-year-old I'd ever laid eyes on, that's for sure. He made Ryan look like a regular dude. What was with all the vampires being amazingly good looking?

"I guess," he replied, wiping his fingers on a paper napkin. "I was twenty–one when I was Turned. That makes me thirty–seven next month."

I tilted my head curiously. "Do you feel twenty–one? Or do you feel almost thirty–seven?"

Sam shrugged. "I guess I don't really feel any particular age. I'm pretty young for a vampire. Ivy's seven hundred years old."

I raised my eyebrows. "That's why she's a raging bitch," I guessed.

Sam laughed. "Grumpy, and with excellent hearing, as well. You've been warned."

"Right. So, can you explain to me how this virus actually works? I mean, I still don't really believe all of this, but you know, just humor me."

Sam nodded. "Sure, okay. Come down to the basement and I'll show you a couple of DNA models I've made."

I stiffened at the mention of a basement, and dropped my half–eaten pizza slice. A basement. Somewhere without windows.

Somewhere I could be locked. Where nobody could hear me scream.

"I'll just talk you through it out here," Sam said swiftly, noticing my reaction. I relaxed again, taking a breath. It was just ridiculous to think that I no longer needed to breathe.

"Do you want the vampire folklore version or the scientific version?" he asked.

I shrugged, picking up my pizza again. "Hit me with both," I replied. "It can't hurt."

"Okay. Vampire folklore first. Back in the eleventh century, this guy is walking down an alleyway, when he's attacked by a mob of drunks. They stab him and leave him for dead. This guy is calling out for help, calling for Jesus or God, but he's clearly bleeding to death. So, anyway, then he starts calling out for *anyone* to help, and this beautiful woman appears in front of him out of nowhere.

"He begs this woman to help him, and she says she will, for a price. He'll do anything to avoid dying, so he agrees. He thinks she's an angel and agrees to give her ownership of his soul.

"She feeds him her blood, and he lives. He falls in love with her instantly. It's only later on that she tells him the truth—she's a demon on day-release from hell, or something like that. And he's just become the first human to be Turned into a vampire through drinking her demon blood."

"That sounds screwed up," I said, pushing my plate away.

"It really is," Sam agreed. "That guy's Caleb, by the way."

"Jesus," I replied, suddenly alarmed. "Can the demon woman help him find me?"

"No." He sounded sure. "She's in hell, where demons belong. She hasn't been back to earth since. Someone closed that little loophole and now she's stuck down there for good."

"Hell," I said. "The Underworld? Is that where I was?"

Sam shook his head. "It usually takes a person a couple of days to reach The Underworld entrance after they die. From what I pieced together, you were only gone a few hours."

I looked around in frustration. "I'm sorry," I said plainly, "but does this not all sound a little crazy to you? I mean, come on. There are vampires? Demons? *Hell?!*"

Sam shrugged. "It's what I've heard. I don't believe one way or another because I haven't seen proof either way. I never believed any of it at first but… you see things. Your perception of what's real changes pretty fast in this world. When you see a person die and then wake up alive the next day, you start to believe some of this crap."

"And the sciencey part?" I asked, hoping at least that would sound a little more believable.

"Right." Sam finally pushed his plate away, seven chewed pizza crusts all that remained of his delicious creation. I stared at the empty plate between us with wistful regret.

Next time I will eat faster.

"Vampires are just regular people that have been exposed to a virus," Sam began. "It's a virus that we carry in our blood. You can't catch it from the air, or from touching something a vampire has touched. It takes a blood transfusion—a big one. Drinking vampire blood isn't enough anymore. You have to have a lot of vampire blood injected straight into your bloodstream for the virus to take hold."

"If vampires were all regular people once, why are they all such assholes?" I interrupted.

Except you.

Sam shrugged. "I don't know. I think it has a lot to do with the type of people who want to be vampires, you know? A normal person doesn't just wake up one day willing to give up their humanity for a chance at immortality. It's people who are already screwed up. Greedy people. People who are dying. People who feel like they don't have any other options. People who get forced into it."

Like me. My head was hurting. I massaged my throbbing temples with my fingertips.

"You okay?" I heard Ryan's voice behind me, and felt a warm

hand on my back. It still irritated the hell out of me, the way he was acting like the good guy in all of this.

"Mm–hmm," I replied, shrugging his hand off of me.

"You thirsty?" he asked, quieter this time.

Sam let out a surprised noise, and I looked up at him. His eyebrows were raised and he looked kind of pissed.

Great, three pissed–off vampires in one day! A trifecta.

"I can't believe you, dude. You say you're trying to help her?"

"Sam, stay out of this." The warning in Ryan's voice was unmistakable.

Sam slid his glass of water across the table so it was in front of me. "If you're thirsty, drink this. You don't need to listen to him."

"Wait." I looked from Ryan to Sam, confused. "Don't vampires need blood to live?"

"Yes," Ryan said.

"No," Sam said at exactly the same time.

"You told me I had to or I would die," I protested through gritted teeth.

"She will go crazy, Sam –"

"Do I look crazy to you?" Sam asked angrily.

Ryan groaned theatrically. "Give me a break. You're … different to everyone else."

"You've been fed a story, Mia." Sam was insistent. "Vampires don't need blood, they simply *like* it, the same way an addict likes their drug of choice. You won't die if you don't drink it. You can just eat and drink exactly the way you did before you were Turned. I've been like this for fifteen years now and I'm just fine."

He did look just fine. Mighty fine, actually. He didn't have that sickly pallor under his skin that Ivy and Ryan possessed. He looked *normal.* I turned to glare at Ryan. "Give me one good reason why I shouldn't believe him."

"What he's saying is impossible," Ryan exploded. "That's a good reason."

Sam pointed to me, but his words were for Ryan. "You think I'm different? *She's* different, man. Look at how together she is. You say she woke up after the change *yesterday*? She should be snapping people's necks right now, having a massacre somewhere, and *look* at her."

I suddenly felt self-conscious. *Having a massacre?*

Ryan did look at me, for what seemed like a long time. "Fine," he said. He went inside and came back with a steaming mug full of what looked like black sludge. He slammed it down in front of me, and some of the dark brown liquid sloshed over the table. "Drink that."

"What is it?"

"It's diluted with coffee. It'll help you feel better."

I pressed my lips together and shook my head. "I don't want it," I said stubbornly.

I saw Ryan's jaw clench, and even though I wasn't trying to read his mind, I could feel the anger and frustration radiating from him. These two obviously had a history.

"Why are you trying to mess this up?" Ryan asked Sam in a measured, even voice that didn't sound half as mad as the way he obviously felt. "I'm trying to do the right thing here."

Sam rose from his chair so the two were eye-to-eye. Well, Sam was about an inch taller, actually, but that's not important.

"What are you up to, Ryan? You don't help people. You *kill* people. Especially pretty high school girls."

He thought I was pretty?

Ryan looked almost embarrassed. "I think I had ... an epiphany."

Sam laughed, slapping his thigh with his hand. "Dude, are you shitting me? Last time you had an 'epiphany,'" he made rabbit ears in the air with his fingers, "you burned Ivy's house down."

"Second time's a charm," Ryan replied coldly.

My feeling that Ryan was generally not a very nice person was being strongly reinforced.

Ivy suddenly appeared behind Sam. She glared at Ryan. "You need to back off, okay? You wanted our help, and you've got it. But you're not in charge here."

Ryan shook his head. "This was a *colossal* mistake. I risk everything for this stupid girl who won't do anything I say, I come home, looking for help from an old friend, and *I'm* the asshole?"

He thought I was stupid? Stupid and pretty all in one.

"You came *home*, Ryan?" Ivy said in disbelief. "This is Sam's home now. Don't start waving your dick around like you own the joint. You burnt this place to the ground, remember? Sam and I rebuilt it, brick by fucking brick. So you can either back off, or get out."

Ryan looked beyond them, to the pool, chewing his lip.

"But she stays," Ivy added quickly. "She's safe here."

"She's mine," Ryan said defensively.

"No, I'm not!" I protested. "I'm nobody's!"

"What I mean is, you're my responsibility," Ryan said quickly. "I didn't mean it the way you think."

I glowered. Nobody said anything.

I threw my napkin down, stood up and went inside without giving anyone a second glance. I slammed every door I could find on the way to the room I had been assigned—I refused to call it my bedroom—and went back to my spot in front of the ensuite bathroom mirror. I studied my smooth neck again, looking for any tiny remainder of the scar Caleb had inflicted, but there was still nothing. My temple was perfectly smooth, no sign of a crushed skull there. My shoulder, the one I had dislocated and later landed on when I fell, felt fine. Better than fine—it had never felt better.

I stepped back so I could take a good look at myself—so I could look at the girl I had become. Everything was the same, but everything had changed. My eyes, normally sparkling blue and full of energy, were now dull and almost gray in colour. Jared had always claimed to be able to tell what mood I was in by the subtle changes in my eye colour, and I had to admit now that he was right. I looked old and tired and washed–up, but if the vampires were telling the truth, I was never going to get a day older—even if I lived another seven hundred years.

At that moment, I heard footsteps approach, and a gentle knock on the door.

"What?" I called out, not really interested in talking to anyone.

The door opened, revealing Ryan. What a surprise. The guy clearly couldn't stay away from me. I looked at him impatiently. "What do you want?"

He looked at my phone, still on the floor where it had landed after I threw it at him.

"You haven't called anyone yet."

I shook my head.

"Why?"

I shrugged, swallowing back a hard lump in my throat. "What am I supposed to say?"

He thought about that for a minute, before sitting on the large windowsill that overlooked the pool.

"I have an idea," he said finally.

"I'm not drinking more blood. Or that coffee," I snapped.

Ryan smiled. "Well, do you want to hear my idea?"

I shrugged, still fuming inside, but too tired to keep fighting. "Sure. Why not."

He gestured for me to sit next to him, and I did.

"Remember when we were in the diner, and I showed you my past?"

I nodded.

"And you seemed to digest that a lot easier than me just telling you things, right?"

I nodded again. "It was like you couldn't lie, even if you tried," I admitted.

"That's right. Here. Give me your hands." He stretched his palms out, and I took hold of them reluctantly.

"Ready?"

"I guess."

I felt the room fade into the background with a kind of sucking *shoooook!* as the memory Ryan was showing me came into clear focus in my mind.

This time was just as bizarre and all–consuming as the first time had been. Except, now that I knew what to expect, I was a little better about receiving all of the information being fed to me.

We were in Ryan's apartment in Caleb's compound in Mexico. I gazed around, wondering what he could possibly show me that didn't involve killing stupid pretty girls and drinking their blood. There was a girl, maybe mid–twenties, holding a blackberry to her ear and obviously waiting for her call to be answered. She definitely didn't look human. Her green eyes practically glowed with supernatural power. She sat on a brown leather sofa next to Ryan, who was poised to listen to whatever conversation she was about to have.

"Sweetie, I missed you last night. I'm back in New York."

That was my mom on the other end of the phone!

A voice that sounded just like mine came out of the scary girl's mouth. "That's okay, I stayed at Evie's. Mom, you'll never believe what happened!"

That's not me, I thought. *How can she sound just like me?*

"Honey, I'm in the middle of a case –"

"I got accepted into UCLA's track program," the Me Impostor gushed over the line. "Full scholarship and everything!"

I heard my mother stop typing for a second, and I imagined her perfectly manicured red nails hovering in mid–air. "That's amazing, honey. You want to come up to celebrate? We could have dinner with Warren at that little bistro in Manhattan, what's it called?"

"Mom, I can't. I have to leave tonight to get there in time. My acceptance letter's been lost in the mail for a week, can you believe it?"

My mom had already resumed her typing. She was a smart

woman, a very successful woman—and I knew she loved me, so I wasn't offended. I'd learnt to accept her the way she was a long time ago.

"That's too bad," my mom said. "Well, will we see you soon?"

"Sure," The impostor said. "Bye Mom, love you!"

I blinked, and felt Ryan let go of my hand as the room came back into focus around me.

"Who was that?" I demanded. "That wasn't me talking—but it sounded just like me!"

"She's a shapeshifter."

I didn't want to ask what that was. Vampires were enough for one day. It suddenly occurred to me how organized this whole charade had been, from me being alone walking to my car, to the fact that they had chosen a weekend when my mother was away to kidnap me.

"How long was I being watched?" I asked Ryan slowly.

Ryan looked out of the window, to the pool and the trees beyond. Day was gradually bleeding into night, the sun just a pale yellow glow amongst the dusk. There was a cool breeze coming through the open window, and I hugged myself against the sudden chill.

"A year," he said, in a perfectly measured, rationed voice.

I took a minute to comprehend that. A lot had happened in the past year. "Was it you?"

"No." I couldn't tell if his expression was one of sadness, or regret. "Not until the last few weeks."

"Right. What about my boyfriend? My family? Do they have any idea?"

Ryan shook his head. "No. Which is why you can call them, without worrying. They all think you're at college, just like your mom does."

I thought about the impostor calling Jared. Had she told him she loved him? Had he told her?

"Sure, why would I worry," I said sarcastically, but I was tired and it came out sounding perfectly reasonable instead of angry and frustrated.

Ryan paused. "I didn't make that up, you know. You've been accepted into UCLA. Full track scholarship. You also got into Brown, Yale, and some pissy little colleges over on the east coast."

I felt my hands start to shake. "Are you joking?"

He smiled. "No joke."

My happiness was short–lived. "But I can't go!" I wailed. "I'm stuck here while your crazy boss tries to find me."

Ryan frowned. "Don't give up hope just yet. Caleb is way too busy to learn anything about his targets. That's *my* job. He probably has no idea where you're even from or how old you are. Plus he's very impatient. If we can throw him off for long enough, he'll get bored and start another project."

I was so ashamed at that moment because I thought to myself: *I wish Caleb would find some other girl instead of looking for me. I don't care if he takes her.*

I don't care if he takes a hundred girls, locks them away, drinks them up and tears at their flesh until they are rotted and hollow and dead inside.

I just want him to leave me alone.

NINETEEN

There was a time in those first few weeks after the change that I thought I would try to escape, but if I did, Caleb would find me.

Please. I just want to go home.

And once he did find me, he would take me again, lock me up and make everyone I love suffer.

But the reality was, he was probably going to make everyone I loved pay eventually even if he didn't find me. *Especially* if he didn't find me.

All I could think of was to hide, in the best hiding spot Ryan had thought of, in a house full of vampires—the only vampires in the world that, for some reason still unknown to me, Caleb couldn't find.

So I stayed where I was. And I prayed that Death would not find me.

TWENTY

I STAYED AT IVY AND SAM'S HOUSE WILLINGLY FOR MOST OF THE time, but there was one night, that first night I was there, when I thought I might try my chances at getting out. I didn't know what to say to Jared or my mom, but I had decided to call Evie, to hear a familiar voice more than anything. I felt like I was losing my identity, and I needed something from home to remind me again who I was.

I was also acutely aware that all of my fellow housemates had exceptional hearing, and I felt claustrophobic enough as it was without sharing my phone call, as well. So, after the house had gone dark and quiet, I grabbed my phone, slid on some sneakers and let myself out through the French doors in the kitchen. The night was humid, little beads of moisture clinging to the blades of grass underneath my feet. I jogged across the huge property, past beautiful old fruit trees, rows of grapevines, and a random old building that looked very much like a steepled church. Even in the darkness, I could see better than ever before, and I briefly wondered why Sam referred to vampirism with words like 'virus' and 'infection' when it seemed more like a bonus than a sickness, at least physically.

I ran for a bit longer, forgetting my phone call for the moment. I just wanted to be alone with my thoughts, to think about where I was and what I was going to do. For the first time in weeks, I felt the breeze on my face, air in my lungs, and a tiny glimmer of hope started to appear. Being surrounded by death had made me realize how much I loved my old life and everyone in it. I was in love. I missed Jared so much it hurt.

Just then, my iPhone beeped, and a text message from a number I didn't recognize flashed onto the screen. I unlocked the phone and started to read.

Bonnie and Clyde, it read. *Hope you're having a great adventure. Caleb sends his regards and says he'll see you both very soon. I like your friends Jared and Evie. They are a real hoot. I bet the blonde would taste great mixed with vodka. And your mom, I'll save her for an early start. The woman has caffeine for blood. Love from Ford. xx*

A second message came through, and appeared to be addressed only to me.

Hey spunky, it read. *Caleb wants to give you another chance. Agree to come back and we'll forget about killing everyone you love. Starting with your boyfriend. xox*

I read the text messages over and over until the strings of words made no sense. I started to shake. I shoved the phone in my pocket and began running again, only this time I was headed for the driveway that led to the street.

I was almost to the end of the driveway when I ran face–first into a wall that I couldn't see. I cried out, flying backwards and landing awkwardly on my tailbone. Pain shot up my spine and I groaned, clutching my back.

"What the hell?" I muttered. I got up, brushed myself off and tried to approach the gates again. But I just couldn't get to them. There was an invisible wall keeping me from getting out.

Just then, I felt someone watching me. I turned around to see Ryan, dressed only in black silk boxer shorts and clutching his phone, making his way down the front stairs.

"What the HELL is going on?!" I screamed. "Why is there an invisible –"

"Stop yelling at me!" Ryan demanded. He looked tired, and I realized he mustn't have slept at all in the days since saving me. Oh well. I hardly cared about *his* comfort.

"I'm trapped, aren't I?" Pissed didn't even come *close* to describing how I felt.

He looked away, clearly embarrassed at being caught out. "Technically, yes. But it's not to stop you from getting out –"

"—It's to stop other people from getting in," Ivy finished his sentence as she walked down the stairs from the front door. She was wearing a red lace negligee that skimmed her knees and left very little to the imagination. The woman looked amazing. And kind of evil.

"I don't trust either of you," I said. "I want to talk to Sam. Sam!" I yelled across the yard.

"He's in the basement," Ivy said, looking bored. "Steel walls, nice and thick. He won't hear you."

"Can't you just do that mind–communication thing with him?" I demanded.

"No, I can't," she replied haughtily. "I'm a defective model."

"Let me out," I demanded.

A defective model? That must be why Caleb can't find us here. The psychic mind stuff doesn't work on her.

"So you can get yourself killed, and us too for helping you? No way. Get over yourself and go to bed." She turned and walked back into the house.

I sank to the ground, tears blurring my vision.

"Mia, come inside," Ryan pleaded with me. He stepped closer, squeezing my shoulders with his cold hands.

"I trusted you!" I said, pushing him away. "Even after you did all those things to me, I trusted you. And you lied to me! All that crap about protecting my family from myself? I *am* a prisoner. You're taking up where Caleb left off. You're keeping me here."

Just then, I felt warm hands on my shoulders. I jumped, turning to see a sympathetic looking Sam. So she had told him to come out after all.

I backed away from Ryan so that I was standing next to Sam. He left one warm hand resting on my shoulder, and unlike Ryan's unwanted embraces, I liked the simple comfort of his touch.

"What is going on?" I asked them both impatiently. "Why can't I get out?"

Ryan's eyes lingered on the gates and he approached the invisible wall I had run face-first into only moments before. He pushed his palm through the air, and it stopped, the invisible wall coming into focus for just a second. It shimmered translucent silver like a mirage in the desert, and by the time I blinked, it had disappeared again.

"Magic. It keeps us all safe," he explained. "Vampires sleep like the dead. We could all take guarding shifts, make sure nobody gets in—but this is easier, and I haven't slept in a week."

"Well, you all come and go as you please," I said. "How?"

"There's a key," Sam said. "I'm sorry someone forgot to give you one. But you are definitely not a prisoner here." He glared at Ryan.

He reached into his pocket and pulled out two small packages, each about the size of a box of matches, wrapped in calico and secured with brown string. They smelled like herbs and reminded me of the hex bag Ryan had made me carry around.

Sam pressed one of the packages into my palm and gestured to the invisible wall. I reached out hesitantly, expecting my palm to bounce right off again, but this time it didn't. I could still feel a slight resistance, but as I stepped forward, the wall shimmered again and rippled, allowing me to step out of the yard to the other side. Sam followed, and together we stood freely at the end of the driveway.

"You want to go for a walk?" Sam asked, holding his arm out for me to grab a hold of. I smiled, relieved.

"Definitely," I replied, looping my arm around his. I didn't wave goodbye to Ryan, who stood silently watching us. *Screw him.*

There were no other houses in the immediate vicinity—Ivy's property must have spanned several acres. When we got to the end of the deserted street, Sam gestured to a park complete with a playground and bright red slide. We crossed the road, and made our way over to the swings. I sat in one, he in the other. I looked around, realizing there must have been a fire recently. All of the trees were charred black, devoid of any greenery save for a few precious shoots of regrowth that dared to peek out from some of the heavy trunks.

"We should have told you," Sam said immediately. "I'm sorry."

I shrugged. "It wasn't you," I said. "It was the other two. I don't trust them."

"Something else is bothering you," Sam said, frowning as he studied my face.

"Where do I start?" I said sarcastically.

"No, really," Sam persisted. I swallowed thickly and handed my iPhone over to him.

He read the messages silently, his pupils growing bigger and his expression more alarmed.

"Did you tell the others?" he asked, handing back my phone.

"No," I said. "I was too busy trying to climb over the magical prison wall."

He smiled then, and it made me feel a little less alone. He really was one of the kindest people I had ever met, human or vampire. Especially vampire. I think he was the only nice vampire I had met at that point.

"Are you considering going back to Mexico?" Sam asked seriously.

"Yes," I replied honestly. "Of course. If everyone I love is going to be hurt, of course I'll go back."

Sam shook his head. "They're bluffing," he said. "Trying to push your buttons. They're in Mexico."

"What if Caleb does send Ford back to New Jersey?" I asked, as the gruesome notion popped into my head. "Ryan said I was watched for a whole year. They know everything about me My friends, my family. The text message mentioned Evie. What if they take her, too?"

"She's your best friend?"

I stiffened. "How do you know?" I demanded.

"Ryan told us about her," Sam replied. "Said she was with you before he took you. Trust me, she's perfectly capable of taking care of herself."

"How?" I said in disbelief. "What is she, a secret ninja or something?"

"She's a witch," Sam replied. "Ryan thinks she knows something is up. And right now, she's casting so many protection spells, all of your family and friends will be safer than ever before."

I arched my eyebrows. "Witch?" I spluttered. "Like Ivy?"

Sam nodded. "Like Ivy."

My best friend is a goddamned witch?!

"You're a doctor," I said. "How can you even believe in witchcraft?"

Sam was thoughtful for a moment. "I never used to, before. But the things I've seen—you can't explain them away with logic. What I've learnt over the years is to never assume you know how things work, because just as soon as you figure the world out, everything changes again."

"Is that what happened to you?" I asked quietly. "Did everything change for you the way it's changing for me?"

Sam chuckled, but it was a dry laugh, devoid of anything good. "I was so young when I met Ivy," he said. "Twenty years old, I was. I was doing so well in college. About to graduate early, with honours, and then go to med school."

"Did you go? To med school?"

"Eventually," he replied, his voice as dry and dead as the burnt trees that surrounded us. "I had to ... wait a few years, until it was safe."

"Why'd you have to wait?" I asked. I needed to know everything.

"The blood," he said, his cheeks flushing pink. "I couldn't handle being around all that blood." He was embarrassed, I realized with a start. Ashamed that he was driven by a desire I was yet to fully understand.

"I don't think about blood," I confessed. "At all. I don't even like it much. Do you think there's something wrong with me, Sam?"

He smiled, little creases curling up at the corners of his toffee-coloured eyes. "There's nothing wrong with you, Mia. It's the rest of us who aren't right."

I stared at my palms. There were no scars from where I had dragged myself over broken glass in that courtyard in Mexico, when I had died. I thought about my death and all the secrets I had yet to learn.

"Did you die, Sam? When you were Turned?"

His face fell then, and it was his turn to stare at the ground. "We all die. We are alive, and then we die, and when we wake up again, we are something else entirely."

"Have you ever killed someone?" I whispered.

He didn't answer me.

TWENTY-ONE

I couldn't wait any longer. I had to call Evie, tell her what was going on. If she thought I was a weirdo, so be it. I couldn't carry the weight of my secret alone for another minute. And if she really was what Sam said—a witch—then maybe she could protect my family when I couldn't.

I must have dialled and hung up at least ten times before I got up enough nerve to let the call go through. She answered on the first ring, the sound of her voice taking the breath out of my lungs.

"Hello?" She answered, and I could hear the suspicion in her tone.

Right. She thinks I'm not me. She thinks it's a shapeshifter calling her from my number.

"Evie," I choked. I burst into tears.

"Holy shit, it's you." Her voice changed completely to one of worry and concern. "Where are you? Are you okay? Tell me, I can come get you. I can help you, Mia. Mia?"

Where to start? What to say? Would she even believe me? I

wouldn't believe me.

"I was—taken," I said falteringly. "I, um, I've been in Mexico. But I'm okay now." *No I'm not.* "Someone helped me get out of there. I'm in a safe place now."

Why was I so reluctant to tell her where I was?

"Are you in Mexico now?" She asked. "I don't think so. You're near the beach, aren't you?"

"How do you know that?" I asked quickly. Was she a part of this?

She sighed. "Mia, there are lots of things about me that you don't know. There are things I can do that other people can't do. I've been trying to find you ever since you disappeared."

The witch thing. Right. "Have I—have I tried to call you before now?"

She snorted. "No, but some bitch pretending to be you called me up. She hung up really fast once she realized I wasn't as stupid as your average blonde."

"Oh. Good." I didn't know what to say.

"Mia, I'm so sorry. Are you—are you one of *them* now?" She didn't say the word vampire, but we both knew what she meant.

I guess she took my silence as a *yes.*

"I should have known they were fucking vampires hanging around school. I should have been more careful." There. She had said the word so I didn't have to.

"It's not your fault, Evie."

"Give me the address. I'm on the first flight out there."

"Whoa," I said quickly. "You can't leave. I need you to protect Jared and my mom. Does Jared know anything?"

She breathed out heavily. "No. Although he's pissed that you left without telling him. What if something happens to you and I'm not there to help you, Mia? I left you alone in a goddamn parking lot in New York the day after I saw a *vampire* in our history class. What was I thinking?"

I pressed my forehead to the cool bedroom wall and closed my eyes. "You were thinking everything would be okay. Just like me."

"At first I thought they'd killed you," Evie confessed. "Only I couldn't find your ghost anywhere."

"My ghost?" *My ghost?!*

"Yeah. I kept waiting for your ghost—your soul—to show up, and it never did."

But I had died. According to Ryan, for a couple of hours, I had been dead.

"I thought I felt you die," Evie said miserably, as if reading my mind. "And when that feeling went away, I realized the vampires must have Turned you, and that it was too late."

My vision blurred as I blinked back something hot. It overflowed, and a single tear escaped, running down my cheek.

"Oh shit," Evie said. "That's not what I meant. You need to come home, Mia. Now."

Another hot tear, then another. "I can't. If I come back he's going to kill everyone I care about."

Evie didn't say anything.

"Hello?" I asked the empty phone line.

"I'm here," Evie replied quickly. "I just –"

"Don't know what to do?" I supplied helpfully. "That makes two of us."

"Why didn't you call me sooner, tell me what was happening?"

I shrugged even though I knew she couldn't see me. "And tell you what? That I'm a *vampire*? Do you know how stupid that sounds to me?"

"It's not your fault," Evie said softly, soothing my jagged nerves. "You didn't know about all this. Most people never do."

"Why didn't you tell me you were a witch?" I asked her. "You've known me for my whole life, Evie, and you never said a word!"

"Would you have believed me?" she asked tiredly. "Or would you have thought that I was crazy?"

She was right. "I just wish I had been prepared, you know? You think for your whole life that the world is one way, and it's nothing like you thought it was. It sucks."

"It does suck. I'm sorry I didn't tell you. I should have told you something, at least."

"Is my m–mom okay?"

"She's good. She's safe."

I pinched the bridge of my nose as another wave of headache crashed into my forehead. "She thinks I'm at school?"

"Yeah." Evie's voice was apologetic. "She's been getting emails from someone who says they're you. And calls, I think."

"I heard. Ryan showed me—it's hard to explain. But I heard one of the calls the shapeshifter made to my mom. She had no idea."

"Ryan. He's the one who helped you escape in Mexico?"

"Yeah," I replied. I omitted the part about him taking me in the first place. I don't know why I was protective of him after what he had done, but there it was.

"And where are you now?" She insisted.

"Los Angeles," I replied, hoping my vagueness would satisfy her.

"Address, Mia. Come on. I need to see that you're alright."

Panic swirled through me. "Please don't come," I begged. "I don't want you to see me like this. I need you to stay with Jared!"

"Okay. Here's the deal. I'm going to promise to stay with Jared, and make sure your mom is protected, and you're going to tell me the address."

My shoulders sagged in defeat. I rattled off the address and confirmed it as she repeated it three times.

"I'm sorry, I have to go," I said. "I'm so tired, I haven't slept."

"Go," Evie said gently. "Sleep. You'll be home soon, I swear."

As I ended the call, I had to wonder if what she was saying was even possible. Surely if Caleb was looking for me, I would have to stay away until he wasn't a threat anymore.

How could I make sure he was out of the picture? How did an eighteen-year-old girl turned vampire kill such an old and powerful creature?

TWENTY-TWO

I couldn't sleep. My bed was comfortable, my pillow just the right height and firmness. I felt queasy, but I was starting to think that the dropping sensation in my stomach would never go away. I just couldn't shut my mind off.

I could hear so many things, including some I probably wasn't supposed to hear. They say a vampire's hearing is most acute straight after Turning, and I was no exception. Ryan was breathing deeply, probably sleeping in the room next to mine. Ivy was in the kitchen. It sounded like she was emptying the dishwasher or something. I could hear Sam in the basement, tinkering with something—probably studying the sample of blood he'd drawn from my arm earlier in the afternoon.

I could hear his every minuscule movement and imagined what he could be doing. Strangely enough, as I listened closer, an entire picture of what he was doing began playing in my head. Almost as if I could see exactly what he was doing, just by listening and concentrating. I was listening with more than my ears—it was like some kind of psychic energy was allowing me to know just what was going on in another room of the house without actually being in there. It was kind of cool. I wondered how much was real, and how much was my imagination filling in the blanks.

I listened and 'watched' from my room as Sam took the small vial of my blood and removed the cap. Using an eyedropper, he drew up a single drop and squeezed it onto a glass slide. The slide carefully went underneath a large microscope, and he pressed his eye to the viewfinder.

A newborn vampire's blood is a peculiar thing to look at, I have since been told. It still has all of the visual markers of human blood, but if you look closely under a high-powered microscope, you will see the presence of a virus, attacking every single cell, burrowing into the nucleus like a hungry worm and recoding the genetic structure that once made that individual a human being. A DNA test is even more telling, and that's what Sam did next.

He slid his chair over to his computer, opened a program with a few clicks of a mouse and dropped another pinprick worth of blood onto a paper swab. This swab he fed into an expensive-looking machine about the size of a commercial photocopier. Sam kicked back in his chair and watched as colored bars and graphs appeared on his computer screen. After a few minutes, there was a knock on the door.

It was Ivy. I knew it even before I heard her speak. Something about her stride, the way she knocked at the door with impatience. I just *knew*.

"Whatcha doing?" Ivy asked, kicking the door shut behind her and following him over to the desk. "More research?"

"Yeah." He rubbed his eyes. He looked tired.

"You look tired," Ivy said, echoing my observations as she brushed a stray hair out of his eyes. She hesitated a little before she spoke again. "You should drink a little, just get a good night's –"

"What have I told you?" Sam exploded. I'd never seen—or

heard—him angry before. "I told you no. The answer is still no."

Ivy's face was pinched with concern. "I'm worried about you, Sammy. You look … sick."

Sam shrugged. "Maybe I'm starting to age, *Ivy*. Maybe not drinking blood is making me human again."

"Shut up," she replied. "I don't want to argue. Show me what you're working on."

Sam glanced at his computer screen again to see the model of my DNA building on the screen, twin helix strands with a ghostly third ribbon intertwined—the vampire virus.

"I'm trying to figure out why Mia's so calm and composed after being Turned less than a week ago." He pointed to the screen. "It all looks normal so far. I'm stumped."

I was calm and composed? I hardly thought so. I felt more like an emotional, sobbing mess most of the time.

"You seem to be developing an obsession over this girl," Ivy said, and when Sam looked at her in surprise, her green eyes practically screamed with envy. *And I wasn't even in the room!* "Walks in the park, dinner together. I've hardly seen you since she arrived."

Sam shook his head. I was flabbergasted. I had been in her house less than twenty-four hours and Ivy was already showing resentment?

"You sound like a jealous teenager," Sam said. "This girl is *different*. I want to know why. I want to help her. I doubt your psychopathic ex is really doing anything to help her."

I started to feel a little dishonest. Didn't they realize I could hear everything they were saying?

"If it were up to you, the girl would starve to death." Ivy's eyes were blazing now. "Perhaps we should try that? I mean, it took you ten years to live without human blood, but hey, she's different."

Sam rubbed his temples wearily. "Go, please. Have an O-Neg or something. Calm yourself down."

Oooh, burn. These two obviously had more issues than the

average couple.

Ivy looked taken aback. "What the hell is that supposed to mean? You think she can go without blood but you want me to have a fucking drink to calm down?!"

They were both yelling now, and Sam stood taller, towering over her. "You've never tried not drinking it," he accused.

"I'm a vampire!" Ivy shouted. "It's. What. I. Do."

"You," Sam murmured in a voice barely above a whisper, "drink blood because you like it. You cut into people and take their blood because you like it. You are the way you are *because you like it.*"

Ivy clenched her jaw, drawing her hand back. Her strike missed, Sam's hand shooting out to catch her wrist mid–air with ease. "Looks like that's not all you've been drinking," he muttered, pushing her away. "Look at you. You're tanked!"

Ivy shook her head, turned and fled up the stairs away from him.

That had been intense. I shook my head, blinked my eyes a few times and waited patiently for the images in my head to dissolve. I tossed and turned, trying to get comfortable, but my mind wouldn't stop racing. Every time I got close to drifting off, another image jumped into my brain. Ivy opening a wine bottle in the kitchen. Sam pacing in the basement. Ryan shifting in his sleep.

I glanced at my phone. Three–fifteen in the morning. So much for vampires being able to sleep soundly. I sat up and swung my legs over the side of the high bed, my feet just touching the cool floor. I padded over to the door and opened it, not surprised when a vampire fell into the room at my feet.

Ryan groaned and rubbed his face wearily. "Where are you going?" he asked.

"Jesus Christ," I muttered, stepping over him. "I'm just getting a sandwich. Go back to sleep."

He didn't follow me, so he must have either retreated to his room or curled up on the hallway floor again. I didn't really care, as long as he left me alone.

As I entered the kitchen, dark except for a lone lamp, I knew I wasn't alone.

"You look exhausted," Ivy observed from the large oak table where she sat. An empty wine glass and a half-full bottle of red wine sat in front of her.

"So do you," I replied. It was a lie. She looked sensational. And drunk.

She shrugged. "I'll sleep when I'm dead," she quipped, smiling darkly. I shifted uneasily from one foot to the other, not sure whether I should invade her space and make something to eat, or just go the hell back to bed.

"There's some cold cuts in the fridge," she said. "Bread's in the pantry."

So she did have excellent hearing as well. Thank God she couldn't read my thoughts on top of that.

"Thanks," I said awkwardly, reasoning that I may as well eat now that she had given me permission. I opened the giant stainless steel fridge and started grabbing salami, cheese, mayonnaise and tomatoes. I found a loaf of bread and a plate and started assembling a monster sandwich. Suddenly, I was absolutely starving again.

I stood at the dark granite bench and ate my sandwich, then another, and a third. By the end I was just eating salami and sliced beef straight from the package and not bothering with bread or condiments. The meat tasted really good, but unsatisfying at the same time—it was too dry, too overcooked for my liking.

"Sam told me you're not craving blood," Ivy said quietly. She had been silent the entire time I was eating, a good fifteen minutes, and I had almost forgotten she was there.

"No," I said after swallowing another mouthful of roast beef. "The thought of it makes me feel sick."

She nodded, taking a moment to think about what I had said.

When she didn't keep talking, I tried to think of something to say, something to break the unbearable silence.

"What kind of wine is that?" I asked.

She looked at the bottle. "Tempranillo. From Spain. You want some?"

I shook my head. "Maybe some other time." After seeing Ryan with his blood-infused coffee, I didn't want to risk spiked wine.

As I was putting everything back in the fridge, I smelled something *really good*. It smelled thick and juicy, like a rare beef roast. I shifted a few things around, packages of salad mix and a bowl of chopped pineapple and strawberries, until my eyes landed on the thing that was making my mouth water.

It was a stack of plastic bags, each holding an equal measure of human blood. I was drawn to them like a moth to a flame, my mouth tensed to rip open the flimsy packaging and suck greedily at the viscous nectar contained within. I stepped back and shook my head, and just as soon as the intense and foreign hunger had consumed me, it was gone again.

It's nothing. You need some red meat is all. You've been living on fries and sandwiches for days.

I slammed the refrigerator shut and jumped as a face smirked at me where the door had been.

"Help yourself," Ivy said sweetly. "There's more than enough to go around."

TWENTY-THREE

This is the point where I wish I could tell you things got better for me. That I took a few vampire history lessons, purchased a vampire cookbook (101 tasty blood-filled recipes!) and packed up my meagre possessions to return to my old life.

Except that's not what happened.

Ivy liked blood. A lot. And she didn't do baggies from the blood bank—she got hers straight from the source. Ryan was the same. He'd drink from a bag when he was in a fix—but once I 'calmed down' enough for him to leave the house (his words), he resumed his normal feeding habits.

Feeding houses. They're everywhere, or at least they were back then. Ryan told me about them, asked if I wanted to come along and get a hit of fresh blood directly from a donor. Apparently the norm was a tube that went straight from a willing blood donor straight into the mouth of a hungry vampire in the next room. You could pay extra to bite someone and get it the old-fashioned way. You could pay even more to drink straight from someone who had just taken a hit of your drug of choice—vodka, heroin, cocaine, valium—so that you could get high at the same time.

I didn't ask either of them which method they preferred—I really didn't want to know. I couldn't think of anything worse than drinking blood, despite the bloodlust that had overcome me when I smelled the stuff in the refrigerator. My stomach was still tied in knots. Sam was having a great time, cooking all sorts of things for me that vampires like Ivy and Ryan weren't interested in. Pasta. Fried chicken. I swear, I was going to be the fattest vampire in LA.

I could tell that it pained Sam when Ivy had to go to these places. So, the first time Ryan suggested tagging along with Ivy, Sam put his foot down. See, I was learning pretty fast that Ivy and Ryan had killed a lot of people together in their time. And they were kind of a bad influence on each other. So, no feeding together.

One night, after I had been at the house for a few weeks, Ivy was on her way out. Sam was already out, which was rare for him, but he had been working on a new research project with a fellow professor and they were going over something that sounded very complicated on campus. So that left me, and my favorite person in the world, Ryan.

Ivy was dressed to kill, in skinny jeans, a black singlet that showed off her ample cleavage, and black leather boots. From my spot on the couch I could see her fussing with her makeup while she waited for her ride. As she stacked on more black eyeliner, I tried to imagine her in one of those feeding houses, drinking blood from a drugged girl. It made me sad.

"Mia," she said. "Remember you were asking me about the wine I was drinking?"

I nodded. I had avoided her as much as possible since the night I'd found her drunk in the kitchen, and this was the first time we had been alone together since then.

"Well," she said, her green eyes sparkling as she handed me a bottle of red wine, "this is it. You should drink it tonight. Let Ryan have some, too."

I felt a wave of uneasiness pass over me, and then it was gone. "Sure. Thanks." I took the bottle of wine and set it on the coffee table in front of me.

"Whatcha watching?" She asked, dropping the eyeliner pencil into her handbag.

"True Blood."

"Cool. Which season?"

"Two," I replied, watching as she stuffed her handbag with a gun, a switchblade and a small make–up case.

She noticed me looking at the gun and smiled. "It's for protection only." A horn honked from the driveway. "Enjoy your show." Ivy called, closing the front door behind her.

I felt like a little kid being left at home while Mommy went on a date. "Enjoy your … blood," I said to the empty room.

Ryan strolled in about halfway through the first episode holding a glass of blood. "Want some of the good stuff in there?" he asked, gesturing to my wine.

"No thanks," I said, sipping my wine.

He shrugged, then picked up the open bottle Ivy had given me and poured some into his glass. Blood mixed with wine. *Gross. Delicious. What?*

"Mind if I join you?" He sat next to me without waiting for a response.

I shrugged. "If you want. Don't you have some girls to kidnap or something?"

"You're hilarious" Ryan drawled, lounging back on the sofa cushions and crossing his bare feet on the coffee table. "*True Blood*? Why are we watching Sookie Stackhouse, Mia Blake?"

I rolled my eyes. "Research."

"Right, you're basing your new life around what you pick up from Anna Paquin?"

"Well, everyone's too busy to answer my questions," I complained. "Or they just like keeping me in the dark. I should just go down to the feeding house and ask some questions."

"No, you shouldn't," he said sharply. "That's the worst fucking idea I've heard all day."

"Oh, really?" I rolled my eyes again and poured myself a second glass of wine.

"Yes, really," Ryan countered. "You don't need to go anywhere. Ask me a question. Ask me … anything."

"Okay. Here's one. Why are you such an asshole?" I shot back.

"It's part of my charm. Why are you such a bitch?"

"I'm asking the questions. How many people have you killed?"

"I don't know. Ask me another question."

Bullshit. I bet he knew down to the exact number.

"How old are you?" I asked, trying a different tack.

"I'm very old."

"Where were you born?" He was so frustrating!

"In a barn," he snickered. "Like Jesus."

"You're not funny. Are you really immortal? Can you die?"

"Everyone can die."

I sighed. "See? You don't answer anything. I'm going for a walk." I got up and started to walk away when Ryan's hand shot out and gripped my wrist like a vice. It reminded me of the other time he had grabbed my wrist. The day I had died. The day I had been Turned.

It made me feel positively nauseous.

"I was born in a village called Rioja, in Spain. My mother was Italian, and my father was Spanish. It was 1191. I'm eight–hundred–and–twenty–one years old."

"You're hurting me," I said, tugging my arm away. He released his grip and let my arm fall at my side.

"I can die, we all can. I won't tell you how, don't want you getting any ideas. But anyway, just about the only thing you can't kill is a demon."

"Demon?" I interrupted.

"Yeah, demon. Like from Hell."

"Hell," I said evenly. "Like the opposite of Heaven?"

"I don't really know about that. I'm not exactly a Christian, if you know what I mean"

I nodded, biting my lip. "But you know about Hell."

He nodded, inclining his head to the side. "Sit. I'm serious. I think it's time you knew what you need to know."

"Will I get fangs?" I asked seriously.

Ryan laughed. "No. Your teeth are really strong, though. You can use them to bite through almost anything."

Gross. I didn't want to think about all the different things I would now be able to bite through with ease.

"Is it true vampires can't have children? Ever?"

He nodded. "Never used to be, though. A recent development. That's why Caleb is so intent on Turning others. Otherwise, the vampires won't survive. Not in these times. There are too many people hunting us."

"Have you ever had a baby?" I asked.

"I'm a man," Ryan deadpanned, "so, no."

"I'm serious!" I said, hitting him with a cushion. He laughed, catching the cushion mid–air.

"I had a child," he said, serious again. "A daughter. With Ivy. She was stillborn. It was a very long time ago."

Born and dead. I couldn't imagine anything more heartbreaking. I wondered if living as long as he had made the pain of losing a child easier to bear, or harder?

"Why did you take the heart from Caleb?" I questioned. "It scares the crap out of me."

"Collateral." He didn't elaborate.

We were silent for a while.

"What's going to happen to me, Ryan?" I asked finally.

"What do you mean?"

I looked down at my hands. "I mean, is he going to find me?"

"No. He's not." He took my hands and squeezed them reassuringly. "He's not going to find you. We're going to figure this out, and then you can go home and forget any of this ever happened."

I shook my head in frustration. "I can't forget, Ryan. I don't even know whether I want to go home! Not if people are in danger. Maybe it's too late."

"It's not too late." Ryan's attempt at comforting me was pretty pathetic, but I appreciated the effort.

I took my hands back, wiping my eyes. "Yeah, well. Let's see how long it takes to get out of this mess before deciding whether it's too late to go back. Ow!" I complained as my back started to throb again. I had landed pretty hard when I ran into the invisible wall (or 'ward' as Ivy called it) and my back had been aching for days.

"How's your back?"

"It's pretty sore. I've been using the heat pack you got me … aren't I supposed to heal fast or something?"

Ryan pressed his lips together, concerned. "You have to drink the blood. Otherwise, you're going to get sick. Sicker than you are now. And your back won't heal, either."

I clamped my mouth shut like a little kid. "Mmm–mph."

"Mia, Sam is different. Even as a newborn vampire, he drank a lot of blood. He was insatiable. His fucking nickname was The Ripper. You need to drink."

"There has to be another way," I said stubbornly. *The Ripper? Sam?*

"There's not. Do I have to force you?"

I narrowed my eyes. "You'd like that, wouldn't you?"

"No, I would not like it. I would like you dying even less, though ..."

Well, what was I supposed to say to that?

"Turn around," he said.

"Why?!"

"Forget the blood for a while. Let's talk about it later. Do you want me to try and make your back feel better?"

"How?"

"I'll massage it a little. I promise I won't try and make you drink blood."

"Fine." I turned around, still watching the television while Ryan's strong fingers started pressing into my skin. A draft of air was getting into the room from somewhere, and I felt goose bumps rise on my bare arms.

I looked to the coffee table, realizing the wine bottle Ivy had given me was empty. Had I really drank that much? On an empty stomach? It was like I couldn't get enough of it. I was feeling kind of woozy, but more than that, I was sorely disappointed that there was no more.

Was there blood already in the wine? Was that why it was so intoxicating?

"Mmm," I said, relaxing my tensed shoulders. I closed my eyes. Ryan was an *excellent* masseuse.

What happened next took both of us by surprise. I breathed deeper as a delightful warmth spread through me, from where Ryan's fingers touched my skin all the way to the tips of my own fingers and toes. A vague feeling of concern was replaced by invisible threads that pulled at me, urging me to get closer to him, to feel that warmth even better. Dreamily, I turned around to face Ryan. Our eyes met for one fiery minute, and then the unthinkable happened.

We kissed.

TWENTY-FOUR

I DON'T KNOW WHO KISSED WHO. IT JUST HAPPENED, OUT OF *nowhere.*

Even as I pressed my mouth against his, I couldn't help but wonder what the hell I was doing. This was Ryan. The bad guy. And all I wanted to do was rip my clothes off and jump into his lap.

"Ryan," I breathed nervously between kisses. "What are you doing?" I was terrified. What was happening here? A voice in my head screamed *Stop*, but that voice was drowned out by something else much more powerful, a primal hunger that rose from the depths of my stomach and coiled around me the way my fingers coiled around Ryan's shoulders.

After a few moments, Ryan pushed me away and looked at me with urgency.

"Are you … drunk?" he asked in a voice barely above a whisper, tracing a line down my bare arm with his fingers.

I giggled. "I think so. Are you?"

He seemed to struggle with that for a moment, looking from

me to the bottle of wine and back again. I leaned forward, arching towards him, and pulled him hard against me, surprising us both with my urgency. His lips were warm and the faint taste of what had been mixed with his wine sparked a thirst in me that needed to be quenched. Without thinking, I bit down on his tongue and moaned as I tasted the same sweet, coppery substance that had brought me back from the dead. I sucked greedily, utterly disappointed when he pulled away.

He drew back. "Your bloodlust is starting," he said warily.

I shrugged. "I don't need a running commentary," I replied matter–of–factly, emboldened by this new feeling that was making me act like a rabid animal.

He pushed away again, and I met his gaze steadily. I could feel the way my eyes burned, the way I longed for what was in his veins as well as the flesh that contained it.

This is it. I really am a vampire. My final acceptance of what I had become was both exhilarating and devastating.

Ryan appeared to be having an internal struggle. I didn't know why, but he kept looking around, to the empty wine bottle, the rest of the room, and back to me. I wasn't patient, though, and I wasn't gentle. My nails gouged his olive flesh, and it took every ounce of self–restraint I possessed to stop myself from pressing deep enough to draw blood.

"I should take you somewhere," he said, to himself more than to me, but it appeared that the bloodlust I was experiencing was also affecting his ability to act rationally. I could almost read his thoughts, could see the change in his expression as he gave in to his own desire and stopped resisting my embrace. *Take me to bed*, I thought to myself, a delicious throb beginning between my legs as I realised he could hear what I was thinking.

A low growl came from Ryan's throat. *Don't tempt me.*

As his mouth crashed into mine I thought of Jared's sweet face and tender mouth and for one rational moment, sadness engulfed me.

What the hell was I doing!?

I pushed those thoughts away. They were worthless now, discarded scraps of the person I used to be. I couldn't feel like this and be safe with Jared—more importantly, Jared couldn't be safe with me. Not with this thirst. Not with this hunger. I could rip Ryan limb from limb and it wouldn't bother me, and he even deserved it, but I couldn't risk going home and doing that to someone I loved.

"You are so fucking beautiful," Ryan murmured, planting kisses down my neck.

"Why did you take me?" I asked suddenly. "Why me? Why not someone else?"

"I did what I was told," he replied, his kisses slowing but not stopping completely.

As his lips grazed my healed neck, Jared's face swam in my mind. "What about *Jared*?" I whispered his name, and it gave me the strength to push Ryan away.

At the mention of Jared, Ryan drew back, a pained expression on his face. I wiped my neck and my mouth with my palm, suddenly devastated.

Nobody spoke. The muted TV continued to glimmer, the only light in the room. The lust and hunger swirled around my chest like a poison that could only be chased away with blood.

"I know you'll try to go back to him," Ryan said finally. "We all try to go back to our human life. But you'll see—he won't understand."

"I won't tell him," I answered numbly, the red haze around me becoming a little less intense. "He doesn't have to know."

Ryan smiled knowingly. "And your unending youth? Your eating habits? Your blood thirst? Your infertility?"

Ouch.

I stared at the TV screen while he kept going. "What about your new routine? Not to mention, were you thinking of moving in with him, with all that blood in your refrigerator? Acting like *this* whenever you get hungry?"

He was right. My cheeks burned with the knowledge that he was right.

He took my hands, and I didn't struggle. "I hate you," I said, my throat thick with emotion. "I could *never* love you. You're *nothing* compared to him." My words were a little slurred from the alcohol, the heat rising in my cheeks equal parts red wine and rage.

He hugged me to his chest, and for a moment I closed my eyes and thought of nothing else except the sound of our hearts thudding against our ribcages. My eighteen-year-old heart, and his eight-hundred-year-old heart, yet they both sounded the same. "People think the opposite of hate is love. It's not. Hate and love are so close, and you know why? Passion. The opposite of love isn't hate. They're closer than you think."

At that moment we could have been any young couple, entwined in front of a movie on a Friday night. If I closed my eyes, he could have been Jared, except Jared was warm and loving and Ryan was cold and chillingly cruel. And if I wished hard enough I could almost believe that I was still me; but the real *me* wouldn't feel like this.

"He'll always be afraid of you," Ryan said solemnly. "He won't understand what you are."

I swallowed thickly, thrilled and frightened. Maybe it was the alcohol, or the small amount of blood I'd tasted when I bit Ryan's tongue, but for the first time since I had awoken from death, I felt *alive.*

"I'll never leave you," he murmured in my ear, sensing me relax as I stopped fighting him. "I'll never be afraid of you." He covered my mouth with his, and I was falling, falling into an abyss that I did not want to resist.

Stop. You have to stop. But I ignored the voice of reason in my head. I couldn't stop.

"Ryan," I breathed. "Are you inside my mind?" Hot hands crawled under my sundress and tugged my underwear down, until cotton slipped over my ankles and was discarded. I pulled at his shirt, lifting it up and over his head.

What I had really meant to ask was: *Are you making me feel like this? Are you compelling me?*

"No". Firm hands picked me up effortlessly, and without a second thought I gripped my legs around Ryan's firm waist.

This is a bad idea. This is the bad guy! But the voice of reason was swiftly drowned by the blood-red heat of desire. It was exactly the same feeling that I had experienced with the blood in the refrigerator—an all-consuming need that engulfed every sense and silenced any reasonable thought I might have had.

He dropped me onto the dining table and in one motion slid his jeans and boxers off. I leaned back on my elbows, still kissing that mouth with such hunger, it scared me. It was like I wanted to devour him all at once. Like I wanted *him* to devour *me*.

He gripped the small of my back, pushing into me in one sure movement, his cock stretching me until I gasped. He wasn't gentle, and I didn't want him to be. He fucked me hard and fast, and I pulled him into me with each stroke, greedy for more, terrified of what would happen once this ended. By then, it was too late to turn back. I kissed his neck, his mouth, anything I could get close to with my impatient mouth. The rhythmic movement of his bare skin on mine felt impossibly good. Better than anything I'd felt in months and months. I had only ever been with one other guy before—Jared—and I struggled to associate how the same act could be so totally opposite to what I'd experienced in the past. There was no love here, no romance—it was violent, it was physical. *Deliciously* physical, the way he drove himself inside me so hard, it hurt. I eyed his collarbone, moving my mouth towards his soft skin, imagining how good it would taste if I just bit down and drank.

But in an instant, everything changed. I gasped as I was beaten to the punch, sharp teeth pinching at *my* neck. I felt anger as my skin broke open like paper. I tried to protest as warm blood oozed from my jugular. Suddenly, any desire I had felt was washed away by revulsion.

The room spun as my blood was siphoned off. The pressure of my blood pulsing into his hungry mouth overwhelmed me. It hurt, like someone had taken a blunt razor and scraped it across my skin and then put an industrial vacuum cleaner onto my exposed artery. And it hurt more because he was taking the one thing I wanted; the one thing I didn't have enough of; the one thing I had been about to take from him.

My elbows went from under me and I sank backwards, laying rigid on the table, my dark lover bent over me. I pulled my neck to the side, trying to disengage his teeth from my skin, but the pain caused by my movement made me gag. I stopped struggling and laid perfectly still, salt water stinging at the edges of my eyes. A horrible dragging feeling scraped through the middle of me. When Caleb had bitten me, he had taken some part of me along with my blood. It had been like a little piece of my soul, torn off in a messy chunk and yanked through me until it belonged to him. But what Ryan was taking from me—it seemed as if he wanted *everything*. It felt like he was ripping my entire *being* out of my body, along with my blood, and claiming my life force for himself. And he was enjoying every minute of it.

Please stop please stop you're hurting me …

He must have taken my stillness as compliance because soon he was sucking harder, until black spots appeared in my vision and I felt myself fading into unconsciousness. Then he shuddered, collapsing on top of me as he came. It hurt almost as much when he pulled his teeth from my neck as it had when he bit into it.

Thank God. It was over. He had taken everything and left me an empty shell, but at least that dragging feeling had finally ceased. At least that animal part of me had been weakened enough to slither away, dormant, and I could think semi–logically once more.

"Off," I wheezed, pushing my palms against the crushing weight on top of me. "Off, off, off!" I started to hyperventilate, taking tiny little puffs of air.

He apparently wasn't listening. "Ryan!" I said, this time very forcefully. "I can't breathe, get off!"

"Vampires don't need to breathe," he murmured, but he slid off of me and went searching for his clothes.

I sat up and moved to the edge of the table, still catching my apparently non–essential breath. It had all happened so fast, I hadn't even taken my clothes off. I looked down, horrified to see my white cotton dress stained with fresh blood—my blood.

"You fucking idiot!" I said, clutching my neck with my hands. "Did you have to bite me?" I looked around, noticing my blood splattered on the floor and smeared across the dining table. I had seen so much blood in the past weeks, it no longer affected me very much. But that didn't change the fact that my neck was burning as it continued to weep.

Ryan ignored me, buttoning his jeans at a leisurely pace. I was about to yell at him again when I realized he wasn't paying attention. He looked … stricken; with rage or confusion, I couldn't be sure.

"Hey!" I said loudly, kicking the oak dining chair in front of me so it crashed onto the floor in front of where he stood. "Earth to Ryan? I'm kind of bleeding here."

The chair smashing into pieces at his feet snapped Ryan out of whatever daydream he was apparently in the middle of. "What?"

I gritted my teeth as my neck continued to burn hotter. "When will this stop?" I pulled my hand away and showed him the damage he'd inflicted.

He went very quiet as he studied my neck. Only a few days earlier, his expression would have looked perfectly composed to me, but now, I could read further than just blank looks. It was like our connection allowed me to see a glimmer of what Ryan was feeling, and he was bewildered as he reached up and touched his thumb to my neck ever so gently.

I did this? he asked inside my mind.

"Yes," I replied slowly. I declined to mention the fact that I had been about to do the same thing to him.

I'm so sorry. I—I don't know what happened.

"That makes two of us," I said blithely.

You're a vampire, he spoke silently. *You'll be fine.*

He fled from the room with speed only a vampire could possess.

TWENTY-FIVE

"I can't fucking believe this," I muttered, fighting back tears. I slid off the table and trudged sticky red footprints all the way down the hall and through my bedroom to the adjoining bathroom.

The first thing I did was stumble over to the bath and turn the hot water on full, fumbling around until I finally got the plug to stay in the drain hole. I avoided looking at myself in the mirror. I purposely left the exhaust fan off, and the mirror fogged up instantly. I had to peel my dress from my skin, it was so sticky with my blood. I balled it up and threw it in the hamper in the corner, refusing to acknowledge the self–hatred that was screaming inside my mind.

Autopilot. One foot in front of the other. That was easier than the truth.

Don't think. Don't think. Just breathe.

Thick steam swirled through the room as I hauled myself over the edge and into the scalding hot water. It burned, but not as much as my neck had burned when Ryan bit me. I started gently washing the wound at my neck, wincing as the water aggravated the smouldering sensation. I stopped and leaned back as a wave of dizziness hit me, and I realized how foolish I had been to wander off, drunk, bleeding and out of my goddamn mind. Silly me wasn't nearly as worried about my ravaged neck as I was about Jared—and something told me what I had just done could cast me two steps back in my struggle to get back to my human boyfriend.

I fucking hate you, I thought bitterly, hoping Ryan could hear me mentally abusing him through our bond. If screwing him had inadvertently screwed my chance at getting back to Jared, I would stake him again, only this time I would get him square in his cold, dead heart.

I really had no idea what had just happened. And I didn't want to think about it, let alone start analysing it in my over-imaginative brain. I had the tendency to overthink things—relationships, grades, *sex*—and becoming a vampire had obviously not quelled that nasty habit. If anything, it had made it worse. I didn't want to think. I didn't want to throb with the pain of invisible bruises where Ryan's fingers had pressed into my flesh. I just wanted to be clean, to wash the blood and the vampire scent off my skin and pretend the last hour had never happened.

Mostly, I never wanted to feel that unrelenting hunger again. It terrified me.

I gasped as another rolling wave of vertigo slammed into me, and I stopped being able to hear my surroundings. I breathed out in a choking little sob, my fingers losing their grip on the high sides of the tub. My vision turned to twin tunnels that were being rapidly eaten away by blackness. Soon, there was no light at all, only darkness.

I think I hit the back of my skull on the rim of the bathtub as I slipped under the water.

Are you okay? I heard Ryan's voice in my mind. I didn't answer. I couldn't. No thoughts or images formed in my still mind.

No emotions tugged at my heart. For those precious moments I was under water in the tub, for all intents and purposes, I ceased to exist.

"Hey!" A hand reached into the water and pulled me upright.

I opened my eyes slowly, taking a moment to focus. "Don't," I snapped, pushing Ryan's hand away. He didn't answer, just grabbed a towel and held it out impatiently.

"Can you, like, turn around or something?" I asked, irritated.

You didn't mind me seeing it all hang out before.

"Excuse me," I said, my tone like acid. "Jesus Christ. Nothing *hangs out* over here, thank you very much."

Bad choice of words. Sorry.

"You're talkative," I said caustically, still entirely more comfortable with using my mouth to speak rather than my freaky mind. "You always make a girl feel this special after you bite her during missionary?" I was being a sarcastic bitch, but in reality I was crushed. I had only had sex with one other person before. Someone I had loved. Someone who I thought might be The One.

I really felt like a major slut.

"I think I passed out," I said, taking the towel.

"No shit," Ryan replied, turning around to give me some privacy. "You've been dead to the world for almost an hour."

I stood up in the tub, goosebumps immediately erupting on my cool skin. I wrapped the towel around myself and tucked it in tightly, stepping out of the tub onto a thick white bathmat that was spattered with my blood. "I hope Ivy has bleach," I said weakly, studying the stained mat. It took me a few seconds to realize what Ryan had said.

"Wait, I was sleeping *underwater* for that long?" I looked at the pink bathwater incredulously.

Ryan nodded. "I came in to check that you were okay." He looked at my neck sheepishly. "And to say sorry about that whole ... situation."

I covered the bite with my hand, suddenly self-conscious. Ryan looked pained.

"You got any sleeping pills?" I asked abruptly, changing the subject. I was sick of talking about blood and I sure as hell didn't want to reminisce about the disturbing sex we'd just had.

"Sure," he said, clearly relieved to talk about something else. He left the room with vampiric speed and I used the pause in conversation to wrap my dripping hair up in a towel.

Ryan returned to the room with a bottle full of bright blue capsules that smelled a little like marijuana. "I don't want to get high," I said hesitantly. I couldn't look him in the eye, so I settled for the ground.

"You'll be fine," Ryan said impatiently, pressing the bottle of pills into my palm.

"What are they?"

"Asphodel. Ground down from the roots of the flower."

I wanted to ask about the pills but couldn't be bothered spending any more time with Ryan. "Okay," I said quickly. "You can go now."

"They're like vampire heroin," Ryan warned. "Don't take any more than two at a time. You can easily overdose on these. And these *will* kill a vampire"

Suddenly, I was intrigued. "Really? Why?"

Ryan's face got all serious, like he always got when he was about to 'teach me something'.

"It's from The Underworld," he said. "The fields of asphodel flowers are what keep demons from leaving The Underworld. It's like poison to them."

"And vampires were made by demons," I added suddenly.

Ryan smiled. "You *have* been listening."

I snorted. "I've been listening. I never said I believed any of it."

But I did believe it, all of it.

I cried for half an hour after we did, well, *it*. At least, for the thirty minutes after Ryan had roused me from my sleep underneath the water in the bathtub. Turns out I really didn't need to breathe after all. While a human would have drowned, I was perfectly fine after spending forty–five minutes unconscious under a foot of water and lavender–scented bubble bath.

I made a mental note to ask again about my alive versus dead status.

I would have cried for longer, but I was so exhausted I just cried myself to sleep. I hid the sleeping pills in my nightstand. I could definitely see vampire poison coming in handy one of these days.

TWENTY-SIX

I HAD NIGHTMARES THAT NIGHT. IT WASN'T SURPRISING. I BLAMED the bloodlust, for awakening something in me that hadn't surfaced before. It threatened to consume me. Part of me thought it would be easier to let it.

My nightmare was a rehash of a story Ryan had briefly told me, when we had first arrived at Ivy's house. The story of the first vampire.

Once upon a time there was a girl. Her name was Talitha. She was an earth witch, the most powerful witch in the world. She only practiced white magic—magic that would not harm, that would only bring light to the world.

Hades, ruler of The Underworld, was on the lookout for a wife, someone to restore the balance in The Underworld and be his equal. The light to his darkness.

One day, a servant told Hades about this powerful witch whose light shone as bright as the sun. Hades was intrigued. He wanted her light for himself.

Hades visited the fair maiden and made her an offer. She could rule the world, he said, so long as it was a world of his choosing. She, having heard a great many terrible things about Hades, refused.

It didn't matter. He took her anyway.

Once a being enters The Underworld, they can never leave. Once Death has claimed them, they belong to Hades for all of eternity. When a soul enters The Underworld, they must immediately drink from the River Lethe, and they forget their sorrows, and their sufferings, and they live in peaceful oblivion.

But Hades was angry that a mere mortal had turned him down—after all, he was one of the most powerful beings in all of creation. She had enraged him. He ferried her to The Underworld, but he did not let her drink from the River Lethe. And so her sorrows and sufferings were not vanquished, and she began her stretch of eternal imprisonment with the full knowledge of the injustices she had suffered.

And so it was, that Hades hid his prized witch, tucked away beneath the world of the living for thousands upon thousands of years. Time passes at a different speed under the world we know, and far too soon Talitha was not the innocent girl she had been when she was taken. Her hatred and rage were so much that even her blood turned black, along with her soul.

So goes the story of the first demon.

There are a ring of fields that encircle The Underworld. They are beautiful, bursting with asphodel flowers. Hades, not wanting to lose any of his prized dead souls, cast a spell that caused the flowers to burn any who touched them.

And so, there is a beautiful young woman who burns her hands on pretty flowers as she weeps, at the edge of the fields for all eternity, trying to free herself from a world she never wanted, trying to get back to the light.

I hadn't thought about the story until it invaded my dreams that night. It was horrible, truly awful, watching in vivid detail as the girl was taken, and imprisoned, and left to rot until she became a true demon. The most horrifying part of the nightmare, though, was right at the end, when the girls' blood turned black. She bit into the soft flesh of her wrist and forced her black blood upon a helpless human, chained in a dungeon not unlike the one I had been locked in in Mexico. As she looked up, her features changed slightly so that I was staring at a bloody caricature of myself. And the young man on the floor beneath her, choking down her blood, looked just like Jared.

I wanted to wake screaming; but something had stolen my voice. As if I were unconscious underwater, I stayed trapped in my nightmare until Ryan shook me awake the next morning. When I looked into his eyes, I knew, inexplicably, that he had shared the same nightmare with me.

TWENTY-SEVEN

"You can't tell anyone about last night," I addressed Ryan the next morning as I walked into the kitchen. He stood at the kitchen bench, dressed in black satin boxers and pouring coffee from the drip machine pot into a mug that said 'I LOVE NY'. I raised my eyebrows in amusement as I read the writing on the mug.

"Tell us what?" Ivy asked from her spot at the kitchen table, biting into a piece of raisin toast. I could practically taste the toast in my own mouth, complete with melted butter, the smell was so overpowering.

I jumped, turning to look at Ivy in frustration. "How do you keep doing that?"

Ivy smiled, not looking up from her newspaper. "It's what I do, pumpkin."

You're the pumpkin, I thought to myself.

Only after midnight, Ryan's voice responded in my head.

I smiled, even after what had happened the night before.

Sometime before I finally fell asleep, I had come to the realization that Ryan probably wouldn't give our encounter another thought. I mean, the guy was a professional. He probably did girls like me all the time.

At our private joke, Ivy scowled and got up from the table. I looked at her plate to see she had eaten all of her bread and left four perfectly square crusts behind.

"A vampire who doesn't like her crusts?" I asked, accepting the cup of coffee Ryan had poured for me. My head was absolutely pounding, and I was planning on lots of coffee and plenty of grease to get me going.

"And I'm still big and strong," Ivy quipped, scraping her left-overs into the bin. She stretched lazily, then put her coffee mug and plate in the dishwasher. I was quickly realizing how anally retentive Ivy was, how much of a clean freak she could be. The striped cushions on the couch had a magical way of being turned every morning so the stripes all ran the same way. I knew this because I kept turning them the other way, to see how long it would take her to notice.

She was starting to remind me of my mother.

Ivy bent down and tied her shoelaces. "I'm going to run down to Santa Monica Pier and back. I won't be long."

I scrunched my face up, calculating the rough distance between Ivy's house and the pier. "That's, like, forever away!"

Ivy smiled. "What can I say? I'm awesome."

"And well versed in teenage vocabulary for someone so old," I agreed.

Ivy didn't answer, just slammed the front door hard enough to make the walls shake.

"She doesn't like me very much," I remarked, taking a mug from the cupboard and pouring myself some coffee.

"Are you kidding?" Ryan replied. "She loves you. This is her being nice."

"I'd hate to see her bad side," I remarked.

Ryan just smirked and sipped on his coffee.

I found a cloth and a spray bottle of disinfectant under the sink and squirted some of the cleaner onto the kitchen table, wiping the cloth over the smooth wood surface.

I can't believe you let her eat breakfast at this table, I thought. *We should burn this table.*

"I already did that," Ryan replied, not amused. "Last night."

"Yeah, well," I muttered. "I'm doing it again, aren't I?"

"I'd say she knows about last night," Ryan said.

"Shut up," I snapped. "I don't want to talk about it."

Ryan smiled cheekily. "It's our unmistakable sexual attraction," he continued, gesturing at himself, then at me. "Your subtle 'Don't tell anyone about last night' probably didn't help things."

"Would you just shut up?" I yelled, and without another thought, I threw the spray bottle at his head.

Normally, this wouldn't have mattered, because Ryan was a vampire and should have moved out of the way with relative ease; and equally, because bottles of cleaning agents are usually stored in plastic bottles. But in this unfortunate case, several factors meant that Ryan was smacked straight in the eye. With a solid glass bottle full of bleach mixed with water—glass that smashed as it collided with his cheekbone. And with bleach that started seeping into the dozens of tiny cuts that littered the left side of his face.

I watched in horror as the bottle smashed into a million tiny pieces, showering the kitchen floor with sharp slivers of glass that sparkled like glitter.

"What was that for?!" Ryan yelled, clutching his bleeding, full-of-bleach eye.

"Oh! Shit!" I yelled, breaking from my trance. I ran over to Ryan, pulling his hands away from his eye, trying to get a better look.

"I am so sorry," I cried. "I thought you'd catch it!"

More groaning.

"What … what should I do?" I asked pathetically.

"Tweezers," Ryan grunted. "Get some tweezers."

I spent the next twenty minutes tweezing glass out of Ryan's eyeball. It was disgusting. I threw up in the trash halfway through the job. My red wine hangover probably didn't help matters.

After I had gotten all of the glass out, I bathed Ryan's eye in warm water, flushing out the bleach while he pouted and sucked a mixture of bourbon and blood through a straw.

"I am so sorry," I repeated after I had finished, being extra careful not to inhale the smell of his blood-spiked drink. "I swear that was an accident. Who keeps their kitchen cleaner in a glass bottle?"

Ryan shrugged, still frowning. "I should stop treating you like a normal person. Just because you act like one, doesn't mean you are."

I sat down at the table, exhausted despite only having been awake for half an hour. "What do you mean?"

Ryan downed the last of his blood infusion and stood up, stepping carefully around pieces of glass to the bench. "You were just a weak girl before. I'm still treating you like that, but you're strong now. Fast. You may still act the same, but you're nothing like you were before."

Before. I pushed every sentimental image out of my mind and focused on the moment I was in. "Where does Ivy keep the vacuum cleaner?" I asked tiredly.

"Get dressed," Ryan said, pouring himself another coffee. "Don't worry. I'll clean this up."

I looked down at my Blairstown running squad t-shirt and frayed denim shorts. "I am dressed."

Ryan rolled his eyes. "I'm serious. Go put those skinny jeans and your striped tank on. Our appointment is in –" he glanced at the clock above the microwave "—thirty-seven minutes."

I didn't budge. "Appointment where?" *And since when do you tell me what to wear?*

"UCLA. And I'm just trying to buy us some time so you don't need to do fifty-three outfit changes before you decide on the jeans and shirt you always wear anyway."

I jumped out of my chair. "Wait. UCLA?!"

Ryan smirked, amused. "I told you. You were accepted. It's orientation this morning."

My exhilaration turned to annoyance. "Why didn't you tell me last night?!" I yelled, forgetting my coffee and running down the hall to my room. I heard the vacuum sucking up pieces of glass as I skipped into my bathroom. I kicked the bloodied bath mat from the night before into the corner. Out of sight, out of mind, right?

I was changed and with fresh makeup on and in the middle of brushing my teeth when the vacuum stopped. Ryan appeared in the doorway that separated my bathroom from my bedroom.

He saw what I was wearing—black tights, a gray oversized t-shirt and camel-coloured leather boots—and flashed an amused smile.

I spat out a mouthful of toothpaste and tossed my toothbrush back in its holder. Turning to face him, I studied his eye. "How's it feeling?" I asked, still feeling really bad.

"Probably as good as your neck," Ryan said, holding my handbag out in front of him. "Come on. We're running late."

I glared at him as my neck throbbed on cue. I turned back to the mirror to make sure my long brown waves covered my healing bite mark.

Satisfied, I took my bag and we both went downstairs to the garage. "Which car are we taking?" I asked, glancing between the Merc, the Range Rover and the other car, which had a name I had never heard of. I waited patiently while Ryan rummaged around the garage, looking for car keys.

"My car," Ryan said. "The black one."

"What's a ... Bugatti?" I asked, wrinkling my nose up as I looked the black car over.

Ryan appeared next to me, keys in hand, and gestured to the car I'd been asking about. "A Bugatti Veyron," Ryan said proudly. "Fastest car in the world."

"Right," I said, getting into the passenger seat and pulling my seatbelt on. "So I guess we won't be late?"

TWENTY-EIGHT

On the drive to the university campus, my exhilaration turned to growing suspicion. "So, Sam works at the same campus we're going to?" I asked Ryan as he drove at a ridiculously dangerous speed down the freeway.

"Yes," he replied, shifting gears again.

"Stop showing off," I snapped. "I hate guys who are into cars. Tell me again what other acceptance letters I got?"

"Brown, Cornell, Washington State, UC. All on a full scholarship. Stanford, Yale, Columbia. All on full-fee programs."

"And you just *decided* that UCLA was the best choice for me?"

Ryan glared at me, and my eyes began to water at the power that was in his gaze. It was because of his age, I realized. Because he had lived for so very long. But I refused to look away, even as my eyes burned.

"UCLA is the *only* choice for you," he growled. "You are being hunted by the most powerful vampire in all existence. You should be at home, under lock and key."

I folded my arms and stared straight ahead. "At home, your home, under lock and key? I might as well be –"

"Dead, I know," Ryan finished my sentence for me. How considerate. "Which is why I'm taking you to your orientation at UCLA, something I'm probably going to regret when we *both* get killed."

"Right," I scoffed.

"Is there something else wrong?" Ryan asked. "Something other than the obvious fact that you *hate* me?"

"I don't hate you," I muttered. "Well, sometimes I do. You just frustrate the hell out of me."

"I would hate me," Ryan answered, "If I were you."

"What would have happened to you, if you had just Turned me and kept going working for Caleb?"

Ryan shrugged. "Nothing, I guess. Life would have just been normal for me."

"And if Caleb finds you now," I asked, "what would happen?" I looked at the steering wheel, noticing Ryan's knuckles turning white from squeezing it so hard.

"He wouldn't kill me right away," Ryan answered calmly, too calmly. "He would likely torture me, throw me in a hole for a couple of months with no blood, until I went insane. Then, he'd probably throw someone down for me to try not to kill. Like a kid, to make it as bad a s he possibly could."

His voice, the way he was sitting, looked perfectly ordinary—too ordinary. I felt the fear that held tight in his throat. And he was terrified.

I put my hand on his arm. I hated that he was right. I hated that, despite how much anger I felt for him, it wasn't the only emotion he made me feel. "That's why I don't hate you," I replied.

"But?" Ryan prodded.

"But I'm afraid of you," I admitted. "Last night? Something definitely wasn't normal. It's like you were compelling me to respond to you. I would never do *that* in a million years."

"I didn't compel you," Ryan replied, his face tight with worry. "I don't know what happened. I'm attracted to you, sure, but I can generally restrain myself from taking advantage of teenage girls."

My cheeks stared to burn. *I'm attracted to you, sure.*

"Is it because we're bound?" I asked, remembering how Ryan had explained our link through his blood that had Turned me.

"I don't know," Ryan replied. "But hey, You're not the first girl I've Turned, not by a long shot. You *are* the first one I've risked everything to rescue. So maybe there's something in that."

It made me wonder, for the next twenty minutes as we sailed down the freeway: Did Ryan have feelings for me? More importantly, did *I* have feelings for *him*?

Half an hour later we were sitting in an open–air amphitheatre, listening to the dean's opening address, when I noticed Ryan wasn't paying any attention to the speech. Instead, he was paying a lot of attention to a hot blonde student sitting a few rows down from us. She was wearing a UCLA t-shirt that looked brand new, and denim cutoffs that showed off her long, tanned legs. She had obviously been keeping up her running schedule over the summer, while I had been sitting in a dungeon and then falling through a plate glass window and dying.

"Oh my God," I said, elbowing Ryan hard in the ribs as the dean walked off stage and everyone around us clapped. "You are *not* allowed to eat my classmates."

Ryan rolled his eyes endearingly. "Relax, kitten. Go, find Sam's office. I'll be a gentleman and introduce myself to this young lady."

I shook my head. "Whatever. I'll meet you back here in ten?"

"It's a date," Ryan smiled.

"I wouldn't date you if you were the last vampire alive," I replied. "Stop acting like we're a couple."

"Would you prefer I went back to being awkward and distant?" Ryan offered.

"Yes," I breathed. "That would make life much easier." I eyed the blonde again. “I mean it, Ryan. Be nice to her.”

“I’ll be a gentleman,” he replied, already checked out of our conversation and striding away.

Sam’s office was pretty easy to find.

“Professor,” I drawled, knocking on the open door. “Mind if I come in?”

A huge smile broke out on Sam’s face, and I couldn’t help but smile back. “Mia!”

“I like your office,” I said, looking around at the mahogany bookshelves that lined the walls and the huge window that looked over the main quadrangle. “It’s … cosy.”

Sam stood up from where he was sitting behind a computer screen, and circled around to the front of his desk.

“You look happier,” he said, studying my face. “That’s good.”

“This place is awesome!“ I gushed. I wouldn’t admit it to Ryan, but I loved this place. The architecture, the chilled-out vibe, the temperature. Even the fact that Sam worked on campus was reassuring, even if slightly suspicious. I told Sam all about my orientation session, how the Dean had said so many inspiring things, and how good my class schedule was.

“Have you told Jared and Evie yet?” Sam asked casually.

I felt my face fall. “No. Ryan only just told me we were coming this morning.”

“You should call them,” Sam said. “You must miss them a lot.”

I smiled painfully. “Like you wouldn’t believe,” I said quietly.

“You should speak to them,” Sam repeated. “It’s not too late, you know. I spoke to Ryan, we want you to go home as soon as possible.”

I immediately got defensive. I mean, all of these people, making decisions—major life decisions—for me? Wasn’t I supposed to be doing that?

“What’s it got to do with you?” I said rudely.

Sam stopped smiling. “I’m sorry, I didn’t –”

“Did you have something to do with me coming here?”

Sam's shoulders sagged. He looked at the ground as if searching for the right answer. "Ryan told me that you got in to lots of colleges. Including this one. He didn't want you going anywhere for a long time. I convinced him that you were going to leave altogether if he didn't let you take control of your own life."

I thought about that for a minute. "Fair enough," I conceded. "Thank you."

Sam smiled again, and I felt my whole body relax. The guy might be brooding and serious most of the time, but when he did smile, it lit up the whole room. "You don't need to thank me," he said.

I grimaced as a wave of nausea snaked through my belly, reminding me that I had yet to eat any breakfast. "Is there a McDonald's nearby?" I asked, clutching my stomach. "I need some grease."

"Big night?" Sam guessed.

I nodded. "Something like that. I swear, I had two glasses of red wine, and I was *stoned*."

"Your metabolism is much different now," Sam said. "Don't forget that."

"How can I?" I replied. "I basically throw everything up that's solid. I'm like a baby."

"That's exactly what you're like," Sam said, smiling.

"Yeah," I said, suddenly feeling small and immature. "Okay, well, I better get back before Ryan kills someone."

Walking back to meet Ryan, I felt a small surge of hope blossom within my chest. I could call Jared. Maybe even Evie and my mother. I could go to school. I could still get back on track and have a life, my life, and most of the things I had dreamed of since I was a little girl.

Almost everything.

My hand slipped down to rest over my stomach, and below that, my barren womb. I suddenly felt a heaviness sweep through me at the knowledge that while I could still act like the old Mia Blake, I was kidding myself if I thought I could just forget everything that had happened and go back to my old life. I felt a longing for the past, and a hollow pain inside my stomach throbbed in time with my aching head.

Ryan and I want you to go home as soon as possible.

Yeah, right. After last night, the crazy bloodlust and the sex, I doubted I'd ever be able to look Jared in the eye again.

TWENTY-NINE

I WAITED A RESPECTABLE DISTANCE UNTIL RYAN HAD FINISHED his conversation with his next potential victim. "Hey, Blake," he greeted me. "Did you find the professor?"

I nodded, following Ryan's gaze to land firmly on the blonde girl's ass. "Oh, really? I was only gone five minutes!"

Ryan smiled. "I'm that good." I felt him glance sidelong at me, while I was still checking Clair out. An image of us entwined on the kitchen table flashed through the bond and I whipped my head around to glare at him.

"Don't," I said through gritted teeth. He must've known I was serious, because he looked at the ground and didn't say—or think—anything more about it. Which was very unusual for him. He normally loved to torment and tease me.

"What's up with all the bruises?" I said, gesturing to Clair as she walked away from us. Her otherwise attractive legs were littered with dark purple and blue circles. It looked like someone had taken a tire iron to her shins.

"I don't know," Ryan said slowly. "Looks like she's had a run in with someone... or some*thing*."

"Let's go," I said, suddenly exhausted. I was still feeling the remnants of that bottle of wine and my head felt heavy and vague.

"Already?" Ryan asked. "Don't you want me to give you the grand tour? We've barely scratched the surface."

A thread of anxiety entered my thoughts. "And why would you be giving the grand tour? I don't see 'Vampire Academy' written on any of the signs."

He shrugged. "I may have attended this university a few times over the years. I've got degrees in Law, computer science, architecture."

I shook my head. "So that's why you chose UCLA as my day pass from prison."

Ryan turned serious. "No," he said, clearly annoyed. "I chose this school because you got a full scholarship. Your little trust fund isn't going to last forever, my dear. You, on the other hand, *will* be around forever, if you play your cards right."

If you play your cards right. Somehow I thought that sleeping with my vampire maker wasn't the right play. I blinked, trying to forget the night before, when I saw Ryan's gaze cloud over as he daydreamed with a frown. Somehow, I knew he was thinking about the very thing I was trying to forget. I glared at him pointedly. He finally noticed and smirked.

That will never happen again, I said sharply through the bond.

Ryan stiffened. "Don't throw anything at my face, please."

I shook my head and attempted to change the subject. "Well, did you get her number?"

"Why? You jealous?" That smirk again, as he unlocked the car.

I started to laugh. I laughed so hard that tears ran down my cheeks. "Yes," I gasped, holding my stomach. "You got me, lover. I'm jea–lous."

Ryan opened his door and slid into the driver's seat, ignoring my sarcasm. "I'm taking her to dinner tonight. I'll probably have to kill her."

I stopped laughing. I quietly opened the passenger door and sat in the car. "*Why*?!"

As soon as I shut my door, Ryan threw the car into reverse. "I think she's working for Caleb."

Fear shot through my entire body. I started to panic as my lungs malfunctioned. "What do you mean?" I asked thickly. "Is he here? Is he coming for us?"

Ryan grabbed my hand and placed it on the gear stick, with his hand over mine. I started to feel that familiar falling sensation, and looked at him incredulously.

You're going to show me something while you drive?

He just smiled wickedly as we drove faster, through suburban streets until we reached the coast. Ryan exited onto a narrow mountainside road that hugged the ocean below. Soon we were going so fast I felt sick. It didn't matter, though. Images and sounds started tumbling through the bond like a motion picture until I could barely see the road past the scenes Ryan was showing me.

The pretty blonde thing at the assembly was on Ryan's mind. He could have sworn he knew her from somewhere, or had at least crossed paths with her before. She smelled familiar to him, not like he had drank her blood or anything, but almost like he had met someone very close to her.

She sat in the bleachers, fussing with her handbag. On closer inspection, Ryan could see her fishing a pen and notebook out.

He walked straight up to her and did his thing. "Do I know you?"

She smiled. "Wow. I haven't heard that one before."

Ryan smiled. "No, seriously. Have we met before?" He put compulsion behind his words this time, always fearful that Caleb could be closing in. Or other people. Ryan Sinclair had made a lot of enemies in seven hundred years.

"No, I don't think so," she replied.

"What's your name?" Ryan compelled, on high alert. This girl could be a distraction, and Mia could be in danger right now. But all he sensed from her through the bond right now was confusion as she tried to find Sam's office.

"Yours first," she smiled, resisting his compulsion with such ease it made him nervous. Then he noticed the small green and white flower tucked into her hair, a flower that stopped vampires like him from compelling humans.

He smiled broadly and stuck out his right hand. "I'm Ryan. And you look awfully familiar."

The pretty blonde girl with dark blue eyes the color of a stormy ocean smiled back at him, taking his hand and shaking it. "I'm Clair," she replied. "And I've never seen anyone like you before."

They chatted some more. Clair revealed she was on the track team on a full scholarship, just like Mia. Ryan felt himself relax marginally as the two chatted about UCLA, running, the weather, and finally, about dinner.

"A poor college student like you must need a good meal," Ryan said cheekily. "Let me buy you dinner on Thursday."

She laughed. "I'm hardly a poor college student. But I do enjoy a good steak."

"It's a date," Ryan said, for the second time that morning. "I'll pick you up at, say, eight?"

"Perfect," Clair said. She wrote her address on a slip of paper and pressed it into his palm.

"Hey, I like that flower," Ryan said, pointing at the asphodel flower in her hair. "Where'd you get it?"

Clair smiled, touching her hair. "My dad loves growing all these weird plants I've never heard of. Did you know California is one of the only places in the world these flowers will grow?"

Ryan smiled to hide his worry. "I didn't, no."

"Well, you learn something every day. I'll see you on Thursday, Ryan Sinclair."

Ryan smiled broadly, ignoring the danger flag at the mention of his last name. He didn't think he had told her his last name, only his first. He thought it was a shame that he'd probably have to kill her.

I wrenched my hand away, dizzy from the vision I'd just seen through our bond. He might have wanted to show me more, but I'd had enough. The car was going a respectable sixty miles an hour now, through suburban streets that were familiar to me now. We were almost home.

I stared straight ahead and didn't say anything else. When Ryan glanced down to change gears as we pulled into the driveway, I tried to hide my shaking hands as I tore little strips of paper off my UCLA class schedule and shredded them with my fingers.

"You're getting my car dirty," Ryan said, but there was no force behind his words. He looked at me, and I was practically drowning in the worried vibes he was giving off.

"Sorry," I said, and folded my arms, staring out of the window.

As I got out of the car, I realized why the car ride had been so abnormally quiet. I had held my terrified breath the whole way home.

THIRTY

A FEW DAYS LATER, ON A THURSDAY NIGHT, RYAN PULLED UP to a nondescript apartment building in nearby Sacramento. I knew because I was sitting in the car with him. After he refused to let me accompany him to Clair's house, I had shared with him my newfound ability to see things in other rooms of the house, even if I wasn't there. He didn't believe me at first, but after I showed him what I had been able to see with Ivy and Sam fighting about me, he changed his mind. Suddenly, despite the risk that we may have been walking into a trap, Ryan was happy for me to keep watch in the car while he confronted Clair.

It was pretty nice digs for a college student. The girl obviously had money, or a rich vampire–daddy renting her a sweet pad. The navy cashmere sweater Ryan wore was just loose enough to conceal the G23 Glock, his favorite pistol, in the waistband of his pants. If *Clair* turned out to be a problem, well, the bullets in that gun were enough to blow her head clean off. Not that I really wanted to think about that, but he had gleefully gone into graphic detail on the drive over. *Thanks for that.*

Ryan adjusted his sweater to fall just right over the Glock that sat sandwiched between his belt and the small of his back. The street was pretty quiet. After a final glance my way, he got out of the car and stood dead still next to it. I knew that he could hear the slightest branch break underfoot half a mile away. I watched as his keen eyes scanned the bank of windows at the front of the apartment block, taking in minute details in each apartment, like seams on curtains and shopping lists stuck to refrigerator doors. The curtains in Clair's apartment were drawn shut, and neither of us could see anything other than the soft glow of mood lighting behind the heavy drapes. He sniffed the air, taking in freshly mown grass on the nature strip, engine oil dripping from the car in front of his, the damp smell of a nearby dog.

Nothing appeared suspicious. It felt fine—which worried Ryan and made me uneasy. It was much better to walk into an ambush when you knew it was there, I supposed. This picture of normality was evidently something he was not accustomed to.

Clair's apartment was on the third floor. Ryan crossed the street and entered the foyer casually. Onlookers wouldn't have been able to catch it, but I had watched as he broke the lock on the door to gain access rather than buzz Clair's apartment. I guessed that the element of surprise was something a vampire held in high regard, especially when a potential trap was involved.

After he disappeared from my sight, I closed my eyes and breathed steadily, letting my other senses take over. Pretty soon a picture started to unfold in my mind's eye. I found it interesting that, as well as seeing what Ryan was doing, I could *feel* what he was feeling and sense what he was thinking. It was almost exactly like the visions he had shared with me—only now we were operating in real time. It was a vision in technicolor, streaming live.

It must be the bond.

The foyer was empty, and Ryan immediately turned towards the stairwell. Elevators were just asking for trouble when one was being cautious—they could trap a vampire easily and permanently. It didn't help that they were normally made of steel and were essentially moveable prison cells that could seal you in and make you undetectable even to a powerful witch like Ivy. It was safer just to take the stairs, and when you lived forever, you could spare the extra few minutes.

Ryan took the stairs two at a time, his arms loose by his sides and ready to react to danger. He sprang forward on the balls of his feet, making it easier to move quickly if required. He had ceased all breathing upon leaving the car, using the extra quiet to open up his supernatural senses and really listen to his surroundings.

Humans were noisy. Ryan was lucky though; he had lived for so long, he was able to filter noise in a way most younger vampires would find impossible. He heard, processed and discarded noises such as people talking, doors opening and closing, a dishwasher humming, someone talking on the phone. I felt him concentrate as he let his supernatural senses reach Clair's apartment, and he listened for what he might find.

Upon reaching the third floor landing, he hesitated briefly. He could hear Clair's breathing, and her slightly elevated heart rate. She was nervous; about a first date or something more sinister, he couldn't tell. She was fussing in the kitchen by the sounds of things, putting groceries or dishes away perhaps. There didn't seem to be anyone else in the apartment.

Seemingly satisfied with his initial scan of the building, he exited the stairwell and made his way down the hallway. Clair's apartment was right next to the stairs, a detail that did not escape his attention. Was it just a coincidence, or had she chosen to stay there because the stairwell offered a quick escape in case of a crisis?

A crisis like a vampire coming to kill her?

He knocked on her door three times and stood back and to the side. If she was going to try anything through the door—like, say, a shotgun or a spell—he would be safely out of the way. He heard footsteps, a lock turning, and then she was standing in front of him with a smile. Both Ryan and I were struck by how pretty she was. Her eyes were big and blue, her hair the color of straw and pulled up in a messy bun.

"Hi," she said radiantly, and he was struck by her effervescence and charm once again. "You're early."

He was half an hour early. It always helped to show up before the enemy expected you, if indeed she was the enemy. If not, she could be a good time for a few hours, maybe something to snack on if the night grew long. He had no doubt of his ability to get her into bed. He could be very persuasive.

I should know. I cringed at his blasé attitude towards munching on the poor girls neck and wondered if he knew his every thought was being streamed directly into my brain. He probably did. It was typical Ryan.

He greeted her with a hello and a kiss on each cheek, immediately noticing the Asphodel flower still in her hair. On closer inspection, I could see that it wasn't an orchid at all. It had the same basic structure as an orchid, but each white petal had a single pinkish line straight down the middle. Thin stalks rose from the middle of the flower, each topped with a cluster of bright orange pollen. It burned Ryan's nostrils and made his eyes water, and in the car I wiped at my own eyes as they, too, began to brim with water. He made a mental note to get the flower away from her, somehow. I hoped he did. It was stirring up my allergies so badly my skin was starting to crawl.

Ryan handed Clair a bottle of wine and stepped inside her apartment. It looked like it had been put together by an interior designer, with not a single thing out of place. He smiled to himself as he realized why he had been attracted to this girl in the first place. It was her striking resemblance to Ivy, and it seemed the similarity ran more than skin deep. Clair seemed to be a neat freak as well.

He followed her into the kitchen, taking a moment to once again appreciate her ass as she opened the wine with speed and efficiency.

Had she worked at a bar? No, he mused, she's too young. But somehow she operated a corkscrew with skill beyond her youth.

"So," Clair said, pouring them both a glass of wine and hoisting herself onto the bench. "Was that your sister with you today?"

So she had noticed me. I heard Ryan wonder if she had noticed what I was. And it hit him, for the first time, that Caleb didn't know that Ryan had Turned me. For all he knew, I was still a human hostage and Ryan was on a bloodthirsty vacation. He was thankful he'd moved the heart to a new hiding spot before leaving the house for his date. After all, it could be that Caleb had zero interest in getting me back, and was only interested in the heart in the jar. He stiffened momentarily, aware that I'd probably shared this revelation as he was having it.

I sat bolt upright in the car. He seemed worried that I might have heard what he was thinking about. There was no point pretending I hadn't been eavesdropping on his every thought.

We'll talk about it later, *I addressed him through our bond.*

"She's just a friend," Ryan answered Clair, swirling his wine and subtly sniffing for any signs the glass was smeared with poison. It seemed clean, so he took a tiny sip.

"Cool," Clair said, her wine untouched. "I thought she might be your girlfriend or something." She blushed a little, and Ryan thought it was a great point of the conversation to test her honesty. With vampiric speed, he stood in front of the bench, his eyes millimetres from hers. My head was still spinning from how quickly he had moved, when he plucked the flower from her hair. He swore as it burned his fingers and threw it down on the bench.

Clair appeared shocked, and I went still as Ryan focused all of his attention on the pretty blonde girl who was most likely going to try and kill him tonight. He had met assassins before. None of them had lived long enough to remember meeting him, though.

"What's your real name?" he pressed, compelling her with his voice and his eyes. His voice was irresistible. I felt sorry for her if she was innocent.

"Clair Madison," she replied robotically, pinned to the spot as he continued to compel her.

Madison. He scanned his memory for any trace of that name, drawing a blank. It was a pretty common name, though, and he certainly didn't know the last name of everyone he'd ever met.

"Are you following me?" Ryan asked. No point beating around the bush, I supposed.

She shook her head. "No." Her eyes were big and round and she wasn't blinking.

"Who are you working for?" Ryan continued pressing her, his power like fingers squeezing the truth from her brain.

Clair's pupils swelled under the pressure of Ryan's gaze, a gaze that he knew could damage her if he wasn't careful. "Valentino's," she said blankly.

Valentino's. He knew the place; they did fantastic pasta. The owners also happened to be a mix of Italian mafia and vampire, although half the restaurants in the city suffered the same credentials. In itself, it wasn't enough to distrust her. It also explained her skill at opening expensive wine.

Ryan smiled broadly, easing off the compulsion. "Well," he said, looking around. "You sure must get some nice tips at Valentino's to pay for this apartment."

Clair smiled, a little more normal but still not all the way there. Ryan fretted that he might have pushed her too far, damaged her frontal lobe. "I'm house-sitting for my uncle. I wish *this was my apartment."*

Ryan raised his eyebrows, gesturing for Clair to drink her wine. "I shouldn't," she said. The fact that Clair hesitated was good, because it meant the compulsion had worn off. "I don't drink a lot. It interferes with … running," she explained.

Ryan excused himself to go to the bathroom. While he was in there, he turned on the faucet and took the opportunity to snoop through her cabinets. In the bottom drawer, he happened upon a cache of painkillers strong enough to kill ten men. Fentanyl. Hospital-grade morphine patches. Even a small bag with what appeared to be some heroin powder in it. There were neatly packaged syringes and a rubber tourniquet, rubbing alcohol and stacks of gauze strips. It must have belonged to the uncle, unless Clair was a junkie. Ryan hadn't noticed anything off about her speech or balance, so he guessed that it belonged to somebody else.

The rest of the evening went pretty well. They ended up staying in. Clair cooked, Ryan ate, and neither of them killed the other. Ryan even got a goodnight kiss from the pretty blonde. He had grown to like her so much over the course of the night that he didn't even attempt to seduce her or take her blood.

Thank goodness, because I was not in the mood to experience some crazy feeding ritual through our bond.

The vibe seemed good. It was normal. It reminded me of home, in some strange way. The simple actions of meeting a friend, having a meal, saying goodnight. Those things had become so foreign to me. It didn't help that I flipped out Vampira-style every time I opened the refrigerator at Ivy's house.

When Ryan finally got back to the car, I was stretched out in the backseat, too aware of everything to contemplate a nap. As he grew closer, I heard a familiar pounding that I'd heard before. The *thumpthumpthump* of the heart in a jar.

"I know about Caleb," I said to him immediately, before he'd even sat in his seat. "I know he might not even care that I'm gone OR if I go back to Blairstown. Why didn't you tell me?"

Ryan started the car and dropped his head momentarily, rubbing his temples. "I need to think about this, Blake," he said wearily. "I don't know what's going on here. Besides, you agreed to stay here with me until we get your bloodlust under control." He shot me a pointed look. "And, spoiler alert, it's *not*."

I slumped in my seat, pissed at him. Mostly because he was right.

We didn't speak for a few moments. I sat sullenly while Ryan eased the car away from the kerb and we drove away from Clair's apartment building.

"I take it you heard everything?" he asked finally, sounding uncomfortable.

"Of course," I replied, still pleased that my new skill of 'seeing' things in other places was apparently something of a rarity. "It was full color and surround sound." I gestured to the folded napkin he was holding, which contained the Asphodel flower he'd ripped from Clair's hair.

"What's up with the flower?" I asked. "I thought I was going to break out in hives or something. It was a *full* sensory experience."

"Oh, really?" he teased. "A *full* sensory experience. Did you enjoy kissing a girl, Katy Perry?"

I pulled a face. "Whatever. I was too busy being bored to death. I thought you were going to come out once you realized she wasn't a threat?"

"She could still be a threat," Ryan said, glancing at me.

"The flower," I prodded. "Can you please throw it out of the window?" I felt my skin getting hot and itchy. "Is this some vampire allergy thing? It feels like I'm standing in the sun all over again."

"It's an Asphodel flower," Ryan explained. "They only grow in a few places, including The Underworld." He shoved it into the glove box between us, and my skin immediately felt a little less hot and bothered.

"Why are you keeping it?" I asked, annoyed that it was still in the car with us.

"I need to show Ivy. She might be able to tell me something about its origins, or where it was grown."

"I don't know why you trust her," I said, without thinking. He laughed.

"What?" I said, a little embarrassed that I had said that about her. He had known her for a lot longer than he had known me. "Am

I being a bitch?"

Ryan smiled, clearly entertained by me. How nice for him. "No, you're being smart. I *don't* trust Ivy. All I know is that she hates Caleb even more than she hates me."

"Why?" I asked, more curious about her than ever. "Why does she hate you both?"

Ryan's smile vanished. "She hates Caleb," he began slowly, "because Caleb took away her entire world. He thought that I was getting distracted by her. So he told her father that we were planning to marry, and where I had hidden her. It's Caleb's fault her father discovered her pregnancy. It's Caleb's fault her father beat her to death before I could get there in time to save both of them."

I didn't know what to say to that. I tried to think of my own father being angry enough to beat me and my unborn child to death. What a horrid way to end one's life.

"And why does she hate you?" I asked.

Ryan was quiet for a long while, and I eventually thought that he wasn't going to answer me.

"I loved her very much," Ryan said, showing a brief glimpse of the pain and rage he usually channelled into being an asshole. "But she consumed me completely. We were no good together. We would go on rampages together, feeding and killing whoever we felt like.

"It was dangerous. We were both becoming … demonic, almost. So one day I left her. I left her all alone and didn't see her for fifteen years."

I raised my eyebrows in disbelief. "And the next time you saw her –"

"—was in Mexico," he finished. "So, yeah, I don't trust her."

I wanted to think about the whole Ivy / Caleb / Ryan issue some more. There was something I was missing, something that involved me. But Ryan's mind was like a well-guarded vault, and I couldn't gain access. Besides, we were home, and we had gotten way off topic during our long-winded conversation.

“Anyway,” I said clearly as Ryan pulled into the garage and shut off the engine. “Caleb. He probably just wants his heart back, Ryan. So why don’t you give it to him and get him off your back?”

He looked at me, really looked into my eyes and studied my face. He reached a gentle hand over to touch my cheek, and left it there. It was such a lovely, innocent gesture amongst all of the other crap that I closed my eyes for a moment. And in that moment, I saw exactly why he wasn’t about to give the heart back in a hurry.

Another vision? Jesus, my brain could only process so much information.

THIRTY-ONE

I WAS NO LONGER IN THE CAR, BUT FALLING THROUGH THE AIR, AN invisible spectator in another time and place.

I blinked several times and looked at my new surroundings.

We stood by a huge underground lake that was as still and smooth as plate glass. The light was dim. The air surrounding us was so cold, the water should have been freezing, but the wafts of steam that were coming off the top suggested that it was warm. The ground beneath my bare feet was cold and damp, stone covered with dark green moss. The cavernous ceiling was at least fifty feet above us and stretched into oblivion, decorated with stalactites that dribbled icy water every so often.

"What's happening?" I asked. Ryan could tell I was freaking out. The feeling I had is so hard to describe. It was as if I was still frozen in the car, a hand brushing at my cheek, and yet I was here, in this cavernous space that stretched further than my vampiric gaze could see. I felt a draft on my bare skin and looked down to see that I was now wearing a thin white dress that looked suspiciously like the one

I had been wearing *that* night. "What the hell am I wearing?"

"Chill out. This is a different way of showing you a vision. You're not just seeing it in your mind, you're seeing it in real life."

I scowled. "And the dress?"

He smirked. "It suits you. We have to fit in, after all."

I studied his new outfit—a white cotton dress shirt with beige chinos—and shook my head. We were both barefoot. "We look like we're about to go to a luau," I said sarcastically.

"A journey through The Underworld, actually," he replied. "Among other places."

I baulked. *The Underworld*. The place where the dead came to rest. I grabbed his arm, terrified.

"Relax," he said calmly, squeezing my hand. "We're not actually here. We're still sitting in the car. I'm just showing you a memory from my own mind, and channelling it into yours."

"Oh," I said, letting my shoulders loosen. "Okay. That's good." And as he said it, I could feel part of my consciousness in the car, almost as if I were able to see two worlds at once, and switch between them at will.

"I want to show you why I think you're in danger," he said. "Why I think Caleb chose you. I didn't figure it out until I was told to Turn you instead of just take your blood. I don't know what he was planning to do to you, but I do know it can't be good."

"Awesome," I said sarcastically. I hated being the last to figure things out, and right now it seemed that I was always out of the loop on everything.

I realized I was still holding his hand and took it back, blushing. I felt like a scared little kid in a haunted house ride.

"Can anyone even see us?" I whispered, gesturing to the dress I was wearing.

"No," he replied. "It's just a memory, remember? Like watching a movie on a 3D screen."

Well, at least I fit in, I snarked, shivering in the thin dress he had chosen for me.

"Oh shush," he said, and in an instant I was dressed in my own jeans and t-shirt. "Watch the bloody show."

And he had meant that literally. I heard a girl's bloodcurdling scream and turned to see a large, hulking man dragging a pretty, young girl by her long, dark curls. He must have been at least seven feet tall and as stunning as he was terrifying. Silver tattoos that glowed in the nightlight were etched all over his luminous skin; skin that shone like gold and fire. His eyes were magnificent—large, black with tiny gold flecks that sparkled with such intensity, it was like looking directly into the midday sun. He had human features but was definitely not human.

"Hades," Ryan supplied helpfully.

"As in the Devil?"

"Mmm-hmm," Ryan replied.

I blinked and continued watching. The girl was screaming, Hades was getting angry and I was nervously bouncing from foot to foot.

He forced the girl up from a kneeling position to her feet.

"What is your final decision?" Hades asked the girl, his voice so loud and full of bass, it shook the air around me.

The girl was a blubbering mess. "Please," she begged. "Just let me go. I don't want to stay down here. I won't marry you!"

Resignation settled in on Hades' face. "Very well. You leave me no choice."

There was a crack, a crunch, and before I knew to cover my eyes, he had snapped her neck like a piece of kindling. All of this had happened in a matter of three seconds and it was only now, after teetering on her feet for a few moments, that the girl hit the ground, dead.

Only that wasn't the end of it. Almost instantly, the girl's ghost (or what I assumed to be her ghost) sat up, delirious, and stepped up out of the body that she had been contained within only minutes before her death. This was both incredible and distressing for me. I thought of the window then, of falling and crashing into the ground, and I edged away from Ryan a little. He gave me a serious look. He knew what I was thinking about, as usual.

He nudged me and gestured to the scene unfolding in front of us.

The girl, who was now a more pale, translucent version of herself, tried to run away. Each time she did, his hand shot out and grabbed her long, dark locks. She finally stopped struggling and looked up into the eyes of Hell incarnate. "Even in death, you will not leave me be?" she pleaded.

This made Hades smile. "Especially in death," he replied. I swallowed back bile as he continued to speak.

"In death, all belong to me. But you already knew this, Talitha Mae." He picked her up and carried her into the darkness of The Underworld until her cries faded into the void.

"Jesus," I said, staring at the body in front of us. It was all too much to take in. I had just watched a girl die—again, after having to watch Kate be ripped apart by Caleb in front of me just a few short weeks ago. I shivered and wrapped my arms around myself.

"Do you know why I showed you this?"

I gulped. "Because I look almost identical to that girl?"

"Bingo," Ryan replied.

I blinked, and the body of the girl who looked just like me was gone.

"What does any of this have to do with me?" I asked, my voice a little too shrill.

"I'm not entirely sure," Ryan said. "But I know you're the key. You, and the heart. That's why I took both of you. That's why you can't leave me, not yet."

That's why I took both of you. His referral to the heart as a person left me extremely concerned.

I started to pace, just like I always did when I was worried. "So you had nothing to do with that?" I asked.

"No," he replied, picking up a stone and skimming it along the surface of the lake. It seemed to skip along the surface forever before succumbing to its murky depths. "It happened before I was even born."

"Then how is it a memory in your head?"

"The same way I have now placed the memory in your mind. Caleb showed me this memory. Talitha, in turn, showed it to him. It is the truth. Vampires are powerful, but we cannot make up things like this. If someone shares a memory with you, you can safely assume that it is true."

I nodded. It was a lot of information to take in, but I thought I was coping remarkably well with it all. Except for the part where I had just watched a young girl, no older than me, *who looked just like me*, have her neck snapped by the bare hands of Satan himself.

"Kosher?" Ryan asked.

I nodded.

"Great." He clapped his hands together and the universe around me changed again. I was suddenly aware of the heat as an unforgiving sun throbbed directly overhead in the midday sky.

"Bet you wish you were wearing that little white number," Ryan deadpanned, smirking at my jeans and t-shirt.

"Bite me," I replied, rolling my eyes.

The Underworld was completely gone, as if it had never existed. We now stood in a narrow dirt alleyway in the middle of two squat limestone buildings. The stench of sickness and death immediately invaded my nostrils, and I had to stop myself from retching. I jumped at the sound of Ryan's voice.

"Do you know where we are?" he asked me. I shook my head no.

"Smack in the middle of the greatest human plague, in the twelfth century. The back alleys where whores go to conduct business and decency goes to die. Welcome."

I wrinkled my nose in distaste. "It smells like ass."

He ignored me, instead gesturing to a pile of debris further into the alley. I took a few reluctant steps, each one bringing me closer to the source of the stench.

I recoiled when I realized what I was looking at. A haphazard pile of rotting arms, legs and faces lay at the end of the alleyway. The faces were the worst. Some of them were bloated or streaked with old blood and almost everything was covered in flies. Rats and mice darted in and out, and I turned away after glimpsing a brown rodent chowing down on what was left of a man's ear. "Oh, shit," I moaned. I wanted to hurl, but I didn't, and I think it was only because we were in spirit form that I kept my baggie of blood down. "Why are we here?"

"You'll see," Ryan said quietly.

A man, no more than thirty years old, dressed in rags and clearly sick with whatever plague had killed the pile of bodies, stumbled into the alleyway. He coughed, tilted his face towards the sky, and squinted his beautiful, sapphire-blue eyes at the unforgiving sun. His mortal eyes had been something wondrous to behold.

"Caleb," I breathed. "He's human."

Ryan nodded. "He's dying."

"Help!" Caleb cried out, stumbling to his knees in the dirt.

As if from nowhere, a young woman stepped out of the shadows of a doorframe overhang and stood in front of him.

"That's the girl from The Underworld," I whispered. "I thought she was stuck there?"

She didn't look as similar to me this time. Her hair was longer and darker, her skin was deathly pale, and her eyes were solid black. She looked positively terrifying and beautiful all at once.

"She was," Ryan replied. "She escaped. She's possessing a human's body."

What's wrong with her?

She's been in Hell for hundreds of years, Ryan whispered through the bond. *She's become a demon.*

"What is your name, love?" she murmured.

"I don't remember," he said sadly.

"Then I shall give you a new one. I will call you Caleb, the chosen one, and you will live forever." She reached down and cupped his face in her hands with such affection, it made her appear human for a short moment.

Caleb let out a small, strangled sob. "Who are you?" he asked in between coughs. "Are you an angel?"

Her rosebud mouth turned upwards in a wicked smile, but her eyes remained dead and black.

"I am Talitha," she said softly. "You belong to me now."

She took one of her long fingernails and drew it hard along the smooth skin on her wrist, until blood sprang to the surface. I looked closer and baulked.

It was *black*. Her blood was pitch black.

She pressed her open wound to Caleb's mouth, and he drank greedily. I cringed as I realized what was about to happen.

He was going to Turn.

Sure enough, he dropped to the ground and began screaming and clawing at his face. I couldn't watch. I looked away.

Thankfully, Ryan jumped to the next scene, rather than making me relive the entire painful and grotesque process of Caleb's Turn.

We stood in a small clearing in the middle of a pine forest. It was nightfall, and things felt eerily quiet, until several pairs of footsteps began thundering through the undergrowth. Caleb and Talitha came into view and stopped in the clearing near us, both panting for breath. It was obvious some time had passed—Caleb was a vampire, though his eyes were still blue, not yet that insipid pearl white they had been when I met him in Mexico.

I heard growling and panting all around us and realized that the beads of light in the dark surrounding Talitha and Caleb were actually eyes.

Wolves?

Hell Hounds, Ryan confirmed.

One of the Hell Hounds stalked out of the shadows and into the clearing, the weak moonlight bringing it into focus a little better. It was huge, much bigger than any dog I'd ever seen, with short, glossy, black fur and teeth that glittered with anticipation.

Talitha was crying. She was a demon, but in that moment she looked like the broken human girl who had been tricked by the Devil. She and Caleb bent their heads together so that their foreheads were touching.

"You know what to do," she said forlornly.

He nodded and kissed her forehead so softly, so gently, that I could not imagine it was the same person that had tortured me and made me bleed.

The Hell Hound leapt into the air, flew in a wide arc, and knocked Talitha to the ground.

"Noooooo!" Caleb yelled, as a second Hell Hound began chasing him away from her. The Hound easily jumped him and forced him down to the ground, all the while a horrific growl emanating from its thick throat.

The Hound snapped at Caleb's throat, and it seemed to take all of his strength to hold the beast just far enough away to stop it from taking his head off.

Talitha was not faring so well. I didn't want to look, but I could hear. The bigger Hound was literally ripping her to shreds. The smell of blood mixed with dead pine needles radiated through the forest, and I retched.

Within seconds she was dead. Faster than I could focus on, the Hound had dragged her ghost out of her lifeless body and fled, quickly followed by the second Hound.

Caleb dragged himself over to her almost unrecognisable body. He appeared to be in shock. With shaky hands, he withdrew a jar and a large hunting knife from his thick fur coat.

When he located her heart by pressing on her breastbone, my heart dropped.

He was going to cut her heart out.

And that's exactly what he did. With trembling hands, he brushed away a single tear from his cheek and then cut into the dead flesh of his lover. After an agonizing and brutal surgery on Talitha's corpse, he held her heart in his hands. He placed the heart in the jar and replaced the lid, then retrieved a small square of paper from his pocket. There were several Latin words written on it, which he said quietly over and over again.

At first I was transfixed by his face, by the way he was saying the words, until I heard a *thumpthumpthump* coming from the jar.

He smiled sadly. His spell had worked. Although she was dead and had been dragged off to Hell by a couple of Hounds, Talitha's heart continued to beat.

THIRTY-TWO

SUDDENLY, WE WERE BACK IN THE CAR.

"No more visions," I said, pushing his hand away from my cheek. "I'm exhausted." I felt sick. How many deaths had I just witnessed from the comfort of leather seats and air-conditioning?

Ryan nodded in agreement.

Neither of us made any attempt to get out of the car. I guessed he was waiting for questions. Really, what he had shown me hadn't answered anything. It had just confused me even more.

"I know it's a lot," he said.

"A lot?" I echoed. "Watching all three *Lord of the Rings* movies in one sitting is *a lot*. That was like taking an acid trip and then getting onto a time-traveling spaceship to Narnia or something." I rubbed my eyes.

"I'm sick of you speaking in riddles, Ryan! Just tell me. What does it mean? The heart. The girl that looks just like me."

Ryan shrugged. "I think Caleb wants to use you to bring Talitha back."

"Back from where?"

He looked at me like I was an idiot. "From *Hell.*"

"They were in love," I said quietly, still shocked that two such cruel creatures could be driven by such a human emotion.

"Yes," Ryan said. "You saw the way she looked at him before she died, such love for someone who was pure evil. She loved him, and he loved her just as much. He's wanted to bring her back from the dead the entire time I've known him."

"How?" I pressed.

"I don't know!" Ryan exploded, slamming the dash with his fist so hard that it cracked. I raised my eyebrows.

Nice one. Isn't this a totally rare car or something?

Ryan sighed audibly and slumped back in his seat. "You have to believe me," he said. "If Caleb has both of you, I don't know what will happen. That's why I took you from Mexico. *That's* why both you and the heart need to stay here, with me."

THIRTY-THREE

I WAS BONE TIRED AFTER OUR EXPEDITION TO CLAIR'S APARTMENT and the visions I'd been subjected to. I called it a night and was surprised when I woke up the next morning in the exact position in which I'd fallen into bed. The energy required to concentrate on receiving psychic information was exhausting.

I was reading through my class schedule, armed with a strong black coffee, when Evie called.

"Hi," I said into the phone, dumping the stack of UCLA papers on the coffee table and wandering into the kitchen.

"Hey," Evie replied. "Whatcha doing?"

"Nothing exciting. You?"

"Just packing a bag," Evie replied, and I heard the excitement in her voice. "I need a lift tonight. I get into LAX at seven."

I felt the blood drain from my face as Ryan entered the room. So he had heard what she said from wherever he had been lurking. Typical.

"You're coming here?" I said finally. "Now? Today?"

I was angry. I was ashamed. I didn't want her to see me like that—a *vampire*.

"Yep," she replied. "Can you pick me up? Or should I catch a cab?"

Ryan caught my eye and shook his head.

"No," I said quickly. "I'll come get you."

"Can't wait to see you!" she said happily.

After promising her I'd be there, I ended the call and looked at Ryan. He must have seen the sheer panic on my face.

"It'll be fine," he said.

I shook my head. "I don't want her to see you," I replied. "She won't like you."

"I probably won't like her either," Ryan reminded me. "Vampires and witches generally don't get along."

I raised my eyebrows in disbelief.

"Except the badass ones," he added. "Like Ivy."

I rolled my eyes.

"So—airport?" Ryan prompted me.

"Oh, yeah," I said, my stomach coming up into my mouth. "You don't need to come. Can I borrow one of the cars?"

Ryan looked at me like I was an idiot. "I *do* need to come," he said. "You could be driving into a trap, remember?"

I thought of the beating heart in the jar. "Okay," I agreed reluctantly. "But prepare to have shreds ripped off you. Evie is… unique."

"Most witches are," Ryan answered. "I'm going out for a few hours. You need anything?"

"Where are you going?" I asked, immediately suspicious. He hardly ever left me alone in the house, so it had to be something important.

"To see our pretty little friend, Clair. I was up all night thinking about how I could possibly know her."

"And?" I pressed.

"I have an idea," he mused. "But I could be wrong. I won't be long."

"Wait!" I said. "What am I supposed to do all day?"

Ryan shrugged. "Order school supplies online. Do something with that rats-nest you call hair. How the hell should I know?"

I ended up nervously pacing the house most of the day. I made lunch, drank some blood-infused soda, and tried not to bite all my nails off. I couldn't comprehend the fact that, in a way, I was meeting my best friend for the first time. The first time as a vampire.

It was a waste of a day. My nerves wouldn't leave me and I kept zoning out whenever I tried to concentrate on reading the UCLA handbook, so eventually I gave up and watched daytime soaps until Ryan got back.

He was in a chipper mood when he returned.

"Did you kill her?" I asked dismally. Maybe that explained his stupid grin.

"What?" Ryan asked, as he added a dash of bourbon to his blood on the rocks. "No. I visited. We talked. Turns out she isn't a threat after all."

He didn't offer any more. "Aren't you going to tell me *why* she isn't a threat?" I asked.

"I wasn't going to," he replied, draining his glass. "But since you asked: I knew her father, a long time ago. She needs a favor, is all."

"Oh," I said, the news not bringing me any relief. "Well, there you go."

"It's almost six-thirty," Ryan mentioned. "You want to go now?"

The airport. Damn. I had forgotten about Evie's imminent arrival for just a few moments. "Crap," I said. "We'll be late."

Ryan grabbed a set of keys from the kitchen bench and started off towards the garage. I hurried after him, grabbing my bag on the way out.

Evie. My best friend in the whole world. I hadn't seen her in almost two months.

Would she even want to be my friend once she saw what I had become?

THIRTY-FOUR

We made it to LAX with lightning speed. My mind was still reeling from the visions of Talitha and Caleb that I'd seen the night before, not to mention the date between Clair and Ryan where I had been a psychic third wheel. But as soon as we arrived at the airport, I forgot about everything. My nerves were on edge and I replayed potential meetings in my head. Would Evie cry? Would I? Would she be afraid of me? Would she try to stake me through the heart? I sure hoped not.

The airport was busy. We parked and went into the domestic arrivals section, Ryan trailing behind me at my insistence. I didn't want Evie to see him until I'd explained him to her properly. I don't know why I cared what she thought about him. Maybe it was because he was all I really had to fall back on if she decided she didn't like Vampire Me. Or maybe it was because I was a vampire like him, and I was linked to him through our bond, and I stupidly cared about him despite everything he had done.

I smelled cheap coffee and sweaty bodies as I got closer to

the arrivals gate. Being a vampire, my senses were so much more acute, which wasn't always pleasant. I tried to focus on finding Evie. I scanned the arrivals board, seeing that a flight from Newark had landed and baggage was available. I started towards the baggage carousels, hoping I would find Evie waiting for her suitcase there.

I was halfway there when somebody grabbed me from behind in a bear grip around my shoulders.

I stiffened, fighting against the grip immediately. It was a guy, and he was tall. I broke free and whirled around, expecting a vampire.

Oh my God. My jaw dropped in disbelief.

It was almost an anti–climax. The moment I'd been wishing for, the one I'd given up hope of ever seeing, was jammed in my face so quickly and violently, I didn't know whether to laugh or cry.

I didn't say anything, couldn't form words. I just stared at him.

"Jared?" I said shakily.

I still loved him just as much as I always had, and that was a relief, to feel something so light and wonderful amidst the darkness that had all but engulfed me.

He grinned like an idiot, his sandy blonde hair all messed up and his deep, brown eyes tired and lined with black circles. "Hey, beautiful," he said affectionately.

"H–hi," I managed to croak back. "Hey, you."

He launched himself onto me in a second giant bear hug, which I returned tightly. He tensed, and I loosened my grip instantly, remembering my newborn vampire strength could probably suffocate him. I hoped he hadn't noticed. My throat got all tight and my eyes started leaking hot, wet tears that flowed faster as I felt his lips graze my forehead. I breathed him in, remembering all the other times I had held him like this. Under his olive skin, I could smell rich copper and chocolate pulsating through his veins—but it didn't overwhelm me the way the others had warned me it would. For that, I was grateful.

We parted eventually, and I took the time to drink him in—from his mussed-up hair that he always left forever before getting a haircut; his almond-shaped eyes that turned from chestnut to ebony depending on what he was wearing; his smooth skin, broken by stubble; his broad swimming shoulders that had been a place for my head to lay many a summer's night; but most of all, the feeling that he was here, and that it felt so right.

"Don't cry, Blake." I smiled as Jared gently wiped my cheeks with his thumb.

"I'm so happy to see you," I breathed. "You have no idea how happy I am."

Was I dreaming? I wasn't, thankfully. But less than two minutes after Jared's arrival, dread was already settling into my bones like an old friend. The others had warned me about relationships with humans—and although I didn't feel the overwhelming urge to feed from Jared, I could still smell the rich coffee and spice scent of blood through his thin flesh, could still hear the steady thrum of his heart beating inside his chest. Pretty soon I felt myself drawn to him, wanting what was inside of him—I wanted *all* of him.

"What are you doing here?" I asked, painfully swallowing my thirst.

"Surprising you," Jared replied with a smile. Oh God, I could have melted hearing his voice after so long. I spotted Ryan ten feet away, watching everything with guarded concern. His presence suddenly brought everything crashing down inside of me. I wished he hadn't come. How was I going to explain him to Jared?

"I just got a text from Evie," Jared said. "She's running late, said we should wait in the car for her."

Evie. Of course. I had forgotten all about her.

I gulped. "In the car?" *With Ryan?*

He nodded.

"I caught a cab here," I lied, knowing that Ryan could hear me.

You are not coming with us, I told Ryan through our bond. *You can follow behind in your car, but you are NOT chaperoning me home.*

I glanced over to see him scanning the airport.

Jesus, Blake, he replied, mimicking Jared's nickname for me. *Catch a cab. Catch a flying saucer. I'll drive at a respectable distance.*

I was so relieved at his cooperation, I didn't berate him for calling me Blake again. Nobody called me that except my friends, and I was sick of him pretending he was one of them.

"That's cool," Jared was saying. He dangled a set of keys in front of me and it took me a minute to realize they were the keys for my car. My Honda Element, the one I'd been walking towards when I was taken by the vampires.

"You drove here?" I asked incredulously. "From New Jersey?"

Jared nodded. " I knew you'd be missing your wheels. There's some weird little towns between here and there."

"I have no doubt," I replied. "So you drove all this way just to bring me my car?"

"And to see you," he replied, swooping in for another leg–tingling kiss that flooded me with warmth.

"Come on," he said, taking me by the hand. "Your chariot awaits."

In the car, my car, I realized I wasn't just frightened by the prospect of Caleb turning up at the airport—I was genuinely nervous to be around Jared. I could feel myself turning inwards, shy and shameful of the secret that coursed through my veins, the secret that separated us from now on. Or did it? Why did it have to spell the end for us? It didn't seem fair; nothing about the last month of my life had been fair.

"So, whatcha been up to? You must have done something other than run and miss me." Jared looked exhausted.

The air was humid, and I could practically feel the positive charge in the approaching storm. Lightning cracked in the distance and I had a horrible flash of falling, of the way my face smashed into the ground two stories below, of the way I pleaded with Ryan not to inject his vampire blood into my veins. My happiness at seeing Jared was instantly engulfed by the abyss of sorrow inside me. I had died. While he was surfing and swimming and missing me, I had *died.* And now I was something else—someone else—entirely.

"I've had the worst flu," I lied, slouching back in my seat. It was eighty odd degrees outside, but I wrapped my hands in my sweater sleeves and tried not to cry. "I've been watching a lot of HBO, actually. I'm a lame tourist."

"Well, at least you have plenty of time to find your feet. You're here for the long haul, right?"

"Right," I answered uneasily. Because I wasn't going home to put my family and friends in danger.

Jared looked pensive. "Are you…okay?" he asked after a few moments.

"I'm—fine," I stumbled. "Why? Do I not seem okay?"

He furrowed his eyebrows. "You just seem … different. Your voice—you don't sound like you. You look sad or something."

I felt my face fall, and I let out the breath I'd been holding. He was probably planning to stay for the weekend. How was I going to keep it together when I couldn't even look at him for ten seconds without wanting to scream about how fucking unfair my life was?

"I just really miss you," I said honestly. "I miss everyone. I miss home. I'm lonely sometimes. This isn't what I thought it would be like, you know? And I'm so glad you're here right now—but I'm already missing you because I know you probably have to leave on Sunday."

I looked away from him then, embarrassed at my vulnerability, my nakedness.

"Mia," he said gently, taking both of my clammy hands and squeezing them affectionately. "I miss you already. You're all I think about. All I want to do is quit Ithaca and live illegally in your dorm room."

That made me laugh.

"But," he continued, "it's only a few years and we can be together all the time. Wherever you want. We'll get awesome jobs and live on the beach somewhere. It'll be epic." He rolled his eyes, making a sweeping gesture with one hand as he said the last word. I had a bad habit of describing everything as epic, and he always teased me for it.

"It just seems like forever," I said lamely, my voice cracking under the strain of my secret burden. *Forever.*

"Give it time," he replied, kissing my forehead, long and lingering. "If you're still not happy next semester—but you will be—then come home. You can live illegally in my dorm room."

Laughter died inside my throat and I gasped as a face appeared in my window. I jumped, shrinking back in horror. We'd been followed. It had to be Caleb. And now poor Jared was going to be dragged into the whole sorry–assed affair that had become my life as a vampire.

We were so screwed.

I let my breath out in a whoosh as Evie smiled through the glass back at me. I unlocked my door and got out, wrapping Evie in a bear hug whilst carefully not smooshing her to death. "You scared the shit out of me!" I said happily, relief slamming into me like a freight train. All the nervous adrenalin circling my body had nowhere to go, and I let out another excited squeal as I released my hug and stepped back to study my best friend.

I don't know how I knew that something was up, but I just knew. Call it my vamp sense, but I felt the smile slip from my face as Evie regarded me with concern.

"I'll go pay the ticket," Jared called as he got out of the car and started walking towards a lit up pay station about fifty yards away.

"Okay," I said. I turned back to Evie and swallowed nervously. I had no words. I felt utterly exposed. I may as well have had VAMPIRE written across my forehead in a poor college boy's blood.

Moments passed.

"I thought you were dead," she said finally, in a tight voice that betrayed her fear.

"Why are you afraid?" I asked desperately. "Evie, it's me!"

"Do you know what I am?" she asked me quietly, nervously scanning the parking lot. I glanced over to see Jared having problems with the pay station. From a hundred yards away, I could hear the coins being spat back out of the slot and an automated voice notifying him to go to the next station to pay.

"You're a girl from Jersey," I answered stupidly, hopping from one foot to another. Why was she looking at me like that?

"I'm a witch, Mia," she said, her voice still razor-like. "I know what you are. You're different now."

I sagged against the car, looking at the ground as tears welled up in my eyes. "Okay. So what am I?"

She didn't want to say it. Her face softened, and she started to cry as well. "I'm sorry I left you alone in the parking lot, Mia. I could feel those vampires—I was trying to draw them away from you. I thought they wanted me. I had no idea it was you they were after."

I gasped in horrified disbelief at what she was saying. That she had known Ryan and the others were there before me. That maybe if we had carpooled that night, none of this would have happened. "You knew they were there?"

She nodded ruefully. "A vamp followed me all the way home. I didn't realize until the next day when you wouldn't pick up my calls that—that they had taken you. I've been looking for you ever since, but someone's put a spell on you that makes you impossible to track down."

Ivy's spell, to protect me from Caleb's trackers, must have also kept Evie from locating me. Ryan silently confirmed this through the bond, irritating me. He just couldn't stay out of my head for five minutes, and it was driving me insane.

I glanced over at Jared again, who was still struggling at the second pay station, when a thought suddenly occurred to me.

"You're not doing that," I said quietly. "Are you?"

Evie looked over at Jared, and suddenly he was walking back towards us, looking a little frustrated. "I had to get you alone somehow," she replied. "I broke his car so my flight would get here before he did. I didn't know he was bringing your car."

"Why did you come here?" I asked suddenly, desperate to know more before Jared joined us.

"I missed my bestie," Evie replied cagily. "Besides, I couldn't let you eat your boyfriend by accident, could I?"

"I'm glad you came," I said honestly, ignoring the part about eating Jared. "I've missed you so much, Evie. So much has happened. So much *crazy shit* has happened."

Jared was almost at the car.

"Why didn't you just call me sooner, Mia?" Evie asked, the hurt obvious on her face. "I could have helped you. I could have been here with you. You didn't have to go through this by yourself."

I shrugged, pain settling in at my temples. Yeah, why hadn't I just called her, or someone, anyone?

Because I was scared, that's why.

"They told me not to. They said I'd be putting you in danger if I contacted you. The vampire who took me—he's still looking for me."

Evie looked confused, but the moment was lost as Jared handed me the validated parking ticket and grabbed Evie's suitcase, lugging it around to the back of the car and opening the tail.

"Later," she said to me, her voice lighter. "We'll talk, you and me. About everything."

THIRTY-FIVE

We picked up burgers and fries at a drive–thru not far from the airport and took the food back to Ivy's house. I was hoping beyond hope that the wards were not up, that Ryan had thought to call ahead and get Ivy to disarm her psychic gate lock. Jared turned the car into the driveway with one smooth motion, and I let out a relieved breath when the gate slid open and we glided into the driveway without resistance.

Ryan had overtaken us a few streets back, and his car was already in the garage when we parked in front of the door. I sensed him in the house and reached my mental tendrils out to him.

Please don't come out, I begged Ryan through the bond. *I have enough explaining to do without you, too.*

Alright, Your Highness. Sam and Ivy are out, you've got the run of the house.

Thank you, I replied silently. Small favors and all that.

"Who did you say you were staying with again?" Jared asked innocently.

"Oh, just some people from the track team," I lied. I felt terrible about being dishonest, but what was I supposed to say? "The dorms aren't available until next month."

"Nice house," Jared said, obviously impressed.

The door was unlocked, and I ushered them both inside. Evie looked positively sick, I guessed from all the magic she could sense. I could feel it and I wasn't a witch, so she must have been positively swimming in spells and the smell of herbs and potions. And probably blood. I know I could smell the sweet stench of the red gold in the refrigerator. Maybe she could, too.

We all ate quickly and silently at the outdoor table, overlooking the pool. I had almost set up plates and napkins in the lounge room, but decided against it at the last minute. I didn't want to sit with Jared on the same couch where I had kissed Ryan, and I sure as hell didn't want to sit at the kitchen table where *It* had happened. As I shovelled fries into my mouth I couldn't help but notice Evie studying the way I ate, the way I looked at Jared, the way I kept glancing nervously towards the hallway where I knew Ryan was eavesdropping on everything we said.

I excused myself when it became clear that Ryan wanted to talk to me.

"Hi" I said casually.

"Are you okay?" Ryan's concerned voice irritated me instantly.

"I'm fine," I said tightly. "You need to stop chattering in my head. Jared is getting suspicious because you keep distracting me. I'll talk to you later."

"I'm coming out," Ryan responded.

"What?" I said, alarmed. "No. You can't. Do not come out of this house."

"Chill out, babe. I'm not going to crash your little reunion. I just want to see the witch, that's all."

"Why?" I hissed. "You got a thing for witches?"

Oh, that's right, he did. He just smiled with nauseating

fake sweetness.

"Spoken like a true stalker," I said, rolling my eyes. "Don't come out."

"I love you, too!" Ryan sang in a high-pitched girl's voice.

When I got back to the kitchen, Evie was sitting at the table alone, and looking at me as if she'd heard the whole conversation. I looked at the kitchen table and cringed inside. "Where's Jared?" I asked, scanning the room.

"Asleep," Evie replied casually. "In your room. Well, I assumed it was your room? The first one off the hallway. It has all your stuff in there. It looks pretty nice for a prison."

I hadn't even heard either of them come inside. Which was weird for a vampire, but still. I had been distracted.

"How is he asleep?" I demanded. "I was gone for, like, two minutes at the most."

Evie smiled indulgently. "I put him to sleep," she said. *Magic.* Of course. I was surrounded by it, and up until a few weeks ago, I hadn't even known it existed.

"Well, that's probably a good thing," I said, although I was pained at the sudden loss of his presence so soon after seeing him again.

"So," Evie said, all businesslike. "We have a few hours before Mr. Tired Eyes wakes up. Tell me everything."

I hardly needed convincing. I hesitated for a split second, then opened my mouth and let everything out in one long go.

I told her. In a voice barely above a whisper, I let open the floodgates and told her every single thing that had happened to me since the last time we had seen each other, the night that I was kidnapped. In some parts, I cried alone; in other parts, like when I told her of my death and rebirth, we cried together.

Except for the night with Ryan. I couldn't say those words, not to anyone. I would die with the events of that night—at least the ones I remembered—locked away in the deepest recesses of my soul.

When I was finished, and I had no more words, I looked at the clock in the kitchen to see that more than two hours had passed. Exhausted, I rose from the table and rubbed my grit–filled eyes. Stumbling across the kitchen, I opened the refrigerator and fished out a bottle of 'tomato juice'. I didn't really feel like it but I knew I probably wouldn't have another chance until Jared left, and I'd never gone three days without blood before. I decided not to nuke the blood, happier when it didn't taste like it had just come out of some poor human's neck as they struggled for their life. It was cold, oddly refreshing, but it left an awful metallic taste in my mouth.

I could feel myself being watched and turned to face Evie, dragging my palm across my face to make sure there was no blood left on my lips.

"Do you like it?" she asked quietly, looking at the red–rimmed bottle. It wasn't like she was just talking about the bottle. It was as if she was asking me if I enjoyed being a vampire.

"No," I snapped. "I don't. Do you like using magic to make my boyfriend pass out?"

Evie blinked, took a step back. I felt my shoulders sag as I realized the compulsion had been coming through in my voice. "I'm sorry," I added hastily, shaking my head.

"It's okay," Evie said. "Your compulsion doesn't work on me."

"You know," I said, turning to rinse the bottle in the sink, "you haven't told me anything about you being a witch. Is it a family thing?"

She didn't answer; and when I turned back, I understood why. I felt the color drain from my face as I locked eyes with my maker.

"I told you to leave us alone," I said in a murderous tone.

Ryan, as arrogant as ever, leaned against the bench, where he'd evidently been languishing without either of us hearing. He was that good.

"Your little boyfriend is still fast asleep," Ryan said lightly, waving his hand. "Surely Evangeline doesn't mind my company? I mean, now that she knows *everything* about us?" He shot a nasty glance at me, and I raised my eyebrows in disbelief at his accusing stare.

"She's my best friend," I said defensively. "I tell her everything. Including what a dick you are."

"Thank you," he replied mockingly. "I've always measured my self-worth on how teenage girls perceive me." He looked from me to tight-lipped Evie, who wasn't saying a thing.

"Can't you just leave me alone for one night?" I asked him, exasperated. "I'm not going to die. And if I do, I promise it's not your fault."

"I wouldn't do that if I were you," Evie said slowly, staring Ryan in the eye. I saw power flare yellow in Ryan's eyes as he attempted to subdue her mentally. He reached his hand closer and brushed her cheek—and incredibly, a white-hot spark extended from her skin, burning Ryan's fingers. He drew back with vampire speed, wrapping his unharmed hand around his smoldering fingers. Suddenly, the kitchen stank like burnt flesh.

"I knew fire was your element," he said, a devilish grin breaking out on his smug face. "The personality gives it away every time."

"Well, look how smart you are," she said icily. "And what kind of vampire are you? The order of Elijah tattoo doesn't look like it suits your personality at all." She gestured to the intricate pattern of black wings and symbols etched around Ryan's wrist.

Ryan was definitely intrigued by my apparent witch best friend. "Do tell," he pressed her. "What kind of personality *do* I have?"

"I know you were following me," she hissed. "For months, I knew there were vampires. And then you took a poor human girl who couldn't even put up a fight? Why not take me and at least keep life interesting?"

Ryan's asshole facade dropped slightly, and I felt his confusion through the bond. "I didn't follow you," he replied, as he looked her up and down. "Though I *would* follow you, don't get me wrong."

"Bullshit!" Evie's voice was getting louder. "I know you were there. I had a vampire tailing me since Christmas last year."

"It wasn't him," I said. "He's confused. He's trying to cover that up because he's a dick, but he doesn't know what you're talking about."

Evie looked at me like I had grown a second head. "You believe him?" she asked in a horrified tone. "You think he's telling you the truth, Mia?"

"He never tells me the whole truth," I said to her while I stared at him. "But I can tell when he's lying. It's part of the bond."

"Great. A fucking vampire bond. Well, I'm going to bed." She flounced into the empty bedroom next to mine, where I had put her bags. A minute later, she poked her head out of the room and addressed Ryan directly. "Oh, and if you try to bite me while I'm asleep, vampire boy, I'll rip your heart out and feed it to a troll."

He smiled and blew a kiss at her. She slammed the door in response.

Ryan and I studied each other uneasily across the kitchen bench.

"She's here to take you home," Ryan said seriously.

"Well, wouldn't you do the same if you were her?" I replied in a voice barely above a whisper. "She thinks it's her fault that I'm here."

Ryan shrugged. "So what are you planning on telling her?"

I set my jaw stubbornly and didn't answer.

"You're going?" Ryan asked, his tone carefully neutral, his eyes flashing with frustration.

"Caleb doesn't even care about me" I hissed, careful not to wake up Jared who was still asleep in my bed fifteen feet away from where we stood. "Have you ever thought that maybe he just wants that goddamned heart back?"

Ryan looked taken aback, and I felt anger rise inside me as his reaction confirmed my growing suspicion.

"Give me one good reason why I should stay," I demanded. "Now. Or I'm leaving tonight."

He scowled, and I could see he understood. I had him backed into a corner.

"If you go home now," he said seriously, "you will die."

"How?" I asked. "How will I die? I want details."

When he didn't speak, I raised my eyebrows to prompt him. "Start talking," I demanded. "You know I'm serious."

"I don't know what he's going to do," he said through gritted teeth. "If I did, I'd be able to stop him!"

He tore his gaze away from me, and I saw the internal struggle he was having. He looked down the hallway one last time, then back at me.

"Please," he pleaded. "Please just trust me?"

I didn't answer him; I just pushed past him and stormed off to my room.

THIRTY-SIX

I COULDN'T SLEEP AFTER THE HORRORS I'D SEEN THE NIGHT before. The stench of blood and rotted souls was still trapped in my nostrils, no matter how hot I made my shower.

Jared was still sleeping off whatever Evie had given him, which was unfortunate. I felt terrible that she had needed to do such a thing, but, of course, she had to if we were going to talk about what was really going on.

About vampires.

I knew she wouldn't be asleep when I knocked on the door at 3 a.m. Sure enough, she answered, still dressed in her day clothes and completely awake.

"You're going to be tired tomorrow," I said, closing the door behind me.

Evie shrugged, avoiding eye contact. "I can't believe I agreed to stay here." Her eyes roamed the room as if it were a dirty den infested with cockroaches, instead of a palatial guest room where the sheets were egyptian cotton and the silk cushions matched the drapes perfectly.

"It's not so bad," I said lamely. Who was I trying to convince? I might have become used to it, but I still didn't want to *be* here. It was pure necessity that had driven me to accept Ryan's deal and stick it out in Ivy's house for a few months. Especially after what had happened with Ryan. The bloodlust that itched under my skin like fire ants. The possibility that I could hurt someone I loved. That I could kill them.

"Don't you think you're a little too comfortable here?" Evie asked point blank. The accusation in her tone was like a slap in the face. The suspicion that I accepted being here, enjoyed it, even.

You should see how comfortable I got on the kitchen table.

"Things are messed up," I tried to explain. "It's not what it seems. I'll be home soon, anyway."

Evie glanced around the room and then grabbed my hand. I felt a jolt of electricity sizzle at my palm and rush through my body, stealing my breath. It was power, I realized, the power of a witch. I stared open-mouthed at my best friend and saw a stranger instead. A stranger whose eyes lit up inhumanly as she spoke in hushed tones.

"He can't hear us," Evie whispered to me. "I cut off your bond for a few moments. Everything we say here stays between the two of us, understand?"

I nodded.

"You need to come home with us tomorrow, Mia. I don't trust this guy. This house, this whole situation … it feels dangerous."

"Of course it's dangerous," I replied, somewhat annoyed. "I'm not a little kid, Evie. I'm here because Caleb wants to kill me!"

I tried to snatch my hand back but Evie was incredibly strong, especially since she was now restraining vampire me. Power crackled through our palms and I felt myself immobilized. It pissed me off.

"Let go!" I whispered angrily through gritted teeth.

"Not until you listen to me," Evie replied in a grave tone. "Mia, I know things. Things about the future."

"Oh, you can see the future now?" I mocked her openly.

Her eyes flashed with what I guessed to be frustration. "If you stay here, you will die. I've seen it, and I've never been wrong before."

I felt all the blood drain from my face as I turned that over in my head.

If you stay here, you will die. If you go home, you will die.

Seemed like no matter where I went, my days were numbered.

My shoulders sagged and I stared at the ground.

"Do you trust me?" Evie asked quietly.

"With my life," I answered honestly. Because I did.

"Then believe me, please. I screwed up and they took you. Don't let me get you killed again."

I sighed, tears blurring my vision. "I want to come home, but I don't. You don't know how this *feels* inside." I clawed at my chest with a shaking hand. "It's enough to drive someone insane. You know?"

There was no need for me to elaborate. She knew why I didn't want to go home.

"I will help you," she said softly. "I'll stay with you at your house, and we can get through this together. There are friendly vampires I know of. They can fill in the blanks for us with blood banks and all that."

I just nodded. It wasn't just the practicalities stopping me from jumping on a plane and flying home—it was this strange feeling, deep in my belly, that said I couldn't leave Ryan. That we belonged to each other.

Evie's face softened. "I know," she said, squeezing my hand. "I know you think you can't leave him. That leaving him would kill you."

"It's stupid," I said.

If you go home you will die.

"It's not stupid," Evie replied gently, using her free hand to wipe tears from my cheek. "It's the way vampires are designed. For survival. The good news is, once you're far away enough that feeling will start to fade."

I nodded because I wanted to believe her.

"Every time you have that feeling," Evie said, "I want you to remember the moment you fell in love with Jared. How it felt. Where you were. Every little detail you can think of."

I started to cry. "Why?" I asked.

"Because," Evie squeezed my hand tightly, "he's the one you should share a bond with. The guy you love, not a vampire who took you against your will and Turned you because he screwed up and you died."

If you stay here you will die.

"Okay" I nodded vacantly.

"Okay what?"

"Okay, I'll think about that every time. And … and I'll come home. Not tomorrow, though. I need a few more weeks to … get this shit under control."

We sat in silence for a while.

If you stay here, you will die. I've seen it, and I've never been wrong before.

"You were wrong once," I said softly.

Evie just nodded, the haunted look in her eyes almost too much for me to bear. She released my hand and the spell was broken. She opened her arms, pulled me into her, and held me while we both cried.

Jared and Evie left early the next morning. Poor Jared was extremely apologetic that he had fallen asleep and thought he must have the flu or something. I felt so sorry for him. The guy had driven cross-country to see me for a few measly hours and I hadn't even put out for him. That last lingering kiss on the front porch before he jumped into the waiting cab was enough to cement my decision to leave immediately.

THIRTY-SEVEN

I LET FOUR WEEKS PASS BEFORE I FELT STRONG ENOUGH TO RETURN home without the crushing bloodlust invading my every thought. I spent those four weeks intensively quizzing Ryan, Sam and Ivy on everything I could think of. I think Ryan took my inquisitiveness as a sign that I was sticking around, and so he relaxed a little on the strict rules and chaperoned outings.

Ryan was gone a lot during that time. He was always visiting Clair. He had really taken to her, and dare I say it, was starting to have feelings for the girl. He started to act differently, too. I took to teasing him about it every time he returned after seeing her. But secretly I was worried. She was human and he was a vampire—what was he planning to do with her?

When he was around, Ryan still acted as if there was no hurry, as if I would be staying in California indefinitely. He kept telling me my bloodlust hadn't peaked yet, that it was only going to get worse.

And he was right, in a way. My bloodlust did get much worse. But not for many months.

If you stay here you will die. That was all I heard in my mind for the entire four weeks.

I thought that I was fine. Fixed. Non–lusty. Safe to be alone with.

It was time to go home.

THIRTY-EIGHT

Once the decision to leave was firm in my mind, there were many things to do. Firstly, I needed a set of wheels. Evie had suggested flying home, but I couldn't risk having my name show up on any commercial airline passenger manifests or travel databases that Caleb might be watching. I couldn't take my own car, the one that Jared had so generously driven across the country for me. It was like driving a red flaming beacon that screamed, 'Here I am, come and get me!'

I also had to time my exit appropriately so that nobody would try to stop me. I doubted Ryan would lock me up again, but I didn't exactly trust him. I knew he had something big planned—he was going somewhere 'important' and could be away for a few days. Ivy was going somewhere mysteriously vague, as usual. And Sam had his teaching commitments at the university. All of this gave me a good six-hour window of time to pack my stuff up and get as far away as I could before anyone realized that I was gone.

Still, the logistics bothered me. I was going to have to stop for the night at some point, and if Ryan was really keen (which he would be) then he'd only have to track me to where I stopped and come get me. I could drive through the night, but that sounded exhausting. The other thing that worried me was having enough blood to drink in case I got my freak on again and felt like biting somebody. I was afraid to be alone on the drive in case I flipped out, but I was more afraid of *If you stay here you will die.*

It was early. I sat at the table waiting for my black coffee and blood to infuse. I hated to admit it, but the coffee component was merely a distraction to mask the plain horror of what I was drinking for breakfast—human blood. Stuff that people donated, from the goodness of their hearts, to help save lives. The stuff that pumped through my boyfriend's veins. And I was putting it in my Nescafé.

Ryan sat down across from me, his own coffee/blood concoction letting off steam in front of him.

"Do you ever wonder whose it is?" I asked.

"What do you mean?" Ryan asked, digging his spoon into a bowl of cereal.

"The blood," I replied. "The person who donated this. They must have thought they were giving it for good, not evil."

Ryan smirked through a mouthful of Cheerios. "Evil?" he spluttered. "Jesus. You're like a nun. Only you put out."

I glared at him in disgust. "You're so fucking hilarious."

I can't wait to get the hell away from you.

"The blood doesn't come from a hospital blood bank," Ryan explained without missing a beat. "Vampires have particular requirements of donors that humans do not. It's about more than blood type. It depends on their diet, their lifestyle, their psychic energy. This stuff is expensive." He tapped on his coffee mug. "Why do you think we limit our intake? Not because we want to. There's only a small amount available."

I thought about that for a moment and my blood ran cold. "A small amount?" I echoed. "So vampires who can't get their hands on this stuff …"

"Get it directly from people, yes," Ryan finished casually.

"Do the people die?"

Ryan shrugged. "Sometimes. It depends."

"So you only drink this blood?" I asked, pointing at his cup. He could tell I was testing him—of course he could, he could read my mind.

"No," he said evenly. Because I already knew. He had drained Kate. He hadn't killed her, though. Caleb had saved her last terrified breaths for himself.

"And?" I pressed. "Do they *die* sometimes?"

"If I take blood from a human, I'm careful. I don't bleed them to death. It gets messy. People would come looking for me."

"What people?" I asked. "I thought you said most people don't even know about vampires?"

"There's a bunch of people who keep tabs on supernaturals like us. Vampires, witches, shape shifters, werewolves, hunters."

"Like a council?" I asked.

"Yes," Ryan replied, draining his coffee mug. "A council of supernatural beings."

"What's it called?" I asked.

He looked at me like I was stupid. "The … council of supernatural beings."

"Original," I remarked.

I thought about that for awhile.

"So are we going to keep pretending your little visit with the witch didn't happen?" Ryan asked casually, fixing his gaze onto me.

I just shrugged.

"That must have been hard. Seeing your little boyfriend? Your pal?"

"Who are you calling little?," I shot back, raising my eyebrows and looking pointedly at the area below Ryan's waistline.

Ryan laughed. "She has a sense of humor!" he cheered, raising his cup and clinking it with thin air. He stood and drained the last of his bloody espresso. "Well, she obviously didn't convince you to leave."

I raised my eyebrows. "Obviously. Doesn't mean I have to be happy about it."

Ryan shrugged. "Well, I'm off. Clair and I are going on a little *sojourn*."

"Don't eat her," I said, trying to think and look as bored as possible. *Hurry up and leave!*

"Jealous?" Ryan asked. "Don't worry, I'll take you somewhere special soon."

"Oh goody," I rolled my eyes. "I can't wait."

I spent the next half hour reading every article in the latest issue of *Vogue* without taking in a single word, while Ryan took his sweet time loading suitcases into his car and grabbing supplies from the fridge.

"You're not taking all that, are you?" I gestured to the baggies of blood he was packing into a small blue cooler bag. If he took it all, I wouldn't have any for the long drive back to New Jersey. And I really didn't fancy trying to pick up a human meal and drinking their blood without killing them.

"I left three for you," he said. "Ivy's picking up more tomorrow, so you'll be fine until then."

I watched as he opened the freezer door and started packing more frozen bags of blood in his cooler. There had to be at least fifty bags of the stuff, each containing a litre of blood. Fifty litres of blood. Where the hell was he going?

My heart sank as I put the pieces together. I stood and walked over so that I was in front of him.

"What are you doing?" I asked quietly.

Ryan looked away, unable to meet my eyes. "It's not what you think," he said.

"It is," I insisted, grabbing at the handle of the cooler bag. "Tell me what's going on!"

Ryan pulled the bag out of my reach and fixed his steely eyes onto mine. "Mind your own business," he said. "This has nothing to do with you."

"You're going to Turn her," I accused. His eyes gave away what he wouldn't say.

"Why?" I demanded. "She's got her whole life ahead of her!" I sucked in a deep breath. "Why would you do that to her?"

"Get out of my way, Blake," Ryan demanded when I blocked his exit from the kitchen. "I mean it. I don't have time to screw around."

"Ryan," I said softly, pleadingly. I put both of my hands on his shoulders, as I asked for the third time. "You've only met the girl a few times. Why?"

Sorrow and pain competed against each other in those dark blue eyes of his.

"Because," he answered finally, "she asked me to."

I was about to argue that that wasn't a good enough reason, when he pushed me to the side and stormed out to the garage. Seconds later, I heard his car peeling off down the driveway and the automatic door closing again with a dull thud.

THIRTY-NINE

I ALMOST CHANGED MY MIND. FROZEN TO THE SPOT, I TURNED that information over and over in my mind. *He is going to make Clair a vampire. To do that, he has to kill her.*

But he hadn't lied to me. If he said she had asked, then it was what she wanted. It didn't make any sense, but I supposed it really was none of my business, after all.

I headed back to my room for what I hoped would be the last time, opened the closet and grabbed the bag I'd packed during the early hours of the morning when sleep had deserted me. I went back to the kitchen, dropped the bag in front of the fridge, and loaded my three measly bags of blood into it. An overnight stop was probably out of the question then, if I only had this much blood.

My breath caught in my throat as I sensed someone else in the room. I turned around and let out a relieved breath. It wasn't Ryan.

"You're leaving?" Sam asked, gesturing to my bag.

I debated whether or not to lie. "You can't stop me," I said finally.

"Who said anything about stopping you?" Sam replied. "I'm

surprised you stayed this long."

"Don't tell the others," I said. "Please?"

"Okay," he said. "I'm sure they'll figure it out, though. Ryan is a very good tracker. He can find anyone."

I sighed. "I know," I said. "I'm just hoping that once I'm home, he won't try to make me come back."

"So when are we leaving?" Sam asked.

I raised my eyebrows. "We? There is no we."

Sam crossed his arms and leaned against the bench. "I notice you have my keys," he said casually.

I looked down at the keys in my hand. "It's the only other car here," I said, a note of desperation entering my voice. "I can't take my car. It's too obvious."

"I'm coming with you," Sam announced. Before I could argue, he uncrossed his arms, plucked the set of keys out of my hand and casually made his way down the hall. "Five minutes," he called. "I'll just pack a few things."

I stood on nervous feet, hopping from side to side, trying to decide what to do. To trust that Sam, a vampire I'd only known for a short time, would deliver me home safely and without an agenda of his own? Strangely, I found myself looking forward to the idea of being alone with him on a cross-country road trip.

Don't get carried away, I thought to myself. *You're never going to see him again.*

And for some silly reason, the thought of never seeing him again hurt. More than I could have imagined. I could kind of see why. Whereas Ryan was the source of all my troubles, and Ivy was cold and aloof, if it hadn't been for Sam's gentle guidance and ability to listen to me freak the fuck out on a regular basis, I would have gone insane the first night I landed in that house. I suddenly understood why the thought of losing him hurt so much. It was because, in my new life, he was the only real friend that I had.

You're going home. You need to forget about him.

Somehow that didn't seem so easy.

I stormed out to the car, irritated that my plan had been sprung before I'd even left the house. I was so terribly bad at anything that required stealth or cunning. I threw my bag in the backseat of Sam's SUV, a sleek black BMW with leather seats and chrome wheels. It looked like a car that Ivy would choose, not Sam. I imagined if he had the choice, he would pick something as ordinary as a second-hand pickup.

"Nice car," I murmured as he entered the garage carrying a duffel bag and a small ice cooler. He must have seen my eyes light up, because he nodded and handed the box to me. "You didn't think three little bags would get you there, did you?"

I shrugged. "I would have had more if Ryan hadn't sniped it all."

Sam's face fell. "That's where it all went?" he asked.

"Well, yeah," I said. "He took a big cooler full of blood bags with him. He's going to Turn Clair in Barbados."

I placed the cooler on the floor behind the passenger seat and closed the door. "I don't know why he has to go all the way to Barbados to do that. It's hardly a time to be getting a tan when she'll be all albino girl."

"Barbados is a hospital," Sam said as he shut the tailgate. "It's in Malibu. It looks like a regular hospital, but it treats anything that falls out of the human category."

"Clair is still human, though," I said. "And how come you're not surprised? Did you know he was going to Turn her?"

I really hoped he didn't know.

"Nothing he does surprises me, Mia. He's done far, far worse than that."

"Oh." I swallowed uncomfortably and hopped into the car, throwing my handbag at my feet. A wave of nausea hit me and I clamped my mouth shut and counted to ten in my head.

You don't need blood yet. You just had some.

"Are you alright?" I opened my eyes to find Sam in the driver's seat, peering at me with concerned eyes. "You're as white as a ghost."

"I'll be fine," I said quietly. I reached down and grabbed a bottle of water from my bag, cracked it open and drank the whole thing in one go.

Stop thinking about feeling sick and you'll stop feeling sick. It's all in your head.

I felt bile rush up my throat and I bolted from the car, barely making it to the garden bed on the side of the driveway before the entire contents of my stomach projectiled out of my mouth and onto a pretty rose bush. Thank goodness the garage door had been open or I would have chundered all over the car bonnet. I felt a warm hand on my back and my cheeks started to burn. *Great, he just saw me throw up. Classy.*

"Here." A fresh water bottle was placed in my grasp. I opened it and took a small sip, swirled the water around my mouth and spat it out.

"Sorry," I said, shaking my head and taking a deep breath. "Let's get out of here."

FORTY

IT WAS SMALL TALK FOR THE FIRST FEW HOURS. SMALL TALK AND me napping. I was so tired, I felt like I could sleep for days. I was tired right down to my weary bones. I awoke just as we were crossing the border from LA into Arizona, in a town called Needles. If I had stayed asleep five minutes longer, I would have missed Needles completely.

"Can we stop?" I asked, rubbing my eyes.

Sam frowned. "It's only been three hours."

I raised my eyebrows. "I need to pee."

Sam shrugged in agreement and turned into a gas station. As soon as I got out of the car I regretted it. The temperature had to be at least a hundred and five, and the sun burned my skin the moment I was outside.

Ten minutes later, I was scratching my reddened skin as we left California and drove into Arizona. The Mojave desert stretched ahead of us, shimmering with mirages of things that did not exist.

"That sucks," Sam said, reaching over and pressing two cool

fingers to the pink flesh at my wrist. The skin stayed white for several moments, indicating a nasty burn.

"I remember that," Sam said. "It took months before I could go out in the sun without getting fried."

They called Sam the Ripper. Ryan's words came back to me like a knife to the heart.

"What was it like for you?" I asked carefully. "In the beginning."

He didn't answer, and after several minutes had passed I guessed that he wasn't going to.

"Have you ever wanted to kill someone? To feel their life force fade away? To take everything from them?"

I thought of Caleb. Of Ryan.

"No," I replied. "Maybe."

He tore his eyes from the road and stared straight at me. The anguish in his gaze was unmistakable and raw.

"I did. I feasted on the suffering of others. The more they hurt, the better I felt. Their blood was like a never–ending river of pain."

"You … hurt people?"

"I killed people, Mia. I killed a lot of people. And worse."

"What do you mean?" I asked. His eyes were glossy, and I wondered if he was going to cry. I've never seen a guy cry before.

"There are things worse than killing someone. I've done most of them."

I swallowed thickly and cracked the window, staring straight ahead. The landscape was barren and desolate, but it looked positively radiant compared to sitting in the car listening to Sam talk about murdering people. I was suddenly all too aware of the fact that nobody knew where I was. Or who I was with. The one person I had trusted in the midst of chaos, and he was telling me this?

Hot, stale air flooded the car, and I closed my window again. I slumped down in my seat and looked limply at Sam, concentrating on the road ahead. I could tell by his expression that he felt me staring, but he didn't turn to look at me. He was clearly locked inside his own struggle.

"Would you do that now?" I asked. "Would you hurt someone again? Would you hurt me?"

He cleared his throat. "Of course not."

"Did you hurt anyone before you were a vampire?"

Now he looked at me. "I know what you're doing."

"What's that?"

"You're trying to pass the blame. Like it wasn't my fault."

"It wasn't your fault," I replied forcefully. "Unless you decided to let someone Turn you, to make you a vampire, then none of it is your fault."

"But what about you?" Sam repeated. "What happened to you that you're so different? You don't even *like* blood."

I blushed, stared at the floor.

"Oh, come on, Mia. A few minor cravings is nothing compared to what I've just described. *Trust me.*"

The funny thing was, I did trust him. Even after what he'd told me. I glanced at his hands and couldn't imagine them being used to inflict misery upon somebody.

"I tried to bite Ryan," I said sheepishly. I didn't need to tell him the rest.

Sam laughed! I felt my face turn even redder.

"Sorry," he said. "I would love it if you bit him. A scar would be even better. God knows he deserves much worse."

I frowned. "You don't like him very much," I said, "do you?"

"Do you?"

I shrugged. "I don't know," I said. And I really didn't. The pull I felt towards him was incredibly intense. If I thought about moving further away from him, it hurt, a dull thud between my temples and a sharp spike in my chest.

"Don't you have that feeling with Ivy? That *pull*?"

Sam's face fell a little. "Not exactly," he said. "I love her, but we don't have that bond a vampire and maker normally share. It's a long story."

"Is that why?" I asked gently. "Why it was so bad for you? Because you didn't have that voice in your head telling you everything would be alright?"

Because as much as I hated to admit it, Ryan's voice inside my head, infuriating as it could be, was the only thing that had kept me sane during those first few weeks after waking up as a baby vampire.

"Maybe," Sam replied. "Who knows? It was a long time ago."

He continued to drive while I thought.

"How old are you, again?" I asked. I knew he had told me when I first met him, but in the murky recesses of my brain, the number had vanished.

"Thirty-seven" Sam said.

"You don't look a day over twenty–one," I remarked.

"That's because I'm not." Sam grinned. "I was Turned on my twenty-first birthday. Well, technically it was the next day, so I guess you could say I am a day over twenty-one."

"How did it—what happened?" I asked, almost afraid of the answer. I still couldn't talk about what had happened to me. Who was I to think that he was any different?

"I was living in New York at the time," Sam began. "Ivy and I had had this huge fight, because she needed to go back to LA and wanted me to go with her, and I couldn't, because my dad was sick and I wanted to be close to everyone and finish school.

"I turned twenty–one in May. My parents threw me a huge party at their house. We were all drinking. Most people were gone by 2 a.m. I went to bed after that. I didn't even wake up and the whole house was on fire.

"All I remember is Ivy dragging me out of bed and jumping out of the window with me in her arms. That was the first time it really occurred to me that there was something different about her. You know … something not human. She had been giving me blood samples for my research at the university, but she always told me it was someone else's blood we were studying."

"Jesus," I said. "What happened?"

"I was dying," Sam said. "Well, I did die, I guess. I had burns to most of my body. Before I passed out, Ivy offered to save me, to give me some of that blood, and when she cut her wrist I knew the blood had been hers. I had watched the virus in that blood completely overtake human blood and change DNA. I didn't want it touching me. I said no."

I thought of falling from that building in Mexico, and being offered the same deal by Ryan, and I shuddered.

"But she did it anyway." He looked terribly sad, clutching the steering wheel with white knuckles.

"And your family?" I probed gently.

"All dead in the fire," Sam replied stoically. "My mother, my father, a sister and two brothers. All gone."

My throat was so tight I could barely speak. Without thinking, I reached out and squeezed Sam's right hand, the one that wasn't on the steering wheel.

"Did you forgive Ivy? For Turning you even though you said no?"

"Of course," he replied. "She saved my life. She loved me."

Something about that story made me terribly uneasy, but I couldn't put a finger on it.

She loved me. Sometimes love makes people do crazy things.

We travelled in silence for another twenty or so minutes.

"I need to go to the bathroom," I said, breaking the sadness that lingered in the air like dead souls.

Sam just looked at me. "*Again*?"

The truth was, my stomach was turning in on itself again, and I was terrified of throwing up in the car while we were doing ninety on the interstate. I told Sam this and he appeared concerned.

"How long have you felt like this?"

I shrugged. "I'm not sure. A few weeks, maybe? It's hard to remember with everything that's been going on. I'm sure it's just part of being a vampire."

He frowned. "It's not something I've ever heard of. And you say you still eat mostly regular food?"

"Sure," I said. "I get cravings for cheeseburgers a lot. I think it's the red meat."

"And the blood? You crave that, too?"

"A few times," I admitted, embarrassed. I almost told him how I had slept with Ryan, but changed my mind. I liked Sam. I didn't want him knowing *that* dirty little secret.

"A few times a day?"

"No," I replied. "Just a few times. Once I wanted to bite Ryan. Another time I smelled the blood in the refrigerator. Other times, it makes me feel clearer, but I don't crave it. It still kind of grosses me out."

"You need to stop and pee a lot for a vampire," Sam mused.

"Gee," I replied. "Awkward much?"

"Sorry," Sam said, giving me one of his enormous puppy-dog smiles that reached all the way to his eyes. "I'm just trying to get a catalogue of symptoms so I can try and figure out what's making you sick all the time."

"I didn't realize it wasn't normal," I said, suddenly alarmed. "Do you think there's something wrong with me? Ryan says I sleep a lot for a vampire."

"You do," Sam confirmed.

"Great, so I'm basically a lazy sloth vampire."

"Cravings. Nausea. Vomiting. Excessive urination. Fatigue. If I didn't know better," he joked, "I'd say you were pregnant."

I laughed. "That's impossible. Vampires can't have babies."

"Plus, it takes two to make a baby," Sam added. "Unless it was the immaculate vampire conception." He was still chuckling to himself when he caught a glimpse of my red face and his smile vanished. "Whoa," he said. "You and Ryan?"

"It was a mistake," I said, shaking my head.

"I hope he didn't compel you," Sam said tightly. "I might have to murder him if he did."

"No, he didn't compel me," I said, burying my face in my hands. "Oh. My. God. I am *so* mortified right now."

"It's no big deal," Sam said. "It's none of my business."

Neither of us spoke for a few minutes.

"In that case," Sam said pointedly. "My earlier diagnosis may have some merit."

"That's not funny," I said angrily.

"I wasn't trying to be funny," Sam said, looking at me seriously. "Mia, it can and does happen from time to time. Don't think yourself impervious to getting pregnant just because Ryan told you so."

My jaw dropped. "You're serious. You're actually serious. This is insane!"

Sam was pulling into a small cluster of shops that I hadn't even noticed.

"Where are you going?" I demanded.

"To buy something," Sam replied. He pulled into a parking bay, shut off the engine and took the keys. "Need anything? Snacks, water?"

"I'm fine," I said. "Thanks." I really wanted to ask him to pick up some kind of hotdog with extra salt, but I didn't want to give his outlandish theory any more fuel, so I didn't.

I pondered Sam's crazy idea while I waited for him to come out of the convenience store. There was no way I could be pregnant—my mind couldn't even comprehend such a possibility. Besides, Ryan was older and wiser than Sam, at least when it came to vampire-related facts. If he said all vampires were sterile, then I believed him. Sam was just being crazy.

By the time he had returned, I was happy again and thinking

about what I would do first when I got home. A visit to Jared, of course, then a quick trip across the Hudson River to see my mom at her work offices in Manhattan sounded good. I still hadn't thought of a convincing story as to why I was home when school was days from starting. I decided to stick with good old–fashioned homesickness as my excuse. Besides, it was true.

Sam handed me a brown paper bag as he got into the car. "What's this?" I asked as I opened the bag, at the same time realizing what the pink cardboard box contained. "Jesus, Sam!"

"Just humor me," he said, starting the car. "Take the test. Tell me how wrong I am. And then we'll never speak of it again."

FORTY-ONE

We decided between us to stop for the night in Santa Rosa, New Mexico. We'd been on the road for over twelve hours and both of us were starting to get pretty tired. We hadn't mentioned the stupid pregnancy idea again, and I had all but forgotten about it when I rushed ahead of Sam and towards the bathroom of our motel room.

"Wait!" Sam said, tossing me the brown paper bag. And then, when he saw my face, he added, "just humor me."

I rolled my eyes and shut the bathroom door.

"Hey, you want some food?" Sam called after me. "There's a Pizza Hut a few blocks down. Do you want me to grab you something?"

"Sure," I replied, taking the cardboard box out of the paper bag and ripping it open. I waited for Sam to leave, and when I heard the motel room door close behind him, I peed on the stick and replaced the cap.

I tossed the test on the counter and promptly forgot about it. I wandered out to the main room, where I had thrown my bag onto the first of two single beds. I decided to take a quick shower while Sam was getting pizza. I took my oversized toiletry bag into the bathroom and locked the door. I had just turned the water on when I spied the pregnancy test sitting on the counter.

Two lines.

I dropped the toiletry bag and fell to my knees, swiping the test off the counter as my knees buckled. I turned the test over, to recheck the helpful little diagram that was stuck to the back. One line—not pregnant. Two lines—pregnant.

I read those words and my entire world came crashing down around my feet.

There are things worse than death. And here I was, in the midst of one of those *things.*

I think back now and still can't believe how calm I was. Now, I realize that I was in shock. I acted quickly, knowing that Sam could return at any moment. I opened my toiletry bag and emptied the entire contents onto the grimy bathroom tiles. Bottles of makeup, nail polish and hairspray scattered everywhere. My eyes fell upon a disposable plastic razor, and I snatched it up. I smashed it under a can of hairspray and fished out the sharp razor blade.

I stood on shaky legs and took one final look at myself in the mirror. I couldn't live through one more thing. Certainly not this. The word *baby* tried to enter my thoughts and I banished it angrily.

Monster.

What had Ryan done to me?

What the goddamn had he put inside of me? It was too much for me to bear.

I didn't want to think about any of it, ever again. I was done. Finished.

I told you to leave me there to die.

And God, how I wished he had.

Deciding to kill myself was relatively simple. It was the only solution I could see to my impossible quandary.

My words to Ryan became a chant that I repeated over and over.

I told you to leave me there to die.

The sharp, dragging pinch of the razor blade took my breath away as I gouged it into the pale flesh of my wrist. Up, not across. How did I know that? It didn't matter. Deeper, deeper. Jesus Christ, it hurt. I cried out and kicked the vanity, trying to distract myself from the pain. I forced myself to think about what I had endured in Mexico, and my Turning, and how this was absolutely nothing compared to the pain I had experienced before.

I watched, fascinated as my own blood began to pump from my artery. Bullseye.

One down. One to go. Only–

"What?" I panicked, watching in utter disbelief as the skin around my wound began to knit together. "No, no, no!" I rubbed my wrist, and underneath my blood was a perfect patch of skin—no cut, no pain, no bleeding, and, most of all, no escape.

Ryan's words came back to me then. *You're a vampire. It will heal in a matter of minutes.*

No escape. Unless …

I skated around the slippery tiles, now slicked with my blood, looking for the bottle of sleeping pills Ryan had given me after pulling me from the bathtub. I had tossed them into my bag at the last minute, and now I was relieved.

These things are like vampire valium.

Yes, but could they kill a vampire?

I unscrewed the lid and shook a couple of the bright blue capsules into my hand, crushing them in my palm.

Bingo.

My skin immediately began to sizzle. No wonder. The thick sludge in the capsules smelled exactly the same as the Asphodel flower Clair had been wearing in her hair. Only this blue gloop looked like concentrate. I climbed into the empty bathtub, clutching the razor and bottle of pills to my chest. I took the razor blade and wiped it against the aqua-colored stuff in my palm, getting as much as possible on the thin blade. I took a deep breath, and repeated my earlier action against the delicate, completely healed skin of my inner wrist.

I screamed. The blue stuff—Asphodel root, according to the pill bottle—immediately entered my bloodstream, and my whole body began to convulse. I leaned over the side of the tub and retched violently. *Vampire poison.*

Sam had been gone maybe ten minutes at this point, and I didn't want him to get back until I was well and truly finished. The bathroom door was locked, hopefully buying me some extra time if he did get back before I bled out.

Other wrist, Blake. Hurry up.

I managed a messy cut on the other wrist before I dropped the razor blade and slumped back in the tub. Everything inside me was on fire. Except my stomach. From my waist to my hips, I felt a buzzing numbness that could have been the stone in my womb dying along with me.

Thank God.

It was going to be over soon, I knew it. The pills were working well, and quickly. I closed my eyes and waited to die for the second time in as many months.

My ears picked up the jingling of keys, and the door to the motel room opened.

"Pepperoni pizza okay?" I heard Sam ask casually. "Mia?"

"Y-yes," I called out weakly. More than anything, I didn't want him coming in until I was dead and finished. *I asked you to leave me there to die.*

Despite being close to passing out, I could still see what was going on beyond the bathroom door. I watched with closed eyes as Sam placed the pizza box on the table and sniffed the air.

He can smell my blood.

"Mia?" he called, a little more urgently this time. He approached the bathroom door. "Everything okay in there?"

"Fine," I managed in a voice barely above a whisper. "Nearly done."

I saw the concern on his face grow. He could *definitely* smell my blood. I saw it in the way he shifted his stance, the way he was literally drawn to it. And there was plenty of it. My wounds were in no danger of healing around the noxious Asphodel that stung my skin and set fire to my veins. There was so much blood, I felt like I was drowning in a river of red.

I asked you to leave me there to die.

"Mia, open the door!" He tried the handle, which I had locked.

"I'm coming in," Sam said, and I heard the door handle crunch as he easily broke the lock with his vampire strength.

Damn. Through my hazy eyes I could make out a pair of shoes, blue jeans, and then I was being picked up by my shoulders, and shaken.

"Mia?" Sam yelled. "Mia!" I saw as he surveyed the room, taking everything in. The razor blade on the floor beside the tub. The poisonous blue goop that I had squeezed from the sleeping tablets. And the blood. It was everywhere. I saw him go pale and wondered if his bloodlust would resurface after so many years. Maybe he would finish me off.

"What have you done?" he asked me. More shaking. I was sitting up now, propped against the side of the bath. Sam grabbed towels and wrapped them around my bleeding wrists. "No," I said, trying to stop him.

"Mia," he said desperately, his eyes boring into mine. "Why would you do this?"

"I have to get it out," I gasped. I started to sob. My head bobbed and black dots started to take over my vision.

"Get what out?" he asked, a look of dread spreading across his face.

I realized I wasn't going to win here. He was going to stop

me from dying, and this thing would still be inside me after they stitched up my wrists and washed the blood away.

"Please," I whimpered, grabbing at his shirt I pointed to the positive test on the floor. "Sam. You have to get it out of me!"

His face fell when he saw what was in my hand. "I was right," he murmured.

And then, "Oh, Mia."

I passed out.

FORTY-TWO

I DRIFTED IN AND OUT. THE ASPHODEL TABLETS WERE CAUSING some wicked hallucinogenic nightmares, so I was trying to stay awake now that Sam had foiled my suicide attempt. He carried me to the car and folded me rather awkwardly into the passenger seat, then ran around to the driver's side. We were on the road and heading west before I could say or do anything. I rested my forehead on the cold glass as we drove through the sleepy night streets of San Rosa. We were a long way from home, at least a ten hour drive even if Sam ignored all of the speed limits. I didn't see how I was going to survive the journey. *Perhaps that was a good thing.*

My wrists throbbed in tune with my hummingbird heartbeat. I had lost a lot of blood. I felt freezing cold and thought that I would probably slip into a coma in a matter of minutes unless I got a transfusion. *How does a vampire even get a blood transfusion?*

Sam was driving and talking on the phone. I could hear the panic rising in his voice.

"I need your help, man!" he yelled into the phone.

Ryan's cocky voice replied clearly, "Oh, so now *you* need *my* help?"

"Listen to me," Sam said, deathly serious. "Mia has hurt herself. I think she was trying to kill herself. She's lost a lot of blood."

"Bring her to Barbados hospital," Ryan said immediately. "It's in your GPS."

Sam looked despondent. "Mia and I aren't in California," he said carefully. "She decided to drive back to New Jersey this morning and I accompanied her."

"What?!" Ryan's voice boomed through the line. "Shit!"

I heard the beep of a life support machine and was amazed to be able to clearly see Ryan's surroundings even though I was hundreds of miles away. The bond apparently worked through a phone line as well. He was in a plush-looking hospital room, sitting beside a comatose, vampire Clair. So she had been Turned. She looked a hell of a lot more comfortable than I had when I had become a vampire.

"She'll heal," Ryan said. "She's a vampire."

"Negative," Sam said. He pulled the car onto the side of the highway and glanced at me. "Something has gotten into her bloodstream. Her blood isn't clotting at all. I've never seen a vampire bleed like this."

"Fuck," Ryan swore. He paused for a moment. "Okay, you need to get her somewhere safe. You cannot take her to a hospital, do you hear me?"

"I know that!" Sam exploded. "Why do you think I'm calling you?"

"Where exactly are you?" I heard Ryan pacing.

"Santa Rosa, New Mexico. On the interstate, five miles east of The Majestic Motel." Sam's jaw was clenched so hard I thought his teeth might shatter.

"Shit. Okay, hang on, I'm thinking. There's a small medical facility there, should be able to accommodate a blood transfusion." He sighed. "Jesus Christ, Mia."

"Address?" Sam enquired impatiently.

My chest was getting very tight. I started sucking in great lungfuls of air.

Vampires don't need to breathe.

Well, we do when we have no blood left in our bodies to transport the oxygen around.

My eyes fluttered shut and my head fell forward, hitting the dash with a dull thud.

"I'm losing her, dude!" Sam was peeling me off the dash as he spoke. "Hurry up or I'll take her to a regular hospital."

"Don't do that!" Ryan yelled.

"Ryan!"

"Okay, okay, I found the address. 67 Villiers Street. It's called Greenmount Medical Supplies. It's a feeding house with an infirmary attached. Go around to the service gate and ask for Valerie."

Sam tapped the address into his GPS and pulled back onto the highway, driving slowly as he watched the red dot on the bright screen.

"Sam, give her as much of your blood as you can spare. Human blood won't work. Ivy and I will helicopter out to you in the next few hours."

"Okay," Sam said. "Wait, Ivy? Don't get her involved, man!"

"I have to!" Ryan answered. "Do you think I know how to fly a helicopter?"

That was the last thing I heard before I passed out again.

FORTY-THREE

I woke up in the infirmary the next morning, in a small hospital–type room. There were clean bandages on my wrists, and my skin had been scrubbed clean of blood. Ryan sat next to the bed where I lay. A thin plastic tube carried his blood from his arm into mine. He looked terrible, and I wondered how much blood he had given Clair before arriving to bleed a little more for me. It was as if he had aged ten years in the space of a day.

I sat up and ripped the cannula and needle from my arm. It hurt, but not as much as ripping my wrists open with a razor dipped in asphodel root had. The small hole in my arm disappeared almost instantly.

So I'm healing again. I must be all better. Goddamn it and fuck it all to hell.

I couldn't bear to think about the fact that a creature had taken up residence inside of me. I didn't think of it as an innocent child. I didn't even think of it as *mine*. It was an invader, a parasite clinging to my insides and sucking the life out of me. It was evil. How could anything good come from a vampire like Ryan?

I wondered if Ryan knew yet. *Of course he did.* Through the bond, I felt his fear, his need to protect me and whatever it was growing in my barren womb.

I immediately put up the walls inside my mind, refusing to let him probe my thoughts any deeper. He jerked back, obviously feeling my rejection like a slap in the face.

"How are you?" Ryan asked, breaking the tense stand-off. "Do you need water? Something to eat?"

"I'm fine," I replied icily, tossing the plastic tubing on the floor at his feet. I decided to get straight to the point. "Why are you even here?"

Ryan scowled and shook his head. "Because I care about you."

I laughed coldly. "You don't care about me," I said. "You don't care about any*one*, or any*thing*, except *yourself*."

"I *do* care about you," Ryan argued. "I want to know why you felt like you had to ..." He stopped mid-sentence, apparently having difficulty speaking.

"... do *this*," he said finally.

I just stared at the scuffed linoleum floor.

"Why would you do that to a *baby*?" he asked finally. "An innocent child who hasn't even lived yet?"

I whipped my head up and glared at him with every ounce of rage that I could muster. I wanted to reach out and rip his heart from his chest.

"Nobody's truly innocent," I said quietly. "Isn't that what you told me?"

"A child," Ryan pleaded, "is the most innocent thing in the world!"

I shook my head. "I want an abortion. I want it out of me. Then I'm going home." I said the last part with plenty of emphasis.

"You're insane," Ryan said, his face getting redder. "You want to kill the first born vampire in hundreds of years?"

"You did this to me," I accused.

"Jesus, Mia," Ryan seethed. "I didn't *do* anything to you. We did this together. The fact that this is happening is kind of impossible."

And then, just to be an asshole, he added, "You threw yourself at me, remember?"

I shook my head in disgust. "Just go away and leave me alone."

"No," he argued. "Your wrists won't stop bleeding, and I want to know why. What did you do?"

"Get out!" I snapped.

Faster than a human eye could follow, Ryan was standing over me, both hands on my head. I felt that familiar drag and tried to push him away. "No!" I yelled, struggling against his fiercely strong grip. But it was useless. He was my maker and, therefore, had a direct link to my mind. I swallowed back tears as I felt him probe into my memories, finding the one at the motel, where I had cut my wrists. It was sickening.

"Stop," I begged. I *wailed*. "You're hurting me!"

He ignored me, surging deeper, until the whole horrific scene had played itself out again. I jerked back, and he finally let me go. My crying bordered on the hysterical. I had never felt so violated in my entire life.

"Asphodel," he breathed. "You could have *killed* it!"

I glared at him through salty tears. "You mean, like you killed Clair? I bet it wasn't like she thought it would be. I bet she *hates* what you've done to her."

"I saved her life," Ryan said quietly, furiously.

"You ruined her life. It's what you do."

"No, sweetheart, the cancer she was dying from *ruined* her life. I was merely trying to prolong it. I owed her father a favour after he saved my ass years ago. *That's* why Clair is a vampire. Not that it's any of your goddamn business."

That knowledge slammed into me like a freight train. He wasn't lying. I thought that he was dooming her, when in fact he had saved her from dying a painful death.

I think I'll keep you. I wasn't convinced of his chivalry, not for one minute.

"You ruin everything you touch," I said. "Get away from me. I don't ever want to see you again."

The sullen smirk across his face made me want to stab him in the eyes. "You're having my child, *dear*. I'm not going anywhere."

I growled. I hated him, despised him, just wanted him out of my space and out of my mind. "I'm not keeping this baby. You can't make me!"

Faster than I could react, a hand whistled through the air and Ryan's fist struck my cheek. I flew back, off the bed, and my skull slammed into the wall behind me. I staggered to my feet, blind with white-hot pain, feeling like my head was going to topple from my shoulders.

When my vision cleared, it was him, still there, trying to compose himself, trying not to beat me to death. "Just do it," I slurred, wiping blood from my mouth with a clumsy palm. "Kill me. Go ahead, hero." And I started to laugh. I felt like I had finally gone insane, finally hit absolute rock bottom, and that it was okay because I truly couldn't sink any further than this.

"I'm not going to kill you," Ryan said, with a look of disgust on his face.

"Doesn't matter" I shrugged, still smiling the wretched grin of insanity. "I'll kill myself. You can't watch me forever."

His eyes flashed black and stayed that way for several seconds. I'd never seen him do that before, only Caleb. It scared the shit out of me. And I had his offspring inside me?

"You wanna bet?" He snarled. "I will lock you up and throw away the key, Blake."

I snapped. Before he could stop me, I leapt forward, clearing the bed between us with ease. I lashed out with my hands, grabbing his shirt collar and throwing him at the closed door. He slammed into the door, his skull smashing the rectangular glass window and his shoulders splintering the wood. I had gone from weak and pathetic to strong and murderous in the space of minutes after being transfused with fresh vampire blood. The feeling of swift recovery and supreme invincibility left me hungering for more. I lunged forward, snapping at Ryan's exposed throat.

The look in his eyes was priceless—he realized that I was stronger than him, even if it was only temporary, and that scared him. I doubted very much that he had ever been scared of me before. He fought with me as my mouth got closer to his neck, and he held me off with dying strength that I knew I could outlast.

"Stop!" Ryan shouted, using our bond to send shockwaves of pain through my head.

"Ow!" I yelled. It hurt. A lot. That pissed me off. A lot. I summoned all of the pain and rage that was swirling in my chest and my stomach and I directed that through the bond, back at him. I wasn't sure if it would work, I had only ever tried communicating via the bond using words and pictures, but it worked alright. Ryan dropped to the ground like a sack of potatoes. He clutched at his head and began to scream.

I smiled.

Ivy rushed into the room. I guessed straight away that she had been listening to everything. She stopped dead in her tracks when she saw my face, and I imagined how I must have looked—electric blue eyes, wild raven hair in bloodied tangles, mascara and tears streaked down my cheeks and blood under my fingernails where I had scratched deep gouges into Ryan's face.

"Stop it," she pleaded. Worried, all of them worried about me and what I might do to the precious monster that *he* had cursed me with.

Ryan continued to twitch and moan.

"Or what? What will you do?" I asked. I was genuinely curious, and a little bit crazy. Would she strike me down with powerful magic? Her eyes darted between Ryan and I.

"You won't do anything, will you?" I was pleased. "You can't hurt me without risking hurting this parasite inside me."

Her face confirmed my suspicion.

Suddenly Sam appeared in the room, and I jumped. Another worried face. "Mia."

"*Sam.*" I mimicked his pitiful tone.

"Stop it." He gestured to Ryan, limp and moaning on the ground. "He deserves it, but not like this. You're better than this. Stop whatever it is you're doing to him."

I tried to stop the flood of black waste that was pouring through the bond from me to him, and choked. "I can't."

It was true. Whatever gate I had opened, I couldn't close it. Hate and rage poured through the bond, making me shiver and making Ryan suffer. The black sludge that was pouring from me into him was starting to make my head hum as well. Panic rose in my throat like bitter bile. "I can't stop it!" I cried. I clawed at my own throat as it started to close and I was gasping for air. Air might not have mattered to me, because I was a vampire and vampires didn't need to breathe, but it still felt like I would smother if I couldn't suck in lungfuls of the stuff.

"You can," Sam said firmly, squeezing my shoulder hard, not enough to hurt but enough so that I had to look at him. "What is it you're thinking about? Is it Caleb? Is it Ryan?"

I shook my head no. Sorrow engulfed me then, and shame. Oh, the shame! I was blaming Ryan for all of this, and he was hardly innocent, but he hadn't forced me to do anything except get in that van three long months ago. And he'd been apologizing for it ever since. Only I'd never been able to forgive him.

It was hate, I realized. All the hate I felt, for Ryan and Caleb and myself—it was *killing* me. And right now, it was killing Ryan.

"You can stop it," Sam said urgently. "Tell me what's happening in your head right now. What you're feeling."

"I hate them," I responded. "I hate this life. I miss everything that I used to have! He's taken it all from me. And now –"

"And now what?" Sam pressed.

"And now I just wish I could die," I said numbly, the fight going out of me. The black sludge disappeared, replaced by a hollow ache that settled in my womb like a cold, heavy stone. I stumbled back, returning to the bed. There was no fight left in me. Ryan scuttled away, still holding his head with both hands, without so much as a backwards glance. Ivy followed, casting a worried look at Sam before she closed the damaged door.

"I want to show you something," Sam said quietly, once we were alone. I didn't argue. He wheeled a large portable machine next to the bed. I realized immediately what it was and baulked.

"You can trust me," Sam said. "I promise."

Part of me did want to see what could possibly have developed inside me over a few short weeks. And knowledge was power.

"Alright," I said dejectedly. How much worse could it get?

I sat on the bed, waiting patiently as Sam fiddled with buttons and switches. "Do you even know how to use that thing?" I asked.

He smiled, as if to say, *There you are*. I didn't smile back, though, instead focusing on the grainy screen in the centre of the machine.

"Shirt up," Sam instructed. I reluctantly pulled my t-shirt up to expose my bare stomach. The gel he squeezed onto my skin was cold and felt gross. He made one final adjustment to the machine and then placed a plastic probe on my stomach.

Neither of us breathed as the contents of my uterus came into focus on the display screen. At first, I couldn't see anything other than a blur of movement, but it very quickly became apparent what I was looking at—a set of arms and legs moving about, a torso and a head.

A baby.

My baby.

I turned my head, horrified and intrigued. "Why is it bouncing up and down like that?" I asked Sam.

He smiled. "Your baby has the hiccups," he said gently.

I have a vampire baby in me and it has the hiccups. The goddamn fucking hiccups.

For what seemed like the thousandth time that day, I buried my face in my hands and cried.

FORTY-FOUR

I DIDN'T WANT A BABY. I DEFINITELY DIDN'T WANT RYAN'S VAMPIRE baby. I had always been *so* careful when I was with Jared. It's funny, sometimes it feels like you can do the right thing your whole life, but it doesn't matter, because fate is waiting there patiently for you to fuck up so it can stick a demon baby inside you. I was past the point of denial, past the point of suicide. Now I was just pissed.

I refused to speak with anyone but Sam from that point on. I was too angry with Ryan, and too scared of Ivy. None of us had slept. I had changed into clean clothes, washed the gel from my stomach. And then it was time to leave.

There was no question of where we were going. It was simply assumed. Sam and I walked slowly to his car and got in, followed by Ivy and Ryan. Nobody spoke, except to give basic directions. We dropped Ryan and Ivy off at a nearby field, where Ivy's chopper was waiting.

And we drove back to Santa Monica.

FORTY-FIVE

I CHECKED MY PHONE WHEN WE WERE BACK ON THE INTERSTATE. Missed calls and texts from Evie, asking where I was. I was listening to a string of panicked voicemails when she called again.

"Hello?" I answered emptily.

"Happy Birthday," Evie said. "Did you get cold feet? I thought you'd be here by now."

It's my birthday today. How did I forget that?

"Something happened," I replied wearily.

"What happened? Did Ryan talk you out of it?"

I wish. "I'm pregnant," I said numbly. What was the point in denying it? She would find out eventually when she came back to look for me.

There was a long silence. I had an idea why. Evie was probably trying to figure out who I had slept with.

"Ryan," Evie spat. "What did he do to you?"

"It didn't mean anything," I said weakly. I sounded *pathetic.*

"This was *consensual?*"

I didn't answer.

"You worthless sucker," Evie hissed. I fought back tears at the hatred in her voice. "I can't believe I trusted you. You lost your soul the day you Turned."

"It didn't mean anything!" I pleaded. *Lost my soul?* "Please, you can't do this to me. I need you. You have to help me fix this!"

There was a long silence.

"Evie?" I asked into the static.

"You stay away from me, you hear?" She was *so* angry. "And Jared. Don't you *dare* try to call him. You don't deserve him."

"What do I deserve then, witch?" I was sobbing.

"I wish they had just killed you." Her voice was heavy; she sounded old. "More than anything, you'd be better off dead."

"Wait!" I cried. "What are you going to tell Jared?"

"The truth!" Evie yelled. "You cheated on him, and you lied to him, and you're never coming back for him. Because this is it for you!"

The line cut out. She had hung up on me.

You'd be better off dead. As usual, she was right.

Don't cry don't cry don't cry–

I started to sob; great retching chokes that racked my entire body. Sam pulled off to the emergency lane and shut off the engine.

"You're not better off dead," he whispered. So he had heard everything. He pulled me close to him and repeated those words over and over again. Maybe he was trying to say them until I believed them. It didn't work, but it did make me feel a little less alone. At least he was still my friend. Maybe my only friend left in the whole world.

"I'm so sorry," Sam said, his voice breaking. He rubbed his big hands in circles on my back as if I was a child. "You deserve better than this."

But it didn't matter what I deserved. Life was cruel. Life was relentless. Life didn't care about pathetic creatures like me.

After a little while, I calmed down. I was too tired to cry anymore. Sam wiped my cheeks dry with his fingers and pushed my hair out of my eyes, his forehead still resting lightly on mine.

"You want food?" he asked quietly. "Some blood, maybe?"

I shook my head.

"I didn't know it was your birthday," Sam said sadly. I didn't reply.

I fingered the thick bandages on each wrist and sighed. A few more minutes before Sam found me and my plan might have worked. Now we would never know. I wasn't stupid; I knew Ryan would never let me out of his sight again. Not until he got this thing out of me alive, anyway.

We continued our drive west. Bright city lights flickered in the distance. I didn't know what city it was, and I didn't care.

A few hours later, Sam asked me again. Food? No. Blood? No.

"I can hear your stomach rumbling," he pointed out politely.

"I'm probably being eaten alive from the inside." I was short with him; I was sick and tired and plain worn out.

That shut him up until evening fell and he pulled into a drive-thru Burger King just outside of town. He ordered a cheeseburger and fries and set them on the seat next to me, along with a fresh baggie of human blood he had retrieved from the icebox in the trunk.

"Please eat something," he implored. His eyes were so kind, so caring. How could I refuse? And yet I did. I turned my better–off–dead eyes outside and ignored my body's pleas for nourishment.

Because I thought, maybe if I didn't eat, if I didn't feed the baby, then it might die. Maybe we both would.

And the nightmare would finally be over.

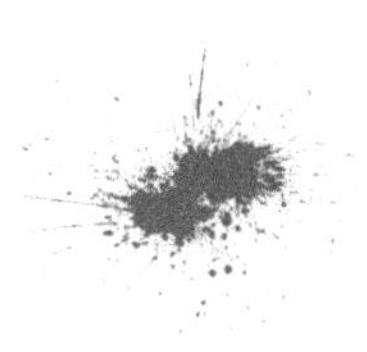

Mia's story continues in The Vessel—Vampireland #2

THE VESSEL

I may be flesh and bone, but my smile hides my corruption.

I may look like a girl, but inside I'm a monster.

I was taken.

I was turned.

I was *saved.*

I was so achingly close to returning to my old life. Halfway, to be exact. But one mistake came back to haunt me, and now I'm trapped in a nightmare.

ABOUT THE AUTHOR

Jessica Salvatore is the paranormal pen name of *USA Today* Bestselling Author Lili St. Germain. And yes, she totally chose 'Salvatore' because in her fictional vampire world, she's married to Stefan. And Damon. And is probably having an affair with Kai Parker.

Seriously, though. Jessica writes about all the things that go bump in the night—especially vampires. She grew up on a steady diet of *Buffy* and *Supernatural* and has met Jensen Ackles and Jared Padalecki no less than three times. If you're a real paranormal buff, you'll understand how freaking cool this is—*and* how seriously she takes her stalking duties.

Aside from paranormal, she writes dark, disturbing romances and nail-biting psychological thrillers that lack vampires, but still have plenty of bloodshed. Her #1 Bestselling Gypsy Brothers series, written as Lili St. Germain, focuses on a morally bankrupt biker gang and the girl who seeks her vengeance upon them.

Jessica (writing as Lili) is also the author of psychological thriller *Gun Shy* and the *California Blood* series.

Jessica quit corporate life to focus on writing and has loved every minute of it. Her other loves in life include her gorgeous husband and beautiful daughter, good coffee, travelling to far-flung locations, and binge-watching episodes of *The Vampire Diaries* and *Supernatural*. Because RESEARCH.

She loves to read almost as much as she loves to write, and has equal love for both her paranormal and her dark romance writing!

If you want to get an automatic email when Jessica's next book is released, sign up here (eepurl.com/cY_O6b). Your email address will never be shared and you can unsubscribe at any time.

Say Hi!

Jessica loves hearing from readers!
You can find her in the following places…

Instagram : smarturl.it/JSalvatoreIG

Website: www.lilisaintgermain.com/vampireland-series

CPSIA information can be obtained
at www.ICGtesting.com
Printed in the USA
BVHW041920130421
604844BV00023B/533